Golden States

Michael Cunningham

Golden States

Crown Publishers, Inc.   New York

Published by Crown Publishers, Inc., One Park Avenue, New York, New York 10016,
and simultaneously in Canada by General Publishing Company Limited
Manufactured in the United States of America
Library of Congress Cataloging in Publication Data
Cunningham, Michael, 1952–
Golden states.
I. Title.
PS3553.U484G6   1984   813′.54   83-25248
ISBN 0-517-55279-5
Book design by Camilla Filancia
10 9 8 7 6 5 4 3 2 1
First Edition

This book is for my family.

The author would like to thank the Copernicus Society for a James A. Michener Fellowship, and the Fine Arts Work Center at Provincetown.

Particular thanks must also be extended to Sarah Metcalf, whose help in shaping this book began with a midnight reading of the first chapter by long-distance telephone; to Gail Hochman, Barbara Grossman, David Groff, Darrah Cloud, and Francis O'Shea.

Golden States

Coyotes were sneaking into the neighborhood like unwanted guests at a party. They lapped water from swimming pools and devoured every cat that had learned to think of dogs as playmates or harmless nuisances. Los Angeles had been dry for months, and as the drought continued coyotes ventured farther and farther into town. Their baying kept people awake at night. In the newspaper, a night watchman said he'd seen a pair of them at a shopping center after midnight, slinking around the Burger King. He said he shouted at them and they took off, but with a peevish attitude, as if they'd been unfairly put upon.

The rain when it came fell miraculously out of a blank white sky. It started as isolated drops blossoming on the dusty streets and quickly gathered weight, drawing rainbows of oil up out of the asphalt.

The sky settled slowly down onto the rooftops, a low green belly still white at the horizon, and for three weeks rain fell straight and heavy as nails, as if to drive the coyotes into the ground. Sulfur-colored water pooled around the foundations of houses, eating away the sandy soil. Some of the fancier homes, on hillsides, had to be sandbagged, and one slid down into a canyon gracefully as a riverboat. It was on the six o'clock news. Two days later a man stood trembling before the camera and told how a roaring wall of mud had taken away his kitchen, including his maid. At night people slept to the steady penetrating thrum of raindrops. A man in Garden Grove told a reporter that he had built an ark in his garage, and when the time came, all he'd have to do was chop the garage roof away. A woman jogger in Tarzana said she saw a coyote swimming across a flood-control channel with something furry in its mouth. She said she'd had no idea they were such good swimmers.

David Stark, age twelve, knew the rain had stopped before he came fully awake. The air in his room was lighter, as if a lid had been lifted off of it. He went to the window in his pajamas. The sky was a clear high silver. Mom stood in the backyard, skimming leaves off the pool. She wore her white robe and carried a long-handled net which splashed like a tossed coin each time she dipped it into the water. The pool was wedged around an old dying tree. Mom refused to have the tree cut down, although it wept parchment-colored leaves into the water and studded the coping with blobs of yellow sap. It kept her busy, clearing the water of leaves.

Janet came into the backyard, carrying two steaming mugs of coffee. The sight of her made David's blood jump. He still couldn't believe she was home again. She gave one of the mugs to Mom and the two women stood close together, saying something David couldn't hear. They held their mugs cupped in both hands, guarding them from the wind. Twin threads of steam rose into the bright air.

David took off his pajamas and put on jeans and a T-shirt

embossed with a picture of Stevie Wonder. It was his favorite shirt, and he wore it so much Stevie's face had faded from chocolate to blue. Before going downstairs he checked his hair in the mirror and tried out different angles of chin, looking for a right way to hold his head. It had recently been pointed out to him that he walked strangely, as if his head was being pulled along slightly too fast for his feet. He tucked his jaw in, reminding himself to just lie back and wait for things to reach him in their own time.

When he got down to the kitchen Janet was there, sitting with her coffee in the breakfast nook. "Morning, Stevie Wonder," she said.

"Hi," he said. He had expected her to stay in the yard longer. Finding her here in the kitchen threw his timing off and invalidated the remark he'd planned about how nice it was to be outside again.

"Rain's stopped," she said.

"Uh-huh." He went to his own chair at the table and patted the backrest, for reasons he didn't quite understand. He'd meant to sit down. Instead of sitting he walked to the refrigerator and took a magnet shaped like a pineapple off the smooth white surface.

"You want some breakfast?" she asked.

"No thanks." He took the magnet and sat in Mom's chair instead of his own. "Can I have a sip of your coffee?" he said.

"Since when do you drink coffee?"

"Well, I like coffee."

Smiling, she slid the mug over to him. It was yellow, decorated with an orange sun, steaming with a black adult life of its own. He sniffed at it, raised it to his lips, and let a drop strain through his teeth.

"Ahh," he said, returning the mug to Janet.

"Good, huh?" she said. He nodded and ran his thumb over the warty surface of the little plastic pineapple. Janet had long dark hair, which she tied into a loose knot at the back of her head. Stray wisps brushed her shoulders. She was not much bigger at twenty-three than David was at twelve, and he thought she looked like him, an idealized female version. She was his half sister, the daughter of Mom's first husband, Ray. Ray had gotten run down along with three other people in a crosswalk in Van Nuys, by a girl driving a Ford van. The girl had felt a spider crawling up her leg and bent down in a panic to brush it off. One of Ray's shoes had been found balanced atop a mailbox two hundred yards away.

"What are you going to do today?" Janet asked.

"Hang out," he said. "What are you going to do?"

"I'm going to sit here in the kitchen all day. I'm going to drink coffee and smoke cigarettes and stay out of trouble."

"Are you still getting married?"

"Looks like not," she said. "The bride has flown the coop."

"Oh." The phrase carried an image with it: a woman in a long white dress soaring like a kite, arms out straight, wind whipping her stiff white veil. David felt his head creeping forward and pulled it back.

Mom came in from the backyard with an unlit cigarette clamped between her lips. "Morning, troops," she said from the side of her mouth.

"Morning," David said. Mom was small like the rest of the family, and she seemed to be shrinking inside her skin, which stayed the same size, hanging empty under her chin.

She poured herself more coffee at the stove. "That rain made mincemeat out of the yard," she said. "The birds of paradise look like they've been beaten down with sticks."

"Well, you were right to hold out on buying an umbrella," Janet said. "It only rained for three weeks."

"This is *Southern* California," Mom said. "I don't even know where they sell umbrellas."

"You need a light?" Janet asked.

"Nope. I'm going to try just holding them in my mouth for a while. Maybe I can cut down that way. Is Rob calling this morning?"

"He said he was going to."

"Do you want to talk to him?" The cigarette waggled in her mouth when she spoke. Her beige hair was crisp with its new permanent.

"No. But I will," Janet said.

"If you don't want to talk to him," Mom said, "I can tell him you're out."

"Maybe you could tell him I've died. Tell him I was sitting here at the breakfast table one minute and the next minute I'd burst into flames."

Mom took the cigarette out of her mouth to sip her coffee. "I had the locks changed after Frank moved out. Not that he ever tried to get back in. I just felt better knowing he wasn't walking around out there with the key to our front door."

Frank was David's father, Mom's second husband. He lived in Spokane now.

David said, "I could stay home and answer the phone today, if you want me to."

"No thanks, friend," Janet said. "I'll have to talk to him sooner or later anyway."

"Reagan's all over the front page this morning," Mom said. "He wants to spend another umpteen billion dollars on bombs. Lord, I don't know what's going on."

"The men have all lost their minds," Janet said. "Present company excepted."

"Better watch out for this one in a couple more years," Mom said.

"David? Oh no, David's going to be the first male feminist. He's going to help save us all."

David grinned and stroked the pineapple.

"I'm going to smoke this cigarette after all," Mom said. "Have you got a match, Janet?"

Janet lit a match for her and held it at arm's length. Mom bent over, the cigarette held between puckered lips.

"Thank you," she said. She sucked the smoke down and expelled brown-gray tendrils of it slowly through her nose. Janet lit a cigarette too. Her smoke meshed with Mom's and made a floating cobweb over the table. David pictured himself flying, with Janet in one arm and Mom in the other, while men with weapons closed in on the house below.

Lizzie came into the kitchen in the nightgown she had just gotten for her tenth birthday. It was pale blue, with wilting blue satin bows over the buttons.

"Morning, Sparkle," Mom said. Janet said good morning too.

David could tell from the set of Lizzie's chin that she was upset about being the last one up. She was always afraid of missing out on something.

"Good afternoon, Lizzie dear," he said.

"Good morning, asshole," she said.

"That's enough of that," Mom said.

Lizzie sat at the table, holding her head carefully erect. She had inherited Dad's wild red hair, and she wore it like an extravagant hat.

"I heard coyotes last night," she said.

"I didn't hear anything," Mom said.

"They were howling under my window."

"Singing love songs," Janet said.

"They ate the Munsons' cat," Lizzie said in a tone of hushed respect.

"They're going to eat *you*," David said.

Lizzie looked at him nervously. She was afraid of coyotes. "They don't eat people," she said.

"That's why you're the only one around here they'd eat."

"You beat off every night," Lizzie told him. "I can hear you."

"What lovely children," Mom said.

"I have to go," David said.

"What about breakfast?" Mom asked.

"I had some of Janet's coffee."

"Oh, you grew up in your sleep. How nice."

"David has never drunk coffee in his life," Lizzie said to Janet.

"Lizzie farts in the bathtub," David said, and he made what he thought was a fair imitation of a fart bubbling up from under water.

"Enough," Mom said. "Both of you."

"Bye." David got up and ran for the front door. As he left Mom called to him, "I'm going to give you your breakfast for lunch. And your lunch too. So get hungry."

Then he was out, free. He saw the neighbor's black Labrador, nosing around the trash cans. He shooed it away, but instead of leaving, it trotted up to him, lolling a pink tongue that looked too big to fit inside its mouth. David patted its head, then whacked it on the rump to make it go away. It went good-naturedly back to rooting in the trash.

He walked through the silvered streets to the meeting place, at the border of a patch of plowed land which would eventually sport a new tract. David's tract was expanding, and several years earlier the great rumbling yellow bulldozers leveled what had been a wild sloping field of sage and yucca. Something went wrong with the money, though, and for now the ground stood naked, stakes and dirty string still indicating the future locations of streets, yards, houses. Behind it rose the ancient hills, shaggy and brown. It had taken on a feeling of enormous age, as if the weathered pegs with their occasional scraps of soiled orange plastic demarked a dead civilization under excavation rather than a new one waiting to be built.

David arrived before Billy did. The tract had turned into a shallow lake, mirroring the pale sky, pegs protruding. He stood on the sidewalk, at the water's edge, and peered over at his rippled reflection against the brown-tinted sky. He was always surprised by the sight of his own face. It didn't look like him.

He nudged the water with the toe of his sneaker, to break it up. Mud sucked at his shoe and he pulled it quickly back out. His face reassembled itself, and he cautiously toed it away again.

Billy came from the opposite direction, the far side of the tract. David could see him walking across the water, kicking up a spume with his high black boots. Billy dressed like a soldier, in camouflage pants and a fatigue jacket. He was small for twelve, even smaller than David, but more squat, his head hunkered down on his heavy rounded shoulders. The first few brown hairs of a mustache rode his upper lip, and you could see ideas quiver in his eyes like minnows trapped behind the pupils.

David had been Billy's best friend since they were both on tricycles. Billy's father left years ago to work on the Alaska pipeline and never came back. Next year, in the seventh grade, Billy would ride a bus to a different school, because he lived on the other side of the district line. David would go to the junior high in the neighborhood, a sleek new building with a white roof like a nun's hat, and no windows at all.

"What ho," Billy called.

"Pip pip," David replied. "Howd'ja do, old bean?"

"Bit of a wet out here," Billy said. He sloshed up to David, walking in his eager, hunched-forward way. Sometimes when he saw Billy, David felt a high, dreamy rising in his belly, and any little thing—the white hairs on Billy's arms, or his quick, businesslike stride—stirred up a wave of pure feeling that immediately dropped down again into guilt and edginess that seemed to last for days. He could not remember just when he had started being so nervous around Billy.

"Look here, old bean," David said. "I've brought you something." Lately he had taken to giving Billy presents. In the past two weeks he'd given him a petrified dinosaur turd from Nevada, a chip of tiger's eye, and a rubber gorilla with fangs and black nipples. Though he'd liked the dinosaur turd and the tiger's eye well enough, the gorilla had seemed to annoy and embarrass him, like a breach of a secret code.

David reached into his pocket and pulled out a fossilized horseshoe crab.

"What is it?" Billy asked.

"A fossil." David was careful not to use its fancier name.

Billy hefted the crab in his palm and scrutinized it with one eye closed. David looked at it too. It was beautiful, a smooth pewter-colored stone with tiny blunt horns and two hooded indentations where, fifty thousand years ago, a pair of eyes had blinked.

"Thanks," Billy said. He put it carelessly in his jacket pocket.

"You're welcome," David said. This one, too, was a failure, but not as bad as the gorilla. It was hard to predict.

"Janet came home last night," David said. "She decided not to marry that guy."

"Bet he's got a little dick," Billy said, holding his thumb and forefinger an inch apart.

"I don't know," David said. "She didn't say what was wrong, or anything."

"Bet he hasn't got any dick at all."

"Well, I don't know—" David felt at a loss. Billy had made up a new way of talking, without explaining how it worked.

Billy started punching the air, doing a little fighting dance that turned him around in circles. "No dick at all," he said, punching away.

"She's going to be a doctor instead," David said.

"You got no dick either." Billy punched in David's direction.

"I do too." When Billy got pulled into himself this way, David might as well have been talking to a whirlwind. His words blew off like dust and leaves.

"I do too," David repeated, just to give himself the satisfaction.

When Billy calmed down, David asked him what he wanted

to do. "Punch somebody," he said. He punched himself in the mouth.

"Shall we go into town and do a bit of sleuthing?" David asked.

"I'm sick of that. We're too old for that."

"Oh. Okay. Well, do you want to go into town anyway?"

"Yeah."

They walked together through the serpentine streets of David's development, Billy stomping into puddles as if to kill them. David walked some feet away, so as not to get splashed, and Billy had to shout in order to tell him the story of how a graveyard in Pocoima had flooded, dredging coffins up out of the ground and floating them down the street like boats. David pretended to believe him, because it was easier than arguing.

They reached the Plaza, which stood like an island city in the middle of its own flooded parking lot. It was buttressed at either end by a Sears and a Penney's, twin buildings of salmon-colored brick, and between them were arcaded walkways lined with lesser stores. David and Billy crossed the parking lot and walked into the arcade, shoulders loose, hands sunk deep in their pockets. David tossed his head to flick the hair out of his eyes, an involuntary gesture he feared might be girlish. He tried to imagine Billy doing it, and couldn't, though Billy's hair was identical to his, a great swoop that extended from a high side part to the opposite ear. David's was always coming untucked from behind his ear and hanging down over his face with an annoying, slothlike life of its own.

The two of them walked the Plaza, checking it out. Things were quiet, mostly mothers out shopping with their kids. The rain had soaked everything. The wood slat benches were dark as maple syrup and the juniper bushes, planted in boxes full of cedar chips, looked drowned. The concrete was covered with the fat limp bodies of worms, some of them big as cigars. A little girl walked on tiptoe among them, screaming.

"I say, bit of a quiet here, eh?" David said, then remembered Billy didn't want to play Mystery anymore.

"Yeah," Billy said. He shouldered an imaginary rifle and shot the little girl, making soft hissing noises with his teeth, like candles being dropped into water. The little girl hopped and shrieked over the worms.

"What do you want to do?" David asked in a deeper voice.

"Kill our enemies," Billy said. He kept the little girl in the sights of his rifle. "We can climb up on the roof of the Penney's and get them in the parking lot."

"How would we get on the roof?"

Billy shot the little girl again, and she sensed it. She stopped jumping around and stared at him. David could imagine what she saw, a miniature soldier standing in combat position, feet planted wide, invisible weapon raised. The little girl stared, not so much afraid as dumbfounded.

"Let's go goof on the people at the Rexall," David said.

"Okay," Billy said. He shot the girl one more time. She watched him incredulously, her head cocked like a bird's.

David and Billy walked to the Rexall and went inside, passing through a stainless-steel turnstile which permitted entry but no exit. The Rexall was full of hard white light, its ceiling lined with luminous panels which gave out a constant faint electrical crackle.

"See any suspicious characters lurking about?" David said, and bit his tongue. In the thin, rubber-scented air of the store he was suddenly aware of Billy's particular smell, a mix of cut grass and gasoline.

"Fuck me," Billy said. "Suspicious characters everywhere."

"How about if we split up and meet halfway? You take the right side, I'll take the left."

"Okay."

"Meet in the shampoo aisle in ten minutes with a full report."

Billy sneered and started off down his designated aisle.

David went to the opposite end of the store. Dead, it was dead today. An old lady browsed the laxatives, which was funny but not good enough to follow up on. A woman in curlers hollered at her baby in a grousing, usual way. David strolled the aisles, looking for someone to be interested in.

When he reached the fourth aisle, he saw a woman who had possibilities. She was thirty or so, with livid yellow hair that had probably been dyed. She wore a red coat, and stood with her weight on one hip, tapping her chin with a long red fingernail. She was looking over a shelf full of rat poisons. David kept on walking, and when he was down the aisle and out of the woman's sight he hurried to find Billy.

"Hey," he said.

"What's going on?" Billy said. He stood in the middle of the housewares aisle with his arms pressed in close to his body, huddled into himself as if he was trying to shrink.

"I believe I've found a woman in a bad predicament," David said. He couldn't help talking in the accent. Any other way of speaking to Billy felt puny and wrong.

"So?"

"She is plainly suicidal. I'd suggest we put a tail on her."

"Hey, forget about that shit."

"What?"

Billy glanced behind, and then leaned in toward David, exhaling a waft of his own odor. His eyes trembled, seemed to be filling with tears. "I've got an Imperial yo-yo in my pocket," he whispered.

"Come on," David said in a lowered voice. "Let's not steal."

"The hell you say. I'm going back for another yo-yo."

"What do you need two of them for?"

"It's easy. There's nobody around."

"I don't want to steal."

"Then don't. Faggot."

"Okay, I won't."

"Okay. See you, faggot."

David turned and walked away, back down the aisle. As he went his hair flopped down over his eyes and he tossed it back automatically, with the same questionable flip of his head. His face burned, and for the remainder of the distance he had some trouble walking. Suddenly his walk felt wrong, and he tried to change it, putting more flex into his knees and turning his toes farther out. It had a certain cowboy quality and struck him as a success.

He checked for the woman at the display of rat poison, but she was no longer there. The shelf before which she'd stood was lined with small yellow boxes, and on each box was a cartoon of a rat laid out on his back, with X's for eyes, and a lily clutched between its claws. He picked up a box and turned it over. On the back side was a black skull and crossbones, with a warning against human consumption. He returned the box to the shelf and set off looking for the woman.

He found her two aisles farther down, contemplating the bath salts. This time, he could get a better look at her face. She had once been pretty. She had the high expectant forehead and shallow chin of a cheerleader. Her face was pitted and ravaged, though, the eyes outlined in black, her bleached hair pulled down in jagged bangs to her brows. She checked over the bath salts with sour efficiency, and held a box of the poison in her hand. As David passed he saw part of the black skull, grinning, from between her glossy red fingernails.

He went and stood by the check-out counter, waiting for her. He took a *True Detective* from the rack and leafed through it. "Woman Held Prisoner Seven Weeks in Bedroom." The grainy photograph showed a puffy-faced woman with a trench coat thrown over her shoulders, weeping in the arms of a rescuing officer, being led from a cottage as cheerful looking as the yellow box of rat poison, with flowered curtains visible in one window.

The girl at the cash register was called Wendy, according to the badge she wore on her blue Rexall smock. David saw her there nearly every day. She might have been fifteen, sixteen at most, and he could tell from the way her thin pale hands darted and trembled that she was in some kind of trouble. Something in the way her fingers hovered over the buttons of the register, nervous as hummingbirds, and in the quick practiced smile that faded the instant a customer's back was turned. She had a helmet of perfect hair that came to two hooklike curls, one on each cheek. Every day David came to the Plaza, he bought a pack of Teaberry gum, and every day she rang up his purchase, handed over the change, and dropped a length of cash-register receipt on the counter.

He stood by the register waiting for the woman with the poison, his eyes skating back and forth between Wendy and the story of the woman who'd been kept prisoner (by her husband, a fat hairless man in a Hawaiian shirt, handcuffed, flanked by detectives). Wendy rang up a pair of tweezers for an old man, slipped them into a waxed paper bag, smiled cheerlessly. David turned the pages of *True Detective*. "Dead Baby Found in Bus Locker." An attendant had heard faint cries, but thought it must be rats. A stupid, lazy man. He could have been a hero.

The woman with the poison stepped up to the register. David slid the *True Detective* back into the rack, picked up a pack of gum, and stood behind her. She smelled of magnolia, a slightly fermented odor. In addition to the poison she was buying bath salts, hair spray, and a package of cocktail napkins. She paid with a twenty-dollar bill. She scowled over her own purchases as Wendy counted out the change and said, "Thank you, come again." Wendy tucked the articles into a bag, and the woman left the store.

David paid hurriedly for his gum. Wendy took his money, smiled, tossed the receipt on the counter. He flipped the gum in his palm, dropped it, picked it up again, and took off after the woman with the poison.

She was walking down the arcade at a fast clip, arms swinging tightly at her sides. David trailed along, keeping himself a good twenty paces behind. When she stopped before the Stride-Rite store, he lingered over a window one shop down, a family of cavorting mannequins done up in snowsuits, their immobile faces haloed with spiky fur, the soles of their boots buried in fake snow that had a wicked crystalline gleam to it, like shaved glass.

When the woman moved on, David moved on too. He paused in front of the shoe store, positioning himself just where she'd stood, trying to see what she'd seen. The window was full of shoes, lined up on graduated green-felt risers like the feet of a chorus. He wondered what exactly had caught her eye. Maybe when she was younger, she'd worn shoes similar to a pair here. There on the highest platform stood a pair of delicate white high-heel shoes, similar to the ones she had on but airier, the toes cut out into vees and lined with a band of silver, the backs held to the ankle by thin straps. He could imagine the woman in her youth, going to parties, dancing and laughing, walking home barefoot after midnight across damp front lawns with her head on a boy's shoulder and the shoes dangling from her hand. He followed her on down the arcade, toward the parking lot, watching her shoes click smartly along on the concrete. He began to wonder if maybe she could be saved.

Under her makeup and bleached hair she was still pretty in an eroded way. The damage could be scrubbed away with soap and hot water. She might just have needed a friend, someone to talk to at night. He could imagine himself sitting with her at a kitchen table, after she'd washed her makeup off, strands of damp hair plastered to her rosy skin. He'd nod judiciously as she talked and talked, the bitterness slipping off her like twine from a package. His nostrils seemed to fill with brine. He walked faster, willing something to happen. The woman had stepped out into the parking lot, skirting the puddles. She pulled car keys from her purse. David stopped at the sidewalk, to gather himself. The woman looked back over her shoulder.

She noticed him. Her hard eyes flicked over his face, and she kept on walking. She unlocked the door of an immaculate white Pinto. David stood pretending to look for somebody who was late picking him up. He tapped his foot and crossed his arms impatiently. The woman backed her car out and pulled away.

David lingered for a while, still tapping his foot, waiting for no one, until the worst of the embarrassment had worn off. Then he went back to the Rexall to pick up Billy.

As he approached he saw there was a commotion going on in front. He had hoped so long for an incident, any incident, that he was a moment in actually seeing it. The scene would not assemble itself. A bald man in a brown suit had Billy by the shoulders and was shaking him in an urgent way, as if trying to rouse him from sleep. Billy's head waggled loosely on his shoulders, his arms hung at his sides. A guard in a blue uniform so dark and new it looked black was jogging up from the far end of the arcade, his neck stiff and his knees pumping. David thought at first that Billy was hurt, then realized he'd been caught stealing.

The guard reached Billy well before David did. As David drew closer he could hear the bald man saying, "—learn a thing or two. People work hard for their money around here, and we don't appreciate it when other people—" Billy had gone limp, his eyes clouded and his jaw loose. David stood to the side of him, just beyond his line of vision.

"Got a little trouble here?" the guard asked.

"Gentleman seems to think he's entitled to what other people have to pay for," the bald man said.

"Well, well. Is that right?" the guard said to Billy. Billy looked at him stupidly, as if he were speaking a foreign language. It seemed to David that this was Billy's punishment for being rude and selfish. This is what you get, he thought.

"Well, let's just see," the guard said. He squatted and dipped his hand into the pocket of Billy's fatigue jacket. He pulled out a yo-yo, which he handed proudly to the bald man.

To accept it the man had to release one of Billy's shoulders, and David thought for a moment Billy would crumple to the ground. Several other people had gathered to watch, middle-aged women and a toddler in red overalls who stared with such open-mouthed rapture that a thread of saliva dropped from his lower lip and dangled an inch above his knees. The guard produced another yo-yo, and another. He held each one aloft for a moment, before the eyes of the spectators, like a grim magician. David heard one of the women make a clucking noise with her tongue. She had a beehive of white hair, and carried a purse decorated with straw bananas. The saliva bead quivered at the kid's knees. David was waiting for it to gather a bit more weight and hit the kid's miniature tennis shoe.

The guard continued to explore Billy's pockets. He offered up for the crowd's consideration a packet of batteries, a mother-of-pearl switch plate edged in brass, a roll of black electrician's tape, and a night-light done up like Popeye, with a yellow plastic pipe protruding from the blank pink ridge of the jaw. David thought, with a certain shock, of how Billy would have sneered at those things if they'd been gifts.

The guard's face was mottled gray, etched with lines so deep they seemed to touch bone, and with the appearance of each new article he mugged a little more for the audience, his small eyes rolling and his brows creeping up toward the shelf of his hair. Billy must have gone into a frenzy of stealing, so exalted by the easiness of it he took anything that fit his pockets. The bald man's square red hand remained planted on Billy's shoulder, and Billy's head lolled to one side.

David glanced over at the glass door of the Rexall and saw Wendy, her cash register abandoned, watching the arrest. She stood hugging herself, and she watched the conjuring of Billy's thefts with pleased fascination.

The last thing the guard pulled out was the horseshoe crab. He turned it over doubtfully in his hand, decided it wasn't merchandise, and slipped it back into Billy's pocket. He said to the bald man, "I'll take him in and call his parents. Can you come along?" "You bet I can," the man replied zestfully, as though he were agreeing to a swim on a hot day. He held Billy's loot cradled in his free arm.

The two men collared Billy and turned him. He stumbled, as if his shoes were too big for him. When the guard steered him around he faced David for the first time. Billy looked at David with blank, terrified eyes.

"Wait a minute," David said in the direction of the guard, but it was weak and useless as throwing sand. The guard seemed not to hear him at all. Billy's upper lip curled back from his teeth, so David could see the full length of his serrated incisors, poking from his purplish gums. Billy hoisted the imaginary rifle, aimed it at David's head, and shot. *Pshiew,* the sputtering sound of the bullet. David felt it, a nervous raw tickle in the center of his forehead. The guard prodded Billy along, and for a moment the guard looked like everything good in the world—order, strength, the rescue of the innocent. Billy let himself be led away. He walked with surer steps, as if he had found the inspiration he needed. David watched him go, two heads shorter than his captors, marching heroically off to the enemy camp.

When they had gone, the woman with the beehive said, "I hope they throw the book at him." Another made the clucking sound with her tongue. A third woman picked up the toddler and carried him off in the crook of her arm. David looked over at Wendy, who was returning to work. In seconds the episode was erased, the witnesses disbanded.

He walked back home. The sky was rising but still white, a deep empty bowl. A bird sliced by overhead, its wings stationary, like an iron cutout riding a wire. Why did he shoot *me?* David thought. He wondered if he should have done something more to help Billy. But what could he have done? How did he slip over into the wrong?

A breeze blew spangles of water from a tree, and one

plopped cold on the back of David's neck. For a moment, he thought the rain was starting up again. An image appeared in his mind, clear as memory. He saw the houses sunk to their rooftops in thick yellow water, sticks of furniture twirling in the currents, the people all drowned, and only the dogs strong enough to swim to safety.

3

Mom made a fancy dinner, to celebrate Janet's not getting married. She set the table in the dining room, with a tablecloth and candles and a silver bowl full of fruit. Green apples, dusty plums, nectarines big as a man's fist, grapes that cascaded over the sides, dangling before their own elliptical reflections. The fruit was piled so high that a nectarine fell from the top as everybody was sitting down. It rolled across the table and landed on the carpet.

"Too much of a good thing," Mom said. She picked up the nectarine and placed it more firmly in the arrangement.

"What is this, lamb?" Lizzie said, "Yuck."

"You like lamb," Mom told her.

"I do not," Lizzie said, lifting her chin. She gave all three words equal stress.

"You liked it last month," Mom said.

"I do not like lamb. I will just eat vegetables."

"Why don't you eat yourself?" David said.

"It looks delicious, Mother," Janet said.

"Thank you."

"Lizzie thinks she's a princess," David announced to Mom

and Janet. "She thinks we're just raising her until the queen comes to pick her up. I heard her say so."

"You did not," Lizzie said.

"I have ears," David told her. "You talk to yourself." It was true. He had heard her in the bathroom a couple of days earlier, whispering, "Oh Mother, I pray you, take me away to my home for I cannot bear to live any longer with natives and criminals."

"I do not," she said, with surprising calm. It wasn't long since something like that would have sent her screaming from the table.

"Enough, you two," Mom said. "Janet, I hope you still like yours medium rare."

"Janet is a vegetarian," Lizzie said. She was developing a scrupulously even tone, as if her voice was a scraper peeling potatoes.

"Was, baby," Janet said. "I gave it up."

Lizzie raised her chin another notch. "Why?" she asked.

"Well, I've been trying to give up a lot of things lately."

"Rob never called, did he?" Mom said.

"No." Janet tucked a wisp of hair behind her ear. Her fingernails were bitten down, raw and bloody looking around the edges. "He will, though. I have a feeling the phone's going to ring any minute."

"Where is Rob?" Lizzie asked.

"He's still in San Francisco, baby," Janet said. "He's keeping the home fires burning."

"Why aren't you getting married?" Lizzie asked.

"Don't ask stupid questions," David told her.

"No, it's okay," Janet said. "I'm not getting married because, well, I don't think I could marry Rob and get into medical school both. I think part of the reason I didn't get in the first time is that Rob makes me feel too comfortable. So I'm setting out to get less comfortable." She laughed. "God, that doesn't make much sense, does it?"

"Yes it does," David said.

"Oh no, it doesn't," Janet said. "I know nonsense when I hear it."

"I understand," Lizzie said.

"No you don't," David told her.

She looked at him coldly. "Do you know what seven times seven is?" she said.

"Don't do that," he said.

"It's forty-nine."

"Mom, Lizzie keeps asking multiplication questions and doesn't give me time to think of the answer. She just knows because they're *doing* multiplication now, and I haven't done it for two years."

"Do you know what six times eight is?" Lizzie said. David put his fingers in his ears and closed his eyes. Mom said something to him.

"What?" he asked her, pulling the finger from one ear cautiously as you'd draw the cork from a champagne bottle.

"Forty-eight," Lizzie shouted. David jammed the finger back in his ear.

The telephone rang. "I think it's probably for me," Janet said. She folded her napkin and went into the kitchen. She didn't pick up the phone until the sixth ring.

"Hello? Hi." Her voice was muffled by the two slatted, swinging doors that led from the dining room to the kitchen.

"Lizzie tells people she was born in London," David said to Mom.

"I was born in London," Lizzie said.

Mom sat still, her fork tilted in her hand, her head cocked toward the door.

"She was born in Glendale, right?" David said.

"No. We've already talked," Janet said in the kitchen.

"Mom, tell her," David said.

"I was pregnant with you in London, honey," Mom said. "But by the time you got around to being born, we were back in California."

"I remember London," Lizzie said, which overrode a sentence of Janet's that had begun, "I don't want—"

"You couldn't," David said. "You were never there."

"I was there."

"Mom?"

"Please stop that," Janet said. "You know how easy it is to make me feel guilty."

"You were there in spirit, honey," Mom said.

"I remember the Tower of London," Lizzie said. "There were little windows, and you could see a river through them."

"That's funny," Mom said. "I did look out a window in the Tower of London when I was carrying you."

"She just saw it in a movie or something," David said.

"There was a boat coming down the river," Lizzie said. "With red smokestacks and a man in a black hat who waved to us."

"Oh, I don't know," Mom said. "I don't remember."

"Do you know," Janet said, "you've used the word *owe* three times in the last two minutes? I don't think I owe you anything."

"We also went to Buckingham Palace," Lizzie said. "One of the guards fainted."

"—any more tonight. Good-bye," Janet said. After a moment she came back into the dining room, running the fingers of one hand lightly over her hair. She smiled, tight-lipped, and sat down at her place.

"Everything all right?" Mom asked her.

"Oh yes. Everything is fine." She smiled down at her plate, at the serving of pink lamb.

"What did he say?" Mom asked.

"He's just a little upset, is all. A man naturally gets upset when his bride-to-be leaves him with a note propped up against the salt and pepper shakers. You know, I don't think I'm very hungry after all. Would you mind if I excused myself and took a little walk?"

"It's dark out," David said.

"I know. I'll be back soon." Still smiling, she got up and walked out of the house.

"I hope she'll be all right out there," Mom said.

"Do you want me to follow her?" David asked.

The telephone rang again. Mom got up to answer it. "No, better leave her be," she said on the way to the kitchen. "I'm sure she'll be back in a few minutes."

David thought maybe he should go anyway. He sat jiggling his legs, uncertain about whether or not to disobey. He looked over at Lizzie, who squinted at him as if he were too small to see clearly.

"No she isn't, Rob," Mom said from the kitchen. "She just stepped out."

David and Lizzie sat listening.

"Well, I don't know," Mom said. "For a little walk, is all. Yes, I'll tell her. Of course. Bye."

David jumped up and ran for the front door. He would stay well behind Janet, hugging the shadows, so she'd never know she was being watched.

Mom called his name, but he got to the door before her voice reached his ears. He had made it, technically. He slammed the door behind him and hoped the gesture would somehow offend Lizzie without offending Mom.

The street was dazzlingly lit, by lamps designed to look old-fashioned, loaded with bulbs so bright it was painful to look into their square, spired housings. The lamps set up a ceiling of light that dimmed the sky and closed the neighborhood in. Lights burned in windows across the street, amber for reading and blue for television.

David crossed over the front yard and peered, cautiously, up and down the street. He could not see her in either direction. He walked a couple of blocks up, and a couple down. She was nowhere. From far away, in the black folds of the hills, a coyote howled. He hated being out alone at night.

He checked again for her. She seemed to have disappeared. Finally he went back home, because he couldn't think of anything else to do.

He paused in front of the house, struck by the hooded shadows the row of miniature pine trees cast against the wall. The Starks' house was Spanish, like all the others in the neighborhood, its rough plaster walls painted the color of a manila envelope. Its red-tiled roof rose to a high off-center peak— inside the slanted living-room ceiling was two stories high, shot through with specks of silver glitter. The houses on either side were not half so nice, and even the one three houses down, which was the same as the Starks', lacked some of the special details they had added over the years. Their front walk was lined with flowers, big brightly colored daisies like the ones in old cartoons that grew leafy arms and legs and did a little dance; by the front door, over the square white doorbell, the family name was spelled out in blue letters on white tiles. A black iron eagle had been nailed above the door, and on the stoop lay a green welcome mat, with three daisies in the upper right-hand corner.

David went inside. "Did you find her?" Mom asked as he entered the dining room.

"No," he said. He had hesitated too long again and failed to be of use to anybody.

"Well, I'm sure she'll be all right," Mom said. "Sit down and finish your ice-cold dinner."

"Lamb," Lizzie said. "Yuck." She speared a sprig of cauliflower with her fork and held it an inch from her mouth. Then she opened her mouth to the exact size of the cauliflower bud, and popped it in.

"What's the difference between Lizzie and a pig?" David said.

"Sit. Eat," Mom told him.

The telephone rang. "I'll get it," David said. He sprinted for the kitchen, and picked up the receiver in the middle of the second ring.

"Hello?"

"David?" A deep voice, crinkled with static.

"Uh-huh."

"This is Rob."

"Hi, Rob."

"Is Janet back yet?"

"No."

"Do you know where she went?"

"No. She went out."

"Tell her something for me, would you, David? Tell her I'll keep calling until I talk to her, every half hour. All night if I have to. Will you tell her that?"

"Okay."

"Good boy."

David sucked in a deep breath. "Don't call her anymore, Rob, she doesn't want to talk to you," he said, and immediately hung up.

Mom was standing in the doorway. "You shouldn't have said that." She stood with her arms folded over her chest. He noticed her arms. Freckled on top, dead white on their undersides, the flesh so soft it favored whatever direction she leaned in. Her thin black watchband bit into the softness at her wristbone.

"I'm sorry," he said.

"My only wish in this whole world right now is for you to go back in there and eat your lamb. Would you do that for me?"

"Okay," he said. He went back into the dining room and said to Lizzie, "The answer is, a pig at least is worth some money."

———

After dinner, he went upstairs and walked softly into Mom's room, avoiding the places in the hall where the floor creaked. Mom's room was not expressly forbidden, but it opened off the dead end of the hall, and there was rarely any reason for going there. Even Mom stayed out of it, lingering downstairs over television until it was time to sleep. Any furnishing that wore out in another part of the house found its way to Mom's room. She had the old watercolors of London hanging still in their chipped blond frames, and the lamps with the Mexican shades, and the chair covered in scratchy green material which, as far as David knew, had not been sat on since it left the living room back in kindergarten. He entered the room with a feeling of abashed humility, the way he would enter an abandoned, walled garden.

The room was dark. David tiptoed to Mom's dresser and pulled out the top drawer, careful not to let it squeak. A cloud of Mom's smell rose like a ghost—her perfume and an under-layer of something sweet and old, like bread gone moldy. In this drawer were stacks of Mom's white underwear, which gave off a hint of light. In the next drawer were sweaters, woolly and neutral-smelling, like a dream of sheep.

The pistol was in the nightstand. The Starks had had it for years, since Dad first brought it home in first grade. It moved from one place to another around the house and finally came to rest here, in the nightstand, after Dad moved out. It had in a way ceased to exist, since no one had spoken about it in years. It simply edged itself into Mom's room like other household objects. David wasn't even sure whether he was supposed to know about it. He did know about it, and checked every so often to make certain it hadn't moved. It lay on its side along with a bottle of aspirin, a yellow envelope full of negatives, a green, spiral-bound memo pad, a half dozen pens and pencils, and a deck of playing cards, held together with a dirty blue rubber band.

The pistol was a dull licorice black, with a surprisingly

slender barrel and a short, nubbly handle. David knew its qualities only by sight. He had never touched it. It had too much slumbering life for that.

He heard movement from downstairs. Lizzie's voice, saying something sour and unintelligible, grew nearer. He hurriedly closed the drawer and crept back to his own room, where he dropped onto the bed and lay waiting for the sound of Janet coming back. He lay with his hands clasped behind his neck, a posture he had borrowed from Gonzo on "Trapper John" and was trying out for himself. On the ceiling hung a *National Geographic* map of the galaxy, saggy at the middle, edged with yellowed tape. A rectangle of starry night sky. Dad had put it up there for him, years ago.

That was before Dad pushed him down the stairs. He knew because he remembered looking up at these same stars when they brought him home from the hospital with the stitches in his head. Dad and Mom had been fighting in their bedroom, and David had stood in the hall listening. He remembered something being said about Janet. Dad threw open the door yelling, "Stupid goddamn lies." David screamed and then he was falling down the stairs. His forehead when it hit the banister made a sound like biting into an ice cube.

That had been years ago. After school got out next month, David and Lizzie would fly to Spokane to spend another three weeks with Dad and his new wife, Marie. Dad was kind to them when they visited. He wore plaid shirts and blue jeans. He had a new laugh, sudden as a spring popping out of a box. David treated him with the wary respect he'd show to a piece of large, dangerous-looking machinery, the precise function of which was unknown.

Time passed. David knew he should be doing homework. On the top of his desk sat a map of California, made of papier-mâché, yellow-green in a brilliant blue ocean. He had become famous with his sixth-grade teacher for his elaborately illustrated book reports and minutely detailed maps and was currently in the process of gluing on cotton balls, real kumquats, and the bearded heads of foxtails to represent crops. With each success, he worried more deeply that the next project would be a failure.

Instead of working on the map he lay listening, aware of his heart and his breathing. He unzipped his pants and started to beat off. When he beat off, his brain shut down completely, and after he finished it was like coming out of a tunnel back into daylight. It left him dazzled and disoriented. He didn't really like doing it but he started doing it now; then he stopped for fear Lizzie might hear him. He lay with his hands folded on his chest, listening to the night. For years he had thought of the map on his ceiling as a map of the universe, until Janet told him that it only charted the galaxy, one tiny piece of all there was. Although he didn't doubt her word, he still thought of it as a map of the universe.

Finally he heard something at his window, a sound so faint it was hardly sound at all but more an agitation of the air, like the whirr of a moth's wings under a lampshade in the next room. He got up to look out the window. Janet sat in the back-yard smoking a cigarette, a small ember that flared and sub-sided.

He walked out of his room and went downstairs. Mom and Lizzie were in the living room watching "Diff'rent Strokes." David walked by unnoticed, went through the kitchen and out the back door.

Janet was sitting in one of the redwood lawn chairs, facing the house, on the thin band of grass that lay between house and pool. Behind her the pool stretched motionless, silver, giving back the sky and the scalloped top of the fence that separated the Starks' property from their neighbors'. The tip of Janet's cigarette hung suspended before her mouth.

"Hello," she said, exhaling a stream of luminous smoke.

"Hi," David said. He went and sat in the empty chair beside

her. The slats were damp and pulpy, and he ran his fingernails experimentally along the arms.

"I was looking up at your window and thinking about you," she said. "And here you are."

"Did you go for a walk?" he asked.

"Well, I didn't manage the walk after all," she said. "I got about two houses down and I came right back here to our own backyard. I've been listening to the phone ring."

"He's called four times," David said.

"I know. He'll call all night if I don't come and answer it. I will, the next time it rings."

"Okay."

She stubbed her cigarette out in the grass, and put the dead butt into her shirt pocket. "I'm not a very good example to you, am I?" she said.

"Yes you are," he told her.

"Sitting out here like a refugee. It's a good thing I brought my cigarettes. You must never start smoking, David, because if you do it will ruin most of your best exits. Half the time you've left your cigarettes behind, and you've got to go back for them."

"Oh," he said.

"Don't mind my blithering. It's nerves, is all."

"Uh-huh," David said.

She pulled her knees up to her chest and dug at a kneecap with her thumbnail. "I'm just afraid I'm going to lose my mind again, is all. I'm making it my spring project not to lose my mind."

"Are you still worried about Ray?" David asked.

"Well, I'd damn well better get over it if I am. It's been fourteen years. And three psychiatrists. You don't have bad dreams anymore, do you?"

"No," David said. Back when he first heard the story of Ray getting hit by the van, he'd had dreams so strange Mom and

Dad took him to a doctor, a woman with her hair pulled back in a thick gray braid. He didn't remember much about the doctor. He did remember that her office was in a children's hospital, where he saw kids no older than he being wheeled down the hallways on carts. He had worried ever since about getting sick.

"Good," Janet said. "You shouldn't even *know* about a thing like that. It isn't fair, a kid your age."

This turn in the conversation made him uncomfortable. He didn't like people talking about taking his knowledge away.

"Look up there," he said, to change the subject. "There's the Great Waldo."

This was an old game. They made up constellations because they didn't know the real ones. "Where?" Janet said.

"See that bright, bright star over there?"

"Which one?"

"Over there." He pointed, squinting one eye and laying his finger on the star.

"Okay. I think I know the one you mean."

"That's the tip of his hat."

"Mm-hm."

"Then his body kind of curves around."

"To the left. I see it."

"No. To the right."

"To the right? There's a tree in the way."

"Are you sure you're looking at the right star? His hat isn't by the tree."

"I don't know, maybe I'm not. I'm going to smoke a joint, do you mind?"

"No."

She took a joint from her shirt pocket and lit a match. Her face in the match glare was like an old photo in an album, and he could imagine himself as an elderly man, looking at Janet's picture and saying, "Wasn't she beautiful?"

"Mom could see us from the kitchen," he said.

"She'd just think it's a cigarette."

He could smell the sweet smoke and see the pale gray thickness of it, drifting over her head. "Can I have a hit?" he said.

"Do you smoke dope?" Her voice was pinched, from holding the smoke in her lungs.

"Yes," David said.

She exhaled, a languid plume. "Since when?" she said.

"Since the middle of fifth grade," he said. It was not quite true. He and Billy had found a couple of joints in Billy's brother's drawer, along with a bone-handled knife and a roll of money. They'd thought about smoking one, but Billy said that Carl, his brother, would probably kill them. Carl had a half dozen uncured snakeskins tacked to the wall over his bed. They had left the joints in the drawer.

"Is that right?" Janet said. "Damn. They get younger and younger. In fifth grade, I was still playing Barbies."

"When did you smoke for the first time?"

"Let me think. High school. Tenth grade."

"I remember you in high school," he said.

"You were pretty little then."

"You were in the science club."

"Well, I pretended to be. The truth is, I was sneaking off to smoke dope with Margie and Luanne."

"What happened to Margie and Luanne?"

"Well, they got married. They sort of faded away."

"Oh. Can I have a hit now?" David said.

"Sure. Is Mother standing at the window?"

"No."

"Okay. Here." She passed him the joint. He pinched it between thumb and forefinger, as he'd seen her do, put it to his lips, and sucked in the smoke, which filled his mouth. He swallowed it, automatically, and coughed it back up. His eyes burned. The smoke hovered for a moment in a rough crescent, and vanished.

"Strong stuff," he said.

"Try another hit," she said. "Pull it straight into your lungs, don't hold it in your mouth."

"I know."

"Okay."

He tried again, drawing the smoke in like oxygen. It seared his lungs but he held it, then let it go in a whoosh.

"Good boy," Janet said. He handed it back, and she took a long, deep drag. The tip glowed, firing its finger of white ash. "Hey look," Janet said. "There's Homunculus the Crow."

"Where?"

"See that big star by the TV antenna?"

"Yeah."

"That's the tip of his beak."

"Okay. And there's his eye."

"No, he doesn't have an eye."

"Yes he does."

"Where are you looking?"

"Right over there. Straight up from the chimney."

"Oh, that's not his head at all. His head isn't half that big."

"Can I have another hit?"

"Sure."

"Where's his body, then?"

"See those two stars over the Munsons' roof?"

"No."

"A little one and a much brighter one."

"I guess."

"That's the spat on his left foot."

David, who had no idea what a spat was, said, "Oh yeah, I see," and gave her back the joint.

"Are you getting stoned?" Janet asked him.

"Yes," he said, though he wasn't sure. A tightness had crept up into his head, and he thought that when he looked straight ahead at the house it loomed big as an ocean liner, its windows blazing. It was hard to tell, when he didn't know what he was waiting for.

"It's subtle," Janet said. "This particular stuff, it just sort of creeps up on you. It makes things funny and a little remote, like you're watching your life from a safe distance."

"I think I feel that," David said.

They sat for a while, looking for constellations. David thought he heard it again, the sound that was no sound, the flutter of the moth's wings.

"Are you thinking about me right now?" he asked.

"Mm-hm," she said. "Why do you ask?"

"I don't know. I guess I must be stoned."

"It's not like what you expect it to be."

"Janet?" he said.

"What?"

He couldn't think what he had to tell her. It had to do with his own actual size, which was bigger than his body. She was safe with him.

"Never mind," he said.

"No, what? Wait a minute, is that Lizzie there?"

"Where?"

"Right there at the back door."

"Is the joint out?" David asked.

"Yes."

"Go back inside, Lizzie," he called.

"No," Lizzie said. She stood in the doorway for a moment, then walked onto the grass. Her blue nightgown shone, as if she were bringing the light of the house outside with her. "What are you doing?" she said.

"Watching the stars," Janet told her.

"Aren't you supposed to be in bed?" David said.

Lizzie positioned herself between their two chairs, spine erect, hands clasped over her belly. The pool was bright behind her. She still couldn't swim; she refused to learn. Whenever

Mom tried to teach her she would pull herself out the first time she got a nose full of water and stand red-faced on the coping, screaming about how she'd never wanted to learn in the first place. If Dad were still around he'd have picked her up and thrown her back in. That was probably why Mom never did. Although it was ridiculous for Lizzie to live in danger of drowning in her own backyard, David had a grudging respect for her determination not to know anything she didn't want to know.

"Mom is all alone in the house," Lizzie said, as if the idea was funny.

"Yes she is," Janet said. "She's going to think her children have all run away."

"I am going to run away," Lizzie said.

"And go where?" David said.

"Nowhere."

"The next time it rains, you're going to get *washed* away," he said.

"Shut up, you asshole." She was afraid of floods too.

"Hey look, you two," Janet said. "There's the Fat Lady of Fargo."

"Where?" Lizzie said.

"Right there. Right up over our heads."

"I see her," David said.

"I see her too," Lizzie said.

"You do not."

"I do. Those three stars over there are her crown."

"I'll be damned," Janet said. "How did you know she had a crown?"

"I can *see,*" Lizzie said.

They all kept quiet for a while, watching the sky. David could not see anything but the usual pinwheels, belts, triangles. "I see her too," he said.

"She's great big," Lizzie said. "Her head is way over by the Munsons' roof."

"Yes it is," Janet said.

"Right," David said. "She's huge."

"And she doesn't have anything on," Lizzie giggled.

"No she doesn't" Janet said. "This is really amazing, Lizzie."

"My feet are cold," Lizzie said.

"Well, I guess we'd better get back inside," Janet said.

"Not yet," David said. "Look, the lady has flowers in her hand."

Janet and Lizzie glanced at one another. "What's nine times seven?" Lizzie asked.

David put his fingers in his ears. "Don't do that," he said, and his voice sounded to him as if he was speaking from a cave. Janet said something, and he unstopped his ears. "What?" he asked her.

"My *feet* are cold," Lizzie said.

"Then go inside. What did you say, Janet?"

"Let's all go in," Janet said.

"That's not what you said."

"Men," Janet said to Lizzie, in a lofty, lecturer's tone, "always want the facts."

"That's not true," David said.

Janet patted his knee. "Come on," she said. "Let's get the lizard inside before she freezes to death."

"Don't call me that," Lizzie said. She had begun hopping on one foot, and shivering.

"Go on," David said. "I'm going to sit here a little longer."

He hoped Janet would send Lizzie in alone, but she got up and slipped her arm around Lizzie's skinny shoulders. "Okay," she said. "See you inside."

"See you," David said.

Lizzie tucked her hand under Janet's belt, glanced over her shoulder, smiled knowingly, and said, "Sixty-three."

James Watt, the secretary of the interior, said we might as well use things up because Jesus was coming anyway, and it would be a shame to leave a lot behind. He was on the six o'clock news, talking from inside his large, immobile head.

Janet laughed, and sputtered cigarette smoke. She, Mom, and Lizzie sat in a row on the sofa, and David lay on the floor, with Watt's pink-orange face flickering on the screen before them.

"That's the best one yet," Janet said. "I still can't believe these men are in power. I keep thinking it'll turn out to be a joke."

"What assholes," Lizzie said.

"Lizzie," Mom said, "I don't know where you picked up this *asshole* business, but I think you'd better quit it."

"Yeah, Lizzie," David said. "You talk like a hooker."

"You look like a used Band-Aid," she told him.

"Enough," Mom said.

David turned back to the television. This morning, he had gone over to Billy's house to see if Billy was all right. Billy's house wasn't in the tract; it and half a dozen others sat in an isthmus of old lemon trees, with the tract on three sides. The air there was dim and sweet from the trees. Billy's house had a porch on which old, matted-looking easy chairs were lined up. Billy had been sitting on one of the chairs when David came up. Before they had a chance to speak Billy stood, raised his imaginary rifle, and shot David, again and again, notching the air with the hiss of his bullets. David had stood for a while, getting shot, then turned indignantly around and come back home.

On television, Watt finished talking. The camera switched over to Weinberger, who was talking to reporters about nuclear capability. He said too many of our bombs were planted in farmland, where the enemy could dig them out. He said we needed a more efficient system.

"The king of the assholes," Janet said.

"Please don't encourage Cattle Annie here," Mom said. "Jeez, how do these men get into office?"

"Elected by the public," Janet said. "Who did you vote for?"

"You know who I voted for. I just didn't think they'd be so . . . I don't know. At least Reagan's not as bad as Nixon."

"Nixon was the worst," David said. He thought he remembered Nixon, from years ago, when everything was as bad as it could be. Whenever he saw a picture of Nixon it gave him a nervous thrill, the same way pictures of Charlie Manson and Hitler did.

"Maybe we should think about moving to Switzerland," Janet said.

"I don't know about you," Mom said, "but I'm too old to learn Swiss."

"When I get older, I'm going to move to London," Lizzie said.

"They'll nuke London right off," David told her. "They'll just polish it off with a couple of extra bombs on their way to America."

"No they won't," Lizzie said. "They'll only nuke America and China and Russia."

"That's enough, both of you," Mom said.

"They won't nuke London, will they?" Lizzie asked.

"I don't know, sweetheart. No. The men in government don't want bombs any more than we do, I don't think."

"There's no point in lying, Mother," Janet said.

"They're going to nuke everybody," David said to Lizzie. "There's going to be nothing left."

"Shut up, you asshole," Lizzie said. She laid her head in Mom's lap. After a moment's hesitation she let the tip of her thumb creep into her mouth.

"Lizzie, I want you to clean up your act," Mom said, stroking her wiry red hair. "I'm serious."

"It must be hard to be ten in an age like this," Janet said.

"It's no picnic being forty-eight, either," Mom told her, smoothing and smoothing Lizzie's hair.

"Well, what can you do about it?" Janet said.

"Oh, I don't know. What can you do about anything?"

A few minutes later, the telephone rang.

"I think it's for me," Janet said. "I'm going to take it upstairs, all right?"

"If you want," Mom said.

Janet left the room. David heard the whisk of her feet on the carpeted stairs, and then the phone stopped ringing. He could hear the tone of her voice but couldn't distinguish the words.

He got up and sat on the sofa, on Mom's other side. He was worried that no one had contradicted him very sharply about nuking everybody, about there being nothing left. "Do you think Janet is scared of Rob?" he asked.

"Oh, no," Mom said. "Well, if she is, she'll get over it. That's what she's here for."

"I know," David said. Lizzie's head rose and fell slightly with Mom's breathing. On television, the news moved through weather and sports to the funny parts. An old woman in Florida showed the camera a ring of burned grass in her backyard, and said it marked the spot where a flying saucer had landed the night before.

"I was just doing up the dishes," she said in a strong, nasal voice, "and there it was." She wore glasses that came to points.

"It sort of glowed," she said, "and it was just hanging out there, don't you know, with the lights going on and off. It was, well, *beau*tiful, and I knew I ought to call Ed, that's my husband, but I just stood there watching it and I felt very, well, relaxed and happy. It was so peculiar. I thought, It can *see* me, don't you know, but I wasn't at all afraid. I felt wonderful. Then I opened my mouth to call Ed and *whoosh,* it was gone."

After everyone had gone to sleep David lay in bed, listening to the nocturnal sounds of the house. Darkness seemed to be the house's natural state. Lamplight hung in the rooms like smoke, resisting the corners, and when the last light was out the house relaxed into itself, the pipes grumbling.

In the hills, close by, coyotes yipped and howled. The rain had not driven them back. Now that they knew how much easy food could be had in the neighborhoods, they were not about to stay in the hills hunting rabbits.

It wasn't long before David heard Janet's door opening. He knew suddenly that the sound of her door was what he'd been expecting, though he hadn't known until he heard it. Janet walked along the hall, past his door. She went softly down the stairs, knowing to step over the fifth tread, which squeaked.

He let some time go by, then got out of bed. He took off his pajama jacket, changed his mind, and put it back on again. Before leaving his room he checked himself in the mirror. He couldn't make out his face clearly in the dark, but could tell that his hair wasn't sticking up at any peculiar angles.

The darkness in the stairwell was deeper and more velvety

than that of the hall, a dark within the dark. He walked down-stairs, stepping over the fifth tread. At the bottom he paused to listen. Janet was so silent he thought she must be hiding, hold-ing her breath. He strained into the still air, eyes wide, as if better vision would improve his hearing. His senses radiated out from him like needles of light, and it seemed that if any one was sharpened they would all grow stronger. Dining room, he decided.

She was sitting at the table in her usual place, smoking a cigarette. The tabletop glowed in the filtered moonlight like old ice. The bowl of fruit, black globes, sat in the middle.

"Hi," David said.

"You should be sleeping," she told him. Her voice was soft and a little too low.

David sat down at his own place. "What are you doing?" he asked.

"Just smoking a cigarette. Watching the wallpaper."

"Oh. Is it okay if I sit with you?"

"Sure."

"Can I have a drag of your cigarette?"

"You don't smoke cigarettes."

"Well, I do, sometimes."

"Sorry. I refuse to contribute."

"What did Rob tell you when he called?"

She blew out a stream of smoke, which hung palely and stretched itself toward the door before vanishing. "Oh, a lot of things," she said. "He still wants to get married."

"Oh."

"And it's all so crazy," she said. "People don't get married anymore anyway, I'll bet nobody else in Los Angeles County is sitting in a dark room right now worrying about marriage."

"They're not?" he said, because he couldn't think of any-thing else to say.

"No. If they're thinking about anything at all they're thinking about—I don't know. Issues. Or drugs. I don't have any idea what other people think about, to tell you the truth."

"You don't love Rob, do you?" David asked.

"That's a tricky question. I guess I always thought love would be more . . . *definite.*" She shook her head. "You like Rob, don't you?"

"Well, I guess so," David said. It was true; Rob was a nice enough man.

"You know," Janet said, "I used to look at him and think, My God, this is it. This is what twenty million American women would give their right arms for. A friendly lawyer with nice hands and scads of money, who loves me and wants to take care of me. This is the Great North American Thing." She dragged deeply on her cigarette. "I got to thinking, if I don't want *this,* what in the world *do* I want? Maybe I don't want anything at all."

"Oh," David said.

"Blithering again, huh?" Janet said. "I keep forgetting you're not thirty-five. What I decided to do, David, is live on my own and try getting into medical school again. Even if I'm not exactly brilliant."

"You are brilliant," he told her.

"I'm not. You may as well know the awful truth. I'm a solid B student, and B students don't ordinarily get to be doctors. But I'm going to study hard, and keep trying. Anyway, it's better than spending my life trying to talk myself into loving somebody."

"You'll meet somebody you love more than Rob," David said. "There are a lot of other people besides him."

"I guess I will. I know I will. Rob's just such a . . . Well, the second awful truth is, I'm not quite what the world calls pretty. I'm not what they're buying this year."

David looked at her and tried to imagine that she wasn't pretty. Although her face was obscured by darkness, he knew it so well he could project every detail from his head. Her nose was longer than most, but it concluded logically over her wide, thin lips. Every feature of hers made sense in terms of every other—her neck was thin, with three deep creases and a pair of cords at the base that moved when she spoke; her forehead rose high above her dark brows, as white and placid as her throat was nervous. Her eyes watched with amusement from pockets of brown-lavender skin that turned, like the colors of a shell, to the pale cream of her cheekbones. She and David looked something alike. There was no way she could not be pretty.

"You are," he told her. He'd meant to say, You are *pretty,* but the word embarrassed him.

"Thanks," she said. "I'm pretty to you. That's nice."

A silence caught, and held. A minute passed.

"Do you want to go to the movies with me after school tomorrow?" David asked.

"No, I don't think so. Thanks. I think I'll just stay around the house."

"Okay. Can't I have just one drag of your cigarette?"

"*No,*" she laughed, and ground the cigarette out in the ashtray. "I think I'll go for a walk."

"It's late."

"I know. That's the best time."

"Can I go with you?"

"No. It's a school night. You'd better go back to bed."

"Well. Okay. See you in the morning."

"Right. Sleep tight."

"Good night."

David left the room and went to the top of the stairs, where he sat down and waited for Janet to leave. This time he *would* follow her. He rested his forehead against the wrought-iron post, which was twisted like a birthday candle. The stairs dropped away beneath him; the house was built over an abandoned mine shaft. He saved himself by clinging to the banister, holding tight while the carpeted treads, still linked, dropped soundlessly into the pit.

This was where Dad had stood, enormous in a bathrobe, one side of which hung open to reveal the whole hairy length of his leg. The ends of the drawstring had hung down below his knees. Janet, who would have been much younger but who had always looked the same to David, had been going out and Dad had hollered to her that she wasn't going anywhere, she was going to stay home and stop slutting around. She'd said, Oh, fine, I'll stay here and slut around with you, and in David's memory Dad had jumped down the whole staircase, one big leap, robe flapping. Janet got the door half open and she and Dad were fighting or hugging in the doorway, there was no telling which. He could picture Janet biting Dad on the lip. A trickle of blood ran down Dad's chin and spotted his bathrobe. Dad had screamed like a woman. This was either just before or just after David was knocked down the stairs. He could not remember which. He could remember that Janet's purse had had fringe that flew in rhythm with her hair as she ran across the lawn, and that a silver car had been waiting for her out in the street.

It was some time around then that she had decided to be a doctor. During the divorce it was all she and Mom had talked about. They'd sent away for college catalogues, Mom insisting on Janet's applying to Berkeley because it was farther away than UCLA. Dad had started pulling up in front of the house at night and sitting there, silent, in his car. Everybody had pictured Janet in a white coat with a syringe, living up north, searching for cures.

David heard her get up with a tired sigh. He lifted his head eagerly to listen. A short silence. Then he heard her walk through the kitchen and go out the back door instead of the front.

He went to his room and looked out the window. Janet had gone to the edge of the pool and was standing with her back to the house, her head bent, looking into the water. The reflection of a streetlight, a false moon, rode skittishly on the surface. She unbuttoned her shirt and shrugged it off. As it fell it disappeared into the dark concrete. Her skin was so white it glowed. She pulled down her jeans and stepped out of them, balancing on one foot and then the other. Her panties were a brilliant white triangle that turned her skin suddenly to ivory. She swung her arms up over her head and dove, and seemed to take an unusually long time hitting the water. For a protracted moment she hung with her body arched, legs pressed together, the dark line between her thighs widening at her underpants. Then the water took her. Her head surfaced and she swam a steady determined crawl, from end to end and back again. David watched over her. Even through the glass he could hear the rhythm of her breathing, a ragged, fragile sound. She was so exposed there, in the water. It seemed as though the noise she made was dangerous, inviting attention the way a wounded animal's lopsided movements attract predators. The bushes that lined the fence cupped their own shadows, spots of darkness so black they seemed to protrude. David listened for the howls of coyotes. He stood at the window until Janet got out of the pool. When she did he saw her breasts straight on. He was so surprised his attention glazed over and he saw them the way he saw photographs, as products of his own imagination rather than inevitable facts of nature. The only naked women he had ever seen were in pictures. Janet stepped out of the water, picked up her clothes, and ran back into the house, her breasts bobbing heavily, implying their own weight and resilience, throwing shadows on her rib cage. He watched with mingled amazement and satisfaction, vaguely taking credit for the invention of her body. He heard her enter the house, and thought of her dripping on the kitchen linoleum, shivering, holding her wadded clothes to her chest. She sprinted up the stairs and down the hall, past his door. He touched his own chest, gently, with the fingertips of both hands. The fact that the Janet who slept one room down was the same person he'd just seen running naked was strange enough to keep him awake until after midnight. If he raised himself up in bed he could see the water of the pool, dark and shimmering.

In the morning he woke and went straight to the window. Mom was in the yard with her net, skimming leaves off the water. Each leaf trailed three fingers in the brightening water. Mom picked them up one by one, with a steady patience. David was sure she was shrinking; her cheeks seemed to have no bones under them at all. He thought, though, that if anything was really wrong, someone would be sure to tell him.

$\mathbf{B}$illy shot David all day at school. He shot him from behind during homeroom class, and again at lunch. When David was crossing the yard on his way to the cafeteria he glanced up at the library and saw Billy standing in a window, shooting him from behind the dusty glass. David smiled and waved, but Billy just kept on shooting. Then David raised his own rifle and pretended to shoot back, but Billy didn't flinch. David felt the weakness of his own bullets. He let the gun drop and walked away, with his shoulders squared and his head held high and his toes turned out, cowboy style. As he walked he could imagine the bullets thudding into his back, dancing him all over the yard.

Without Billy there was nothing to do after school. Other kids were not interested in him, and a few held mysterious grudges. A boy named Benny Richter once tore to pieces the intricate cover David had made for a report on the lost city of Troy, with broken columns cut out of *National Geographic* and the face of a fashion model he imagined to look like Helen. The scraps of the cover fell at his feet, and before the wind took it he saw the woman's lips, offering a kiss from a ragged-edge triangle of skin. With Billy mad at him he had no real friends at all, and after school he just went home.

When he got there he found Janet back in the pool, swimming laps. She had on a two-piece bathing suit. Mom was still at work and Lizzie was up in her room, dancing so hard to her Michael Jackson album she set the hall chandelier abuzz. David went out and sat beside the pool, with his knees tucked under his chin. Janet swam strong determined laps, head down, sucking air every second stroke, her face an agony of exertion. At either end of the pool she did a flip turn, pushing off underwater and streaking back the way she'd come. Her bathing suit was two turquoise bands in the paler turquoise of the water. David counted fifty laps.

When she was done she clung for a while to the edge of the coping, gasping for breath. She smiled at David, unable to speak. He asked if she was all right, and she nodded. She stroked her way over to the ladder, hoisted herself out, and bent to one side to squeeze the water from her hair. David could see the herringbone stream of water that washed down her spine and disappeared into the bottom of her suit, emerging in twin slick movements on her thighs.

Still panting, she came and sat beside him. "Hello," she whispered.

"Hi," he said.

She drew her knees up to her chest and sat the same way he did. She smelled scoured and bleached.

"You're a good swimmer," he told her.

"I just hate to have to stop," she said.

"What did you do today?"

"Besides swimming? Nothing. What about you?"

"Nothing," he said.

She nodded, and they both stared straight ahead at the peaked roof of the neighbor's house, which sliced up over the fence, a reversed duplicate of the Starks'. Behind it, the sky was a limpid, even blue.

"You shouldn't swim alone," he said.

"Well, I'm not alone anymore. You want to come for a swim?"

"I don't think so," he said. "I'll just watch you." He worried about the way his right nipple had sprouted a single dark corkscrew hair. It didn't look right. He thought he would keep his body private until it looked more symmetrical.

"All right." She stood and walked to the deep end, her wet hair clinging to her back. Her back was thin, the buttons of her spine prominent enough to throw small rounded shadows. She paused at the pool's edge, swung her arms, and dove in, cutting the water straight, barely raising a splash. David watched her swim back and forth, ticking off the laps with grim efficiency.

The telephone rang inside the house. David ran into the kitchen. He could hear Lizzie jumping around upstairs, to the rhythm of "Beat It." He picked up the phone.

"Hello."

"Hello, David? It's Rob."

"Oh. Hi."

"Is Janet there?"

"Um, no."

"Do you know where she is?"

"Well, she went out."

"Do you know where she went?"

"I think she went out with a friend," David said.

"What friend?"

"Well, I think she went out with a friend from here."

"Who's that, David?"

"I don't know. His name is Billy."

"I see. Who is Billy, David?"

"I don't know."

"Is he an old friend of Janet's?" Rob asked.

"I think so."

"I don't think I ever heard about him."

"Well, everybody around here knows him. He was in the marines. Now he's studying to be a doctor."

"What do you know? And Janet went out with him?"

"Uh-huh. I think so."

"I see. Well, just mention to her that I called, all right?"

"Okay."

"Been a pleasure talking to you, David."

"You're welcome," David said, and hung up. His face was flushed and his nose ran a little, the mixture of shame and giddiness he always felt when he told a story. This one was a mistake—he'd surely be found out. But he'd worry about that later.

He checked the kitchen window. Janet was still swimming. As he watched her he slipped his hand up under his shirt and pulled at the single hair that sprouted from his nipple. He thought about werewolves. Wolfman movies had always scared him more than any other kind; something about a man, normal and nice as anybody, turning suddenly into a monster. Monsters that stayed monsters were one thing. They were themselves and you were you. He tugged at the hair his body had grown, and considered plucking it out, but decided it would hurt too much.

Janet was still swimming when Mom got home. Mom worked in the school superintendent's office, making reports. David had no idea what the reports were about.

"Another day, another thousand dollars," Mom said as she came into the kitchen. She carried with her a gust of her work-smell: perfume and mimeograph ink. She set her purse down on the kitchen counter. The purse drooped into its own loose weight, like a sack of jelly.

"Janet's out there swimming," David said.

"I see." Mom washed her hands at the sink, with dish soap. "And you're the lifeguard?"

Embarrassed, David went to the refrigerator and took a deep swallow from the milk carton.

"I told you not to do that," Mom said. "You leave crumbs on the spout."

"I didn't leave any crumbs," he told her. "Mom, do we have to go see Dad this summer?"

She took the dish towel from the handle of the refrigerator and dried her hands slowly. David noticed that she had thick blue veins in her hands. The veins settled and unsettled themselves under her skin.

"I thought you liked going to Washington," she said.

"Well, I don't, really."

"I think you'd better go anyway. Your father will be hurt if you don't."

"Uh-huh." David rearranged the magnets on the refrigerator. There were five of them: a pineapple, a peach, a plum, a bunch of grapes, and a wooden ladybug. "When did Dad push me down the stairs?" he asked.

"He didn't push you down the stairs, honey. It was an accident. He was mad at me, and he accidentally bumped into you because he wasn't looking where he was going. He would never have pushed you down the stairs on purpose."

"Uh-huh," David said. He felt with his fingertips along the top of his forehead, where the scar was, a thin straight line like a length of fine wire buried beneath the skin.

"He really would rather have died than hurt you. Remember how he carried you out to the car? I thought he was going to kill us all, getting you to the hospital."

"I guess so," David said. He remembered the trip to the hospital, with his cherry-red blood all over Mom's blue dress and Dad sitting clenched at the wheel, blasting the horn at anybody who got in the way. Dad had driven up on the sidewalk for a block, with the horn pressed down. It had seemed like the end of the world.

"He loves you," Mom said. "He'd go crazy if you didn't come up to see him."

"Uh-huh." He worked the magnets into a straight line. Upstairs, Lizzie executed a dance step that rattled the plaster. "She's going to break the ceiling someday," he said.

"Well, if she does, you catch her for me," Mom told him.

David could imagine doing it, catching people as they fell through the ceiling like laundry through a chute. "Was Ray a good dancer?" he asked.

"Ray's feet weighed about ten pounds each, rest his soul," Mom said. "It was like dancing with a bear in combat boots."

"Oh."

"Not that that stopped us," Mom said. "We used to go dancing all the time. I just kept a good supply of bandages in my purse. Ray thought he was a good dancer."

"Uh-huh." David liked hearing about Ray. The main thing he knew was that Ray had been funny. Once when he asked Mom if Ray was a better husband than Dad, she had glanced up over David's head as if Ray himself stood there and said, "Well, he knew better jokes, I'll tell you that much."

There were pictures. Ray with his big broad face and big body upside down, doing a cartwheel at the beach; Mom in a black bathing suit, with curly gray hair and black lips. David's favorite picture was the one of Mom, Ray, and Janet taken when Janet was three years old. This one was in color. They were standing in front of the toothy grille of their car, an old Chevy Ray had named the Flying Dutchman, and all three of them wore baseball caps. They had bought a miniature cap for Janet. Mom stood with her arms folded over her chest and one hip cocked, playing tough, and Ray held Janet encircled in one giant arm. You could tell what they'd meant to do—they were all supposed to look mean, like ballplayers. Janet had giggled, though, and Ray, too, had just started busting up when the shutter clicked. Mom's dark mouth strained to hold in a laugh that must have escaped a moment later, twenty years ago. David studied and studied the picture, taking in its minutest detail, as if it were a relic of a lost civilization.

He went to the window to watch Janet swim.

"Don't you have homework?" Mom said. "What about the epic map of California?"

"I'll do it in a minute," he said. Out in the pool, Janet's arms sliced the water.

"I'll watch Janet," Mom said.

"Well, we both can," he told her.

Rob called during dinner. Though David tried to answer it, Janet got there first.

"Hello?" she said. David stood close by her in the kitchen, making no pretense of not listening. Janet rolled her eyes for him, to indicate exhausted patience with the caller.

"What do you mean, 'back?'" she said. "I've been here all day."

David went to the refrigerator and took the peach-shaped magnet into his hand. He ran his thumbnail thoughtfully along the cleft. A peach was like an ass.

"No," Janet said. "Who would I go with?

"*What?*"

She listened, and laughed. David inched into the cool, humming vicinity of the refrigerator. Janet was looking straight at him now, her head level and her dark brows low over her eyes.

"Well, I don't know where anybody would get an idea like that," she said, "but it's not true. Of course it isn't."

David backed right up to the refrigerator, passing the peach from hand to hand. His elbows pressed against the slick, perfect surface of the door.

"No," Janet said. "What do you think, I've got a waiting list? *No.* In the pool, if you really want to know. Swimming about a thousand laps, so I'd be tired enough to sleep." Her face had darkened, and a pair of red bruised-looking patches appeared on her cheeks. She twisted the telephone cord around her fingers.

"No, I don't think you can," she said, looking piercingly at

David. "Because I don't want you menacing my family, is why. My word should be good enough."

She listened, wrapping the cord around and around her fingers. "Well, I'm sorry to hear that," she said finally. "No, maybe I'm glad to hear it. It makes things clearer.

"I think it's time for this to stop now. Really. Good night.

"You only make it worse, Rob. What's the point?

"I can't. No, honey, I do. But I don't. Oh shit. Good night."

She pushed the cradle down and stood another moment with the dead receiver still at her ear. "You made up another story, huh?" she said to David.

He nodded.

She replaced the receiver and leaned against the counter, holding one elbow with her opposite hand. She regarded him in the solemn, black-eyed way she used when she was mad or puzzled—her chin dipped down, her mouth tense at the corners with an edgy tightness that could tip over into laughter.

"So what's my new boyfriend like?" she said.

"I don't know."

"What made you think of a marine, is what I'd like to know."

"I don't *know,*" he said helplessly.

"A marine who's studying medicine." She shook her head. "You're really something, you know?"

"I know."

They eyed one another, and David, in a fit of nervousness, held up the little peach for her to see. "Cyanide," he said. He put it in his mouth and pretended to swallow.

Her lips trembled, held firm a moment; then she laughed. Success. David crossed his eyes, clutched at his heart and dropped to the linoleum.

"Be careful," Janet said, coming to him. "You'll really swallow that thing."

David stayed on the floor, with his eyes squeezed shut and the tip of his tongue sticking out the side of his mouth. The magnetic disk on the peach bled an iron taste into his mouth.

The floor smelled of ammonia and, distantly, of dust. Janet squatted beside him. She brought her own smells, chlorine and musky perfume.

"You shouldn't have lied," she said. "It isn't fair to him."

David opened his eyes. Why was she worried about *him?* He took the peach out of his mouth. "I'm sorry," he said, a little flatly.

She rested her hand on his shoulder. "Next time," she said, "think of something better for me than a marine. Okay?"

"Okay."

"Is anybody in there coming back to dinner?" Mom called from the dining room.

"Tell her to send it to the starving Armenians," David whispered.

"Nope. Come on now, up." She took his hand and together they got to their feet. David snapped the wet peach back into place on the refrigerator.

"Coming," she called.

The telephone rang.

"I'll get it," David said.

"No," Janet told him. "I'm sure it's for me. You go on out and finish your dinner." She took him by the shoulders and propelled him, gently, to the door. When he balked at the threshold, she smacked his rump.

"Go," she said. "I'm not fooling."

He passed unwillingly through the swinging doors into the dining room, where Mom and Lizzie sat at the table. "It's about time," Lizzie said.

"Shut up," he told her, and hung around the doorway, listening. Mom and Lizzie listened too.

"I knew it'd be you," Janet said in the kitchen. "Listen, you're going to have to ... What? Oh Rob, don't cry. No. Come on, honey. Stop. Really. No, there's no one. Really."

Mom pulled her attention back to the table with a visible

shift of her eyes. They were vague and unfocused, then they turned to needles.

"You going to eat, or what?" she said to David. "Come on, sit down right now."

David sat, his ears straining after Janet's voice.

"I don't know what keeps you alive," Mom said. "It must be sheer force of will, I can promise you it's not vitamins. I don't know how you're going to find the strength to go out there and support me in my old age if you don't permit an occasional vegetable into your bloodstream. It's nothing permanent, remember. They're just passing through—"

She went on, in a loud voice, despite the fact that David willed her so hard to be quiet he could feel the heat radiating from his face. Her talk drowned out Janet's voice and she didn't stop until Janet came back into the room, smiling, her eyes damp and pink.

"Pardon me, everybody," she said, and swiped at her nose with her index finger.

"It's okay," David told her.

"No, it's not okay," Janet said. "I don't want to keep on disrupting everybody like this."

"Yes, we're getting very disrupted," Lizzie said.

"You don't even know what *disrupted* means," David said.

"Yes I do."

He opened his mouth to ask her for the definition, and stopped. She might actually know it; she knew a lot of words you wouldn't expect her to. Instead, he said, "You're going to have to go to Spokane by yourself this summer, because I'm not going."

"Yes you are." Her eyes clicked over to Mom. "He's going, isn't he?" she said.

"I think he is," Mom said. "I think you both are. Matter of fact, I'm pretty sure of it."

"If David doesn't go, I don't have to go either," Lizzie said.

"I thought you liked going to see your father," Mom said. A moment of stiff, social silence followed.

"Well, we do," David said.

"*I* don't," Lizzie said. "We never did."

"Shut up, Lizzie," he said. "You don't know what you're talking about. She doesn't know what she's talking about."

"Well, kids, you have to go to your father's," Mom said. "He'd be so hurt if you didn't."

"If you don't go," David said to Lizzie, "he'll come down and get you."

Her eyes widened, and her lower lip tucked itself in as automatically as a flower closing. She looked at her plate. "I'm not going to eat any of this succotash," she said.

"You don't have to eat it," Mom said. "Is it really that awful, going up to your father's?"

"No," David said.

"Lizzie?"

Lizzie shook her head. "I *hate* succotash," she said. "Why do we always have to have it?"

"We haven't had it since Valentine's Day," Mom said. "Listen, you just have to go to your father's. It's not me saying so, it's the court."

"We *know*," David said.

"We know," Lizzie added softly.

"Well," Mom said, and said nothing further. After a while, she asked Janet, "Are you all right over there?"

Janet's eyes had dried and taken on a hard sparkle. "Oh sure," she said. "Just going through a little adjustment."

After dinner was finished and the dishes put away, David sat in his room working on his map of California. He heard Janet go into her room. A few minutes later Mom came upstairs and tapped on Janet's door in her careful, determined way, as though she were breaking open the shell of a soft-boiled egg. David heard Janet's voice and then Mom's, clearer, saying, "Can I come in for a minute?" The door opened and closed.

Mom's voice, like Janet's, was reduced to wordless sound; an oboe. Janet's was a clarinet. The two of them talked on, and though David tried to hear them through the wall the words couldn't be fathomed. He listened to the murmur of their voices, and glued foxtails and cotton balls onto the places where the state was most fruitful.

Dad had taken up shooting when he lost his job. David remembered going with him once to a practice range, where he shot at targets tacked to bales of hay. A red ring inside a blue one, with a black circle the size of a heart at center. David had been only five or six, and Dad wouldn't let him shoot. He remembered Dad's hands on the shotgun—long brown fingers that might have been carved from a lighter, finer-grained wood than that of the gun. Although he saw Dad every summer, his clearest recollection was six years old or more. Dad stood with his feet wide apart, aiming the long gun, his profile intent. Sunlight picked out each red hair on his head, and a white aura outlined his hooked nose and heavy, square chin. David had never seen him so still before. For a long moment he was able to look at Dad's face as intently as he examined his own body. Dad's eyebrow, darker red than his hair, the color of an Irish setter's coat, had a single thread of white in it which David had never seen. A giddiness had risen from his belly to his head, the same tingling weightlessness he felt going over the top of a ferris wheel. He loved Dad. The gun cracked, a sharp clean sound. After he was through, Dad gave David the target for a souvenir. The target had five ragged holes shot through its small black center. It was still taped up on David's wall, by the bed, five dots of white plaster shining through the black like stars.

Janet went swimming again that night, as he'd thought she would. He waited up for her, watching, after Mom and

Lizzie had gone to bed. He stayed on guard and did not beat off.

This time Janet wore her bathing suit, which looked gray in the darkness, and carried a towel draped over her shoulders like an athlete in a locker room. When she dove, the splash she made lingered surface. David could see the suggestion of her shape, blue-white, as she swam a lap underwater. Before she surfaced, he was downstairs. As he passed through the kitchen, his belly went queasy with anticipation. The pilot lights on the rangetop glowed blue, like the light on television, and for a moment in passing them he was a photograph of himself, moving through a picture of his kitchen. He stepped outside into the smell of the damp grass and the disturbed water, and the sound of Janet's breathing.

He stood for a while beside the pool, waiting for her to see him, but she swam with her head down, grinding out the laps. Finally, David peeled off his jeans and stepped cautiously into the water at the shallow end, wearing only his shorts and a T-shirt. He had planned on Janet's asking him in; he had even put on clean underwear. The water was warm, warmer than the air. Rising to David's thighs, it felt languid and heavy. He sank to his shoulders, keeping his head above water, since he thought he looked stupid with his hair plastered down. Janet kept on swimming, still unaware of him. He stood crouched at the shallow end with the water lapping around his neck, unsure about how to approach without scaring her. The moon of the streetlight shimmied on the unsteady water, and David could feel the rhythm of Janet's swimming. The water was alive with her. He worked himself closer, hoping she would notice him. As she passed he felt the wake of her legs. The effervescence they left behind clung to his own legs, tiny bubbles that fizzed like tadpoles against his skin. His cock got hard, with its perverse independence, and though he willed it to go limp again it wouldn't obey. He edged a bit closer to Janet and as she pushed off the shallow end her arm slid against his belly. She came up sputtering, the air whistling out of her. "It's okay," David said in a loud whisper. "It's only me."

Janet was a moment in orienting herself. He could see the dark oval of her open mouth. "Only me," he said again in a soft voice. "Everything's okay, it's only me."

"Shit, you scared me," she said breathlessly. "I just thought —God, I don't know what I thought. All my worst fears seemed to have come true."

"I'm sorry. I was trying not to scare you." He felt ridiculous, just his head bobbing before her like a talking beach ball.

"It's okay. I'm glad you're not a shark."

"I couldn't sleep," he said. "So I decided to go swimming with you."

"Well, good." She stroked to the side, her arms and legs rippled by the water, her belly slightly luminous below the bra of her bikini. David couldn't think of just what to do. He feared that his stiff penis might work its way out of his underpants and float before him. With a mournful thought of his hair he took a breath, ducked underneath, and swam to the deep end.

The bottom of the pool was netted with undulating shadows, a granular blue darkness. Swimming through it was like a dream of flight. When he reached the far end he surfaced, took a breath, and went back under. Janet was swimming toward him, also under water, her hair billowing, black, framing the pale blue of her face. Bubbles bloomed from her and floated lazily to the surface. David swam straight at her and she jack-knifed to pass under him, a movement slick as a dolphin's. He felt her slipstream all along his body as she swam beneath. They came up at opposite ends of the pool, then dove and crossed over again, with David brushing the bottom and Janet passing above. As he went under he blew out of his nose and mouth, to tickle her. His head felt light and prickly, and when he shut his eyes a green phosphorescence burst under the lids. He moved carefully, to keep himself tucked into his underpants.

When he came up he found Janet floating on her back, her hair adrift around her. He floated too, close by her, and found that with his ears under water he could hear the swishing of her arms as she gently paddled to keep herself afloat. Hearing only the steady suck of the water, he watched the night sky. The stars stood out in piercing relief, and for the first time it occurred to him that they were actually hanging in space. He thought he could see the band of the Milky Way, a soaring ghostly belt, and the faint sounds of the water seemed to be the sounds of space as well. He felt like he could rise into space the way he'd rise through water, with a slow patient buoyancy. For a moment it was clear to him that every single thing, every person and animal on earth and every alien being on the millions of planets within his sight, all moved to the rhythmic swooshing of the same water. He was connected to them. He seemed to lift up out of his body and suddenly the stars were *there,* right before his eyes, nothing like the twinkling specks he'd grown up with but blazing, breathing, unnamable, alive. In a panic he blew out his air and sank. The water closed up over his face and he let himself drop into the deepening blue. He watched the bubbles of his own expelled oxygen and saw the stars scattered on the water's surface.

When he came up again Janet was pulling herself out of the pool. She sat perched on the edge of the coping with her legs dangling and said, "Think it's about time to go back inside?"

David nodded, and swam to the side. He wondered if she had felt the melting upward, too. Maybe it was an ordinary experience, so common that no one ever mentioned it. He wanted to ask her, but couldn't couch it in words. He had no idea of what to call it. He docked himself next to her, propping his elbows on the coping beside her legs. Beads of water shone dully on her stomach and shoulders.

"This was good," she said. "It's good to have another body out here with me."

David thought she might have felt the nameless thing, and

was telling him indirectly. "Yes," he said. "It was really, um, *great.*"

"I've got a towel here," she said. "Come on out, I'll let you have it first."

"No thanks," he said, reluctant to return to the open air in his small, odd body. "I think I'm going to stay in a little longer."

Janet looked up at the sky, kicking her legs idly in the water, setting up a suction David felt on his hips and thighs. "Pretty night," she said.

"Yes," he said, and then he said, "Yes," again, with greater force.

"Will you be okay out here alone?" she asked him. "Mother will be terribly upset if she comes out here tomorrow morning and finds you floating face down."

"I'll be okay," he said.

"Maybe I'll stay and watch you anyway," she said.

"No. Go inside. I mean, I'm really okay. I'll get out in just a minute." He wanted her gone now. He was afraid of losing the moment by saying something stupid. "Really," he added.

"Well, okay. Knock on my door when you come up, all right?"

"Uh-huh."

She bent over, patted his cheek, and got up, the water running off her legs. She picked up her towel, which David knew to be yellow though it looked white. She rubbed herself with it, and David thought he could feel its bristle on his own skin.

"Good night," she whispered.

"Janet?" he said.

"What?"

"I don't know."

"Come on," she said.

"I forgot what I was going to say."

"Well, tell me at breakfast if you remember it. Night."

"Night."

"I'll leave you the towel."

"Okay."

As she walked across the grass to the house, David's belly took on its queasy lilt again, the sensation of joyful nervousness. Once she was safely inside he floated on his back again, in gentle circles, scooping the water with his cupped hands as if blindly hunting its subtle shapes. The stars were beautiful in their usual way, cool and remote. Though he tried to melt up again he stayed where he was, inside his own body. He wondered if Janet had been the crucial element, if her presence had somehow charged the water with an electricity he himself lacked.

When he got out he took the towel from the lawn chair Janet had hung it on, and checked it for her scent. All he could smell was the chlorine and the laundered odor of the terry cloth. He dried off carefully, as if he was using the towel to cover himself with paint. Then he picked up his wadded jeans and walked back through the kitchen, past the blue lights of the stove.

When he reached Janet's door he hesitated a moment, and rapped with the knuckle of his index finger. "Okay. Good night," she whispered from inside. He had hoped she'd open the door.

"Good night," he whispered, and in case she hadn't heard said, "Good night" again, a little louder. Then he was embarrassed at having said it twice.

David sat in homeroom class not looking at Billy, who he knew was shooting him from the back of the room. By alphabetical arrangement David sat in a front seat, a vulnerable position. He kept his eyes fixed on the teacher in a show of attention so intense he couldn't distinguish a word she said. The teacher's name was Miss Mullin. The class called her Moons Mullin for her enormous breasts. David watched her write the names of Spanish explorers on the blackboard. She called the class *people*. "Listen up, people," she said, and David's attention glazed over as he watched her with bright-eyed enthusiasm.

Miss Mullin's skin was pitted in the hollows of her cheeks, and the fever-colored powder she wore caught there in little orange flakes. The powder ended at the top of her white neck, which made her look as though she had invented her own head. As far as David knew, he was the only person in school who liked her. She was ridiculous, no doubt about it, but he could see the sorrow in her small brown eyes. Every now and then somebody called up to say there was a bomb hidden at school, and when the bell rang three times, the bomb code,

Miss Mullin would roll her eyes, throw the chalk down, and say, "Okay, people, line up." They'd all go stand in the playground waiting for the school to explode while Miss Mullin stood at the head of the line, unafraid, talking to Miss Linden, who was her friend. Sometimes David imagined grabbing her and pulling her out of range, shielding her with his own body while bombs rained down on the building.

Miss Mullin wiped the names off the blackboard and put more names in their place. History moved forward toward the present. When the bell rang, David bolted out of his seat. In art class he'd be temporarily safe from Billy, who went during art period to a special class for people with low marks in cooperation.

Art was the finest, most dangerous class. The teacher, a squat, hook-nosed woman named Mrs. Pilegi (Mrs.: someone was *married* to her), kept after everybody to let himself *go*. When she said the word *go* she made a snap-wristed, clawing gesture from her breast to the class, as if she were tossing them a ball.

Today they were making collages, with string and scraps of felt and dyed rice. David sat on a stool near the window, as far as possible from the notice of others, and stuck grains of rice to his drawing, a man catching a woman on a trapeze. As he worked he tried to keep people from looking at him and tried to keep his tongue from creeping out the side of his mouth. He carefully glued grain after grain of blue rice to the woman's leotard. Then he came to her skin. The only flesh-colored rice was too pink, and he debated over whether to make her skin plain white or the gaudy pink. He favored white, but without any coloring it looked too much like *rice.* He realized his tongue had inched its way out between his clenched lips. He pulled it back in again. Mrs. Pilegi, who had been circling the room in her orange-and-pink flowered smock, came up behind him and crowed, "My, what cautious work. Why don't you make the skin purple, David? Go a little wild."

"Well, okay," he said. He placed a few purple grains along the woman's cheek.

"See? She doesn't have to look real. You can have fun with her. See?"

"Uh-huh," he said. When Mrs. Pilegi had moved on, he dug the purple rice out with his thumbnail. Mrs. Pilegi was the only one of his teachers who seemed to notice him, and to take an interest in him. She was the only one he didn't like.

Lunch came next. The lunch yard was open territory. David and Billy had always sat together in a far corner, where the chain-link fence ran into the rippled aluminum flank of the Quonset hut where art classes were held. The two of them would sit eating their sack lunches on the warm, mica-flecked dirt, making up stories. David supplied the plots, with Billy putting in action sequences whenever David let things get too bogged down with lovers and fancy sentiments. They traded their lunches nearly every day, Billy taking David's peanut-butter-and-jelly sandwich and giving him the peculiar sand-wiches his mother made. Billy's mother would put anything between two slices of white bread: shreds of gristly gray meat, orange cheese from a tube, sometimes just potato salad. David had pretended for so long to like the sandwiches that at some indeterminable point he really did start liking them. At least they were always surprising.

Today, he couldn't decide where to go. He didn't want to sit in the old corner, but every other area was somebody's province, and it would be strange to just sit down among a group of friends like he was one of them. Holding the limp, rolled top of his paper sack, he stood in the doorway to the yard and scanned for Billy. The cafeteria, which smelled of green beans and disinfectant, was only for people who bought their lunches; sack lunches went into the yard. David was sur-prised at how few places there were to hide. In his mind the world was full of gullies and caves and mountain peaks which would shelter you if only you could elude your enemies long enough to reach them. The stories he told himself almost always hinged on a secret safety zone. At the moment, though, he stood facing the fenced-in yard, and there was no possibility of sneaking off anywhere else.

He went back to the old corner because he couldn't think of anything else to do. He sat himself down with his back against the fence, its links biting him through his shirt. He opened the sack and pulled out the expected contents. A sandwich, a warm speckled banana, three cookies in a Baggie.

He was halfway through the sandwich when he saw Billy walking around the border of the yard. Billy had on his fatigues and his camouflage jacket. He carried a lunch sack and walked with quick gliding steps, like a stalking cat. Other people fell out of his way, because Billy had that kind of reputation. He turned briskly at the corner and came straight for David, his head hunched down low as his shoulders. David forced himself to keep on eating his sandwich. Billy passed by and stared at David as if he were an unpleasant surprise. He moved along and did another circuit of the yard. David watched him the way he'd watch a zoo animal with strange, insistent habits. Billy paced around the yard and on his second circle he stopped just short of the place where David sat and squatted down, his arms rigid between his knees, his fingers splayed on the dirt. He stayed there, ten feet away, watching David with narrowed, shining eyes. David ate his sandwich. He thought of offering some to Billy, but knew it would be stupid. Billy rocked slightly on the balls of his feet. His body pulsed like an engine revving. David thought about getting up and going elsewhere, but he had no place to go. He peeled his banana with elaborate care, as if he was demonstrating the correct procedure. It's *Billy,* he told himself. My best friend. It seemed to him there must be something for him to do or say, a sentence or two that would make things normal again. Billy was waiting. David felt like a boy in a story; a boy who meets up with a monster that asks him a riddle, and will tear him to pieces if he gets the answer wrong. It's Billy, he reminded himself. To keep calm, he focused his mind on small details of Billy's life. Billy carried a 1929 silver dollar in his pocket, David's gift. Billy worried that his cock would never grow to a decent length, and was now checking the mail every day for the enlarging device he'd sent for from one of his brother's magazines. Billy always claimed he'd kill anybody who hurt a friend of his.

As if it were the logical sum of these facts, David thought, He loves me. The idea came to him in a foreign voice, like someone whispering inside his head. He looked at Billy. He opened his mouth, but nothing came out of it. Billy watched him with avid eyes that were not like Billy's at all. After a while he opened his own lunch and ate it in huge, rending bites. David wondered what kind of sandwich his mother had made today.

The two of them stayed where they were until the bell rang to signal the end of lunch. David got up, dusted off the seat of his pants, and joined the others who were obediently heading back inside for the afternoon's classes. At the doorway he glanced back and saw Billy still crouched in the same spot, his neck craned to watch David's departure. He loves me, said the voice inside David's head. David thought he should have come up with a way to bring Billy around. He could have told him— what? It was too late now anyway. Science class started in four minutes. Today the science teacher was bringing in a life-size rubber man, with organs you could take out and put back in again.

To get home from school, David walked down the Vista Arcadia, a wide boulevard that led to his part of the neighborhood. Vista Arcadia was lined with blue-gray pine trees so big their branches intertwined and made a tunnel of the street, admitting only dimmed, sluggish sunlight. Like the tree in the Starks' backyard, they were left over from the old estate, the ranch of a movie mogul whose girlfriend, according to the stories, crashed her plane through the roof of his house. The man had raised peacocks, and the peacocks dispersed into the hills when the land was sold to developers. The birds had long since died off. Although Mom said it wasn't possible, David swore he remembered seeing a peacock land in the backyard once when he was very young. It had been evening, and the bird flapped down out of the dusky sky, stood for a while on the grass, and opened its tail, showing off its galaxy of brilliant blind eyes. David thought that was his first memory.

As he passed under the trees, he heard a sputtering sound from above. He looked up and saw Billy high in a pine, straddling the crotch of a branch, shooting him. David could see the black waffled soles of Billy's shoes, and the bill of his army cap. David stood gaping, unable to decide what to do. Billy stopped shooting him, and pulled a pine cone from the branch closest to him. The cone came loose only after some effort, and David could hear the feathery sound of needles falling to the pavement around him.

"Hey Billy," he said, too softly. He called again, "Billy," in a louder voice. "Come on down," he called. "We don't have to be enemies. Let's forget it."

Billy bit at the top of the pine cone, as if he were pulling the pin of a grenade. He lobbed it down at David, who jumped out of the way. The pine cone bounced toward him as if in pursuit. Each time it hit the concrete it made a hollow wooden sound, like the plock of a Ping-Pong ball. Billy started counting. "One two three . . ."

"We don't have anything to fight about," David said.

"Four five six . . ."

"I'm not mad at you."

"Seven eight . . ."

David ran. He was barely out from under the tree when Billy reached ten, and hollered, "Ka-boom." Billy shook the branches of the tree, and a shower of needles fell.

Janet was swimming when David got home. He stood in the kitchen, watching her, drinking milk from the carton. Mom didn't get back from work for another hour, and Lizzie had Brownies today, although she was likely to get kicked out any time for swearing at the other girls. David stood with his belly pressed hard against the edge of the sink, feeling the comforting rise and fall of his own gut as he sucked in deep swallows of milk.

He expected the telephone to ring and it did, so soon after the idea came to him that he thought he'd picked up vibrations the bell gave off at the first microsecond's contact with an impulse coming through the wire. He got it in the middle of the first ring.

"Hello."

"Hello, David?"

"Hi, Rob."

"Hi. Let me speak to Janet, please."

"Well, she isn't here."

"Where is she?"

"Out."

"Out where?"

"I don't know."

"Did she go out by herself?"

David let a good long pause go by; he counted silently to three. Then he said, "Um, I don't know."

"You do know, don't you, David?"

"Nope."

"Is it the same man she went out with yesterday?"

This time he let the silence hang for a count of five.

"Nope."

"I see. Did she happen to mention when she might be back?"

"Uh-uh."

"All right. Okay. Thank you for your help, David."

"You're welcome," David said. "Bye."

"Good-bye."

After he had hung up, he returned to the window in time to see Janet lifting herself out of the pool. Her body glistened with water. David wondered how he'd be able to make her laugh this time, when she found out he'd done it again.

Rob didn't call that afternoon and didn't call in the evening. David spent hours in edgy anticipation, listening for the tiny quickening of the silence that preceded the telephone's bell. It rang only twice. Once for Mom, the doctor's office, and once again during dinner. The second time it was a friend of Janet's, calling from San Francisco. David caught as much as he could through the door, but between Mom's talking about the various things that concerned her and Lizzie insisting over and over again that the other girls in Brownies were all assholes, he was able to pick up only fragments.

Janet said, ". . . from you. Good. Oh, I'm okay. Holed up in . . . you know. Of course he is. It kills me, it really does, but if a little . . . no, none. Of course I have. I just know it's the right . . . Uh-huh. Every day but today. I *did.* You know how he is, though . . . Mm-hm. . . . A lot of swimming. Well, it's the next best thing for putting you to sleep. Really, you should try it . . . classes in the fall. No. But I've got to give (a shot? a shit?) . . . back to the fold. Right. Okay, thanks for calling. I'll keep you posted. Okay. Bye."

After that, there were no more calls. The evening passed. Mom and Janet watched television, the smoke from their cigarettes drifting along the ceiling. Lizzie finished her homework in fifteen minutes, watched "The Muppets" with Mom and Janet, then danced to her Michael Jackson album until Mom made her go to bed. David passed nervously from his room to the kitchen to the living room and back again. He watched bits of television on the wing. Fonzie was adopting a juvenile delinquent. David went back up to his room and when he came down again the stupid blonde on "Three's Company" had a date with her boss. David liked TV and welcomed even the worst shows with the same kind of grudging affection he'd have shown to feeble-minded, slightly embarrassing aunts and uncles.

Before "Three's Company" was over, he wandered back up to his room. He stood at the window, with the silent pool stretched out beneath him. Along the fence Mom's row of white petunias blackened the bushes behind them the way flames deepened darkness. He listened for the sound of coyotes, but they weren't out yet. Far away a car horn bleated. As David stared through the windowpane he began to think someone was out there, watching him. He couldn't fix on any one point. But somewhere, in the thick blackness of the junipers or behind the tree, an intelligence sat outside looking in as surely as David was inside looking out. He peered another minute into the stillness, then went downstairs to the tune of a 7-Up commercial tinkling from the living room. He patrolled the kitchen and the dining room, checking to make sure the windows were locked. He checked the front door too. The living room was trickier. He had to check the window there without arousing suspicion.

"What's into you tonight?" Mom asked when he came and stood behind the sofa. "You haven't stayed in one place more than two minutes all evening."

Sometimes it annoyed him that she kept such close track of his doings. She made him smaller by noticing him all the time. The irritation caught in his throat like a lump of dough.

"I'm okay," he told her.

"There's something in the air tonight," Janet said. She was sitting compactly, with her knees hunched up to her chin. "I feel it too. Maybe it's the full moon."

"The moon was full two weeks ago," Mom said. "There can't be more than a sliver tonight."

David went to the living-room window and, after a moment's hesitation, parted the drapes. There was no leering face pressed to the glass.

"What are you up to now?" Mom said.

"I'm looking for the moon," he told her. The more she irritated him, the more important it seemed that the house be made fast against whatever lurked outside. He checked the latch, and found it fastened.

"If I'd known kids were going to be this jumpy," Mom said, "I'd have gotten goldfish instead."

The house wound down for the night. Lizzie was already in bed, and David put on his pajamas and pretended to go to sleep. Mom came upstairs after the news. She gave a dry, papery sigh at the top step, and her footsteps, measured but light, one foot falling a little harder than the other, diminished down toward her room. Janet stayed in the living room with the television, watching Johnny Carson. David could hear the heightened rhythm of laughter and applause. He wondered if she would go swimming. Every now and then he got up and walked to the window in his pajamas. The yard was unchanged. The two redwood lawn chairs sat facing the house. A line of yellow light rimmed his door and he went and stood with his ear to the wood. He could make out a man's voice on television. The voice droned, paused, exclaimed; for a moment it sounded like a live man downstairs. David cracked his door open. Applause drifted up the stairwell, and a man hollered, remotely, "Thank you, thank you, I love you all."

He went back to bed and lay on top of the blanket, with his legs straight out and his arms at his sides, palms up, as if to cup sound. The television rattled on. His mind dulled with the effort of listening and after a while he thought thickly that his body had risen a fraction of an inch off the bed. His thoughts were a heavy line he followed up, up into brightness. He saw, vividly, a gypsy pedaling a bicycle on a red dirt road. Then he was asleep.

He woke later, with a start, surprised at having slept. The

light was gone from around his door. He jumped out of bed and ran to the window, to see if Janet was swimming. He found the pool smooth and empty. Sleep clung to him, and everything was strange. The world had moved an inch or two off center, so that all its qualities were usual but wrong—nearly perfect imitations of themselves. The trees's splayed roots hugged the edge of the coping like sleeping snakes. The moon, which had risen and was no more than a sliver, just as Mom predicted, skated on the water beside the brighter, aspirin-colored sphere of the streetlight. David watched the scene in dumb wonderment. This was his yard.

He felt more than saw something in the shadows. His attention crept toward the far corner, by the fence, where a small triangular thicket of oleander and birds of paradise bloomed. Something there. He thought first of coyotes. He searched for the spark of an eye or a tooth. For an instant the garden was ordinary, and then his eyes shifted focus and he saw a man standing in the bushes. The man was no more than a shape, shoulders and head. He fell out of focus, turned into oleander with branches that suggested a man, and when he came back into focus there was no doubt. A man, standing outside, watching the house.

David paused, mesmerized. It was a man, it wasn't, it was. He drew closer to the glass, so close his breathing made a blotch of fog. The man moved. David was out of his own room, down the hall and through Mom's door in an instant.

The sound of Mom's breathing filled her room. It *was* the room. David crossed the black floor through the breathing darkness to her shape under the blankets, and jostled her shoulder. She coughed, and when she stirred she sent up a sweet-sour, sleeping smell.

"What?" she said. "What is it?" Her eyes shone in the darkness and she was suddenly terrifying, an undersea creature wrongfully disturbed. David lost his voice.

"Um—" was all he could manage.

"What is it, honey? Are you sick?"

"There's a *man* outside," he said, and his voice squeaked on the word *man*. "A man," he repeated.

Mom sat up and said, "Where?" All the sleep had gone out of her voice.

He's standing out by the pool," David said.

"Is he trying to get in the house?" Mom asked.

"I don't *know*." His voice cracked again.

"Where were you when you saw him?" Mom's voice had descended into the throaty, rolling calm it took on during ca-tastrophes. When Dad pushed David down the stairs, she had picked him up and said in the deep, calm voice, "Take us to the hospital quick," as if it was something they did every day.

"In my *room*," David said. His own voice out of control. "He was *standing* out there *looking* at me."

"Are you sure?" Mom said.

"*Yes.*"

"Okay. Let's call the police."

She got out of bed in her nightgown and followed David to the door. He controlled an impulse to make her go first into the hall. When he stepped out, the stairwell lay ahead of him like a pit, with the phone on the other side. He made it past the stairs to the telephone table, taking speedy little steps, urged on by the cloud of Mom's warmth and odor. He picked up the receiver and handed it to her. She dialed one digit.

"Operator? The Rosemead police, please." She paused. "Emergency," she said, and laid a hand on David's shoulder to counterbalance the word.

"Hello? This is Beverly Stark at one oh one Buena Vista. We have a prowler."

David was impressed with her competence. She knew just what to say to the police. He liked the word *prowler* too—a good shrinking word, like a dog's name.

"Outside," she said. "No, I don't think so. Fine. Thank you, sergeant."

She replaced the receiver. Now they were alone again, back in danger. He wondered if he heard a stealthy scraping from below. He thought of the gun in Mom's nightstand.

"Just stand right here," she said to him in a hushed voice. "We won't wake up the others. We'll just wait for the police to get here, okay?"

"Okay," David whispered. He ached to say, "Let's get the gun," but couldn't. The gun was hidden away, unacknowledged; it did not exist and would not exist unless Mom herself summoned it up. She held his shoulders, and he slung his arms loosely around her bony hips. This reminded him of another time, shimmering at the edge of memory, when he and Mom had hidden in the dark together, waiting for help.

The door to Janet's bedroom opened, and she stood in the black doorway, her legs invisible beneath her white nightgown. She floated like a ghost.

"What's going on?" she asked in a whisper.

Mom motioned her over, and she came. "David saw somebody out in back," Mom said in her collected voice. "The police are coming."

"Oh," Janet said. She crossed her arms over her chest and Mom lifted one hand off David's shoulders to touch her shoulder, too.

"Do you think we should wake up Lizzie?" Janet whispered.

"Lord no," Mom said. "She'd go after him with a baseball bat."

Janet laughed, a thin whistling laugh that forced itself through her nostrils. She started to speak, when the pulsing red light of a police cruiser bled suddenly through Mom's open bedroom door.

"Saved," Janet said. Before Mom or David could move she started down the stairs. David followed her, and Mom came right behind.

David was right behind her when Janet opened the front door and stepped into the dazzling beam of a flashlight. The light delineated her body like an x-ray. It held her pinned at the threshold, and flicked off. Her nightgown turned solid again.

"Evening," a gravelly man's voice said. "You report a prowler?"

David and Mom squeezed themselves in on either side of Janet in the doorway. A patrolman stood on the front stoop. He had a square, handsome face in which only the mouth moved.

"I guess we did," Janet said.

"I reported the prowler," Mom said, working her way in front of Janet, taking charge. "I'm Beverly Stark." David noticed, as he sometimes did, her habit of announcing her name to people as if she expected them to have heard of her.

"My partner's in the back," the patrolman said. Behind his broad body the revolving light of a cruiser stained the front lawn pink and gray and pink again.

"Thank you for coming out," Mom said. She covered herself with her arms. She was so tiny before the uniform. David stepped around and stood between Mom and the patrolman.

"I was the one that saw him," he said.

"Tell me what you saw, please," the policeman said.

David glanced nervously back at Mom, who nodded. "I saw a man by the pool," he said. "Over in the bushes by the fence." In a fit of embarrassment, he spoke these sentences to the policeman's square, black shoes.

"What was he doing?" the policeman asked.

"He was just standing in the bushes," David said. "Looking at me."

"Looking at you?" the policeman said. "How could you tell in the dark if he was looking at you?" The policeman wore a wristwatch big as a silver dollar. The black hairs of his wrist curled up over the metal band.

"Well, I couldn't, really," David said. "But he was standing there *looking.*"

"Was he trying to get in the house?"

"*Yes,*" David said, and his voice cracked.

"Was he?" Mom asked. "Are you sure, David?"

"No," David said. "I don't know." He couldn't imagine how he had worked himself over into the wrong.

The partner returned from the back, walking behind the puddle of light his flashlight cast on the ground. "Negative," he said. "Nobody's there." He was younger than the other, but shared his wide, well-cut face. They might have been brothers.

"Looks like a false alarm," the first one said. "Nobody saw him but the boy here."

"It's not a false alarm just because nobody's standing back there with an *ax,* for God's sake," Janet said. "If David says he saw somebody, he saw somebody."

"Right," the partner said. "Anyhow, there's no one on the premises now."

"Did you check the windows?" Janet asked with irritation.

"The windows haven't been tampered with," the partner said. "If you like, we'll come in and check the house."

"Please," Mom said. "We'd all sleep better."

The three of them hung back to let the police enter. The police brought with them into the house their smell of after-shave, fried food, and leather. They split up, running the beams of their flashlights all over the dark rooms. David followed the partner, who had not been so skeptical about his story. The partner walked briskly through the living room and the kitchen, shining his light here and there, surprising everything with light. There was the milky green glass of the television, there the shiny leaves and grotesque shadow of the rubber plant in its brown plastic pot. In these slashes of light the house looked haunted, a mute witness to murders.

After the police had gone through with their flashlights they turned on the lamps and checked again, upstairs and down, looking into every closet. They opened the door to Lizzie's room. She didn't wake up. David wondered with a chill how often they found somebody hiding in closets, or in little girls' rooms.

When they finished their circuit they met back at the front door. "Looks like everything's all right," the first one said. David stood hating him. He hoped to find a big black man in the hall closet as soon as the police were gone. Then he crossed his fingers and glanced at the ceiling, to cancel the wish.

"Thank you for checking," Mom said.

"No trouble," the man said, looking at David as if it had actually been a lot of trouble. "Part of our job."

Janet squeezed the back of David's neck, reassuringly. "Keep it safe for democracy, men," she said.

"We get a call we answer the call, miss," the partner said. "We don't pick and choose. You never know when people are really in trouble."

"I know," she said in a subdued voice. "Don't mind me, I'm the crazy daughter they keep in the attic. Thank you for coming, really."

The partner let his flashlight beam creep along the floor and stopped it short of Janet's feet, where it quivered. "Apology accepted," he said, and a smile broke, startlingly white, in his heavy face.

"Yes, thank you, you've been grand," Mom said. "Come on now, crew. Back to bed."

"No trouble, ma'am," the partner said. He shifted his focus to Janet and added, "Just call me any time there's trouble."

She said thanks and smiled, in the particular way she sometimes did, her head cocked and her brows lifted skeptically.

"Bye," David said. He said it too loudly. He said "Bye," again, at the right volume.

"Evening," the first one said, settling his mouth in a grumpy, doglike way. They both left, and the first one closed the door firmly, with a finality that suggested the outdoors was private property, and the Starks were being evicted into their house.

"Assholes," Janet said.

"Is it you Lizzie gets it from?" Mom asked.

"Hey, Lizzie slept through this whole thing, didn't she?" Janet said.

"What I wouldn't give to sleep like that," Mom said.

David thought with satisfaction of how angry Lizzie would be to have missed out. She always fought sleep like death itself but yielded to it, when it took her, so completely that she slept through earthquakes and thunderstorms. She always instructed everyone to wake her up if anything important happened.

"You know," Janet said, "it's sort of cold in here."

"Well, what about a shot of brandy?" Mom said.

"Good idea."

"Can I have one too?" David asked.

"Oh sure," Mom said. "Maybe you'd like a cigar too."

They all went into the kitchen. Mom took a bottle from the cabinet and poured brandies into two juice glasses. The glasses had pictures of sliced oranges on their sides.

"You said I could have one too," David told her.

"You can have a sip of mine," Mom said. "A *small* sip."

David took the glass from her and raised it cautiously to his lips. The trick was to swallow as much as possible without spitting it back up. He let some seep in and held it on the back of his tongue, a thick brown taste that burned. To get rid of the burning he swallowed, which only pulled the liquid heat in a line down through his throat and chest. His eyes filled with tears, and it was a while before he could regain enough breath to say, "Ahh, that's good."

Mom took the glass back from him, and held it aloft. "Cheers," she said with a faint smile.

"I really did see a man in the backyard," David said.

"Sometimes it's hard to tell in the dark," Mom said. "Don't worry, you were right to tell me about it."

"I think there was a man in the backyard," Janet said.

"Well, maybe there was," Mom said. "He's gone now."

"Right," Janet said.

"There's nothing to worry about," Mom told David.

"Can I have another sip of your brandy?" he asked.

"No. What are you, a midget in disguise? What have you done with my little boy?"

"I don't know," David said. He slipped his fingers between the buttons of his pajama top and plucked at the single wiry hair that grew from his nipple.

"If we have another Peeping Tom, let's not call the police," Janet said. "Let's just deal with him ourselves."

"If we have another Peeping Tom," Mom said, "I can stand in the window and show him a thing or two that'll send him into another line of work."

"Mother. There's a child present."

"Him? He's practically thirty."

"Well then, he can have some of my brandy too," Janet said. She handed David her glass. In his excitement he took too deep a swallow. The liquor seared his throat and came right back up again. He sputtered it all over the table. The burning buzzed in his nostrils.

Mom said, "Whoops," and patted him on the back.

"Listen," Janet said.

"What?" Mom asked her.

"Nothing. My imagination."

"Did you hear something?" Mom said.

"Nope. Drink your brandy. I've been turning into a nervous old maid these past few weeks."

"I've been turning into a nervous old maid since 1972," Mom said.

"What did you hear?" David was finally able to ask through his choking.

"Nothing," she said. "Don't listen to me, you'll get as crazy as I am."

"Let's just go to bed," Mom said. "Squeeze your eyes shut tight and before you know it it'll be morning."

"Right," Janet said.

"David? Hit the sack, school day tomorrow."

"Okay," he said.

For a long moment before going upstairs, the three of them kept still, listening. Deep in the house a pipe gurgled, a rude froggy sound like male digestion. They all laughed and went to bed.

7

David slept patchily and woke with the first light. A bird piped outside, a single repeated shrill like metal twisting on metal. He'd had a bad dream, a variation on the monster dream, which was already dispersing into his blood as he woke.

He got up and went to the window. It was a violent sunrise, the sky burning orange at the horizon, setting fire to the scraps of cloud that hung behind the black branches of the tree. The pool blazed pink, and wisps of steam rose up into the warming air.

He put on his jeans and T-shirt, checked his hair, and went downstairs. The house held its darkness. When he walked out the kitchen door the new light cut through his clothes, brilliant and cold. His breath ran before him in darts of vapor. He walked around the pool and checked for footprints in the little corner garden. Nothing. He went out through the gate and around the side of the house, and found no prints in the dewy grass. The man was gone. David crossed the lawn and stood at the edge of the sidewalk. He turned to look at the house. Its pale yellow face stood blue with the sun behind it; the windows were black as tar paper. He looked up and down the street. On the Starks' side the houses were all shaded, blue or gray depending on their daylight colors. On the other side the houses burned, pure white or deeper white.

He walked down the street, checking it out. The bird screeched again, and he wondered what kind of bird it was. Everything in the world had a name. He resolved to learn more of them than he knew; he didn't even know the name of the tree in his own backyard. He thought he would feel less strange and overwhelmed by things if he knew better what to call them. As he walked along, he speculated over the names of the trees that lined his street. Under the trees were cars, and he ticked off their names. Cougar, Firebird, Country Squire, Rabbit.

When he first noticed the man sleeping in the car a chill shot through him. The fact that someone was *in* one of the cars, with his head propped against the window, impressed itself upon him. He jumped, and the blood rose singing to his head. A man. There. His focus blurred, took in nothing but black hair inside a brown car, then sharpened again.

It was Rob. He sat behind the wheel, asleep with his head reared back and his mouth half open. David approached the car cautiously. He had seen Rob plenty of times before, most recently at Christmas, but didn't remember his head being so big. The sun caught Rob's face in profile, turning his beard stubble the color of copper wire. He wore a gray suit, and a dark red tie covered with little circles like wagon wheels. The top button of his blue shirt was open, revealing a riot of illuminated red hairs that turned black and burnt-looking as they disappeared into the shirt.

David could not think of what to do. His first impulse was to call the police. His second impulse was to get Mom. But if he woke Mom, Janet would know about it too, and she had a bad habit of feeling sorry for Rob.

Hesitantly, almost against his will, David crossed over to the driver's side and tapped on the window. He tapped too softly, and Rob didn't stir, so he tapped again, this time too hard.

Rob jolted awake and looked frantically at David. When he turned David could see that he had a black eye, swollen and dark as a plum, yellow at the edges.

David jumped back. He recovered himself a moment before Rob did, and took a half step forward. He could not think of what to say.

Rob thought of what to say. An opaque shallow-bottomed sureness rose into his good eye, replacing the terrified glitter, and he rolled down the window and said, "Morning, David, my friend."

David stood hovering between courtesy and murder, his own eyes bleary with an agitation that was like tears. Rob's face was fattish around the jaw, and his lips were too red for his white, white skin. He was not, David thought, what you could call handsome.

"What are you doing?" David heard himself ask.

"Sleeping," Rob said, and grinned. His small teeth were as square as products off a factory line. When he smiled he showed a stripe of puffy darkish gums.

"What happened to your eye?" David said.

"Minor altercation," Rob told him. "You should have seen the other guy."

"Oh. Well, you shouldn't sleep here."

"Question of zoning?" Rob scrubbed his good eye with his finger.

"Janet doesn't want to see you," David said.

"Is that what she told you?" Rob opened his eye again. He looked at David as if he could see something meaningful on David's forehead.

"Uh-huh," David said to the curb.

"Well, sometimes women don't mean just exactly what they say, or say just what they mean. What if you and I went and had a cup of hot chocolate somewhere, and talked about women?"

"Did you drive down from San Francisco?" David asked.

"Yes I did. I stepped out of my office and got in my car and came straight here from work. That's just what I did."

There was something of Janet in the way he spoke. David couldn't put his finger on it; it had to do with rhythm, or something. Rob smiled again, showing his teeth and gums in a proud, satisfied way, as if he'd swallowed Janet whole.

"Oh," David said, shifting his weight from foot to foot.

"What do you say to a cup of hot chocolate?" Rob said. "I'll buy."

David hesitated, then said, "Okay," because he couldn't think of how to say no to anyone as big and insistent as Rob, and because he was flattered to be asked by anyone to do anything. His cheeks burned with the knowledge that his vanity made him too easy.

"Good," Rob said. He patted the passenger seat beside him. "Hop in."

"We can walk," David said. "There's a place over at the Plaza." He silently congratulated himself on staying out of Rob's car, which he noticed was a Celica.

"Okay," Rob said. He opened the door, stood, and stretched. David had not remembered him being so tall. Rob's spine cracked, and he rubbed his neck. "Jesus," he murmured. "Never let yourself get as old as I am, my friend."

"Okay," David said. He turned and set out walking toward the Plaza, anxious to put a little distance between himself and Rob's height. Rob caught up with him in one loping stride.

"Nice morning," Rob said.

"Uh-huh," David said, hurrying along.

"What are you in now, the fifth grade?"

"Sixth," David said.

"Oh. Sorry."

"It's all right."

They walked the rest of the way in absorbed silence. Rob walked in a loose-footed, reared-back way that didn't match his suit or his haircut. David could hear him breathing, in short breathy snorts like a horse. David thought with pride of how he could probably outrun Rob, even though his hips barely came up to the middle of Rob's thighs.

The Plaza when they reached it was nearly empty, its parking lot vast and sun-dazzled. The Burger King stood apart, at a remove from the Plaza proper, sharing a corner with the Cinema Twin. It alone was open for business, its glowing yellow sign made pale and greenish by the sky. David made to push open the swinging glass door but Rob reached over his head and touched it first, opening it for both of them while David's outstretched hand pushed empty air. He nearly stumbled on a ribbed rubber mat.

Hardly anyone was in the place, just a few men in suits, men with a certain sad, displaced look. The Burger King was spotless, all its surfaces scrubbed clean and its floor swept, the plastic wood-grain tables and molded orange chairs looking content and natural in the absence of people. It was a pretty sight.

David and Rob went up to the counter, to order from a sharp-nosed woman whose name, according to her badge, was Faith. "What'll it be, my friend?" Rob asked.

"Coffee," David said. Rob looked at him doubtfully, eyebrows lifted, and David said, "Coffee" again, this time directly to the woman named Faith.

"Okay. One coffee and one tea," Rob said. "You don't have any herb teas, do you?"

"Nope," Faith said scornfully. David agreed with her. To ask for something like that at a Burger King was stupid.

Faith rang it up on the register, and David reached automatically into his pockets, though he knew he didn't have any money. Rob raised his hand, flat, like a cop stopping traffic, and said, "On me." David felt a tick of gratitude for which he was instantly ashamed.

When Faith brought the coffee and the tea, two cardboard cups sealed over with white plastic lids, Rob gave her a limp dollar bill from his wallet, which had cowboy designs stamped onto it. Curlicues and steer skulls. David put his hands around one of the cups, absorbing its heat, which made him feel stronger. He took his cup, along with the white plastic tubs of cream and the envelopes of sugar, and guided Rob to a table at a window on the neighborhood side, overlooking the slant tile roofs and sun-gilded TV antennas of home.

In silence, they peeled the lids off their cups, which yielded with small sucking sounds. David poured the two creams and all four envelopes of sugar into his. The cream turned his coffee a mottled khaki, and he lifted it tentatively to his lips. The smell and heat assaulted him. Eying Rob, he let the coffee creep against his upper lip. It worked its way between his teeth, and he summoned every thread of will he had to keep from grimacing.

"So. I'll bet you're surprised to see me," Rob said.

"Uh-huh."

"I'm a little surprised to be here." He grinned and glanced around the Burger King, pleased with himself for being there. In the fluorescent light his black eye looked worse; it looked like something he was dying of. David squinted one eye and focused on Rob's bad side.

"You're going to miss work today," David said.

"I've always suspected the practice of law could go on without me for a day. How's Janet?"

"She's okay."

"Has she been going out a lot?"

David looked into his coffee. He knew he ought to confess, but he couldn't. He couldn't stand to topple that far over into the wrong. "I don't know," he said.

"Well, I'm here now," Rob said. He looked doubtfully at the

backs of his hands, as if he suddenly wondered whether he was really here at all.

Neither of them spoke for a while. David noticed that his coffee was unsteady in the cup, and realized he was jiggling his legs furiously against the single post that held up the table.

"Sometimes you have to take action," Rob told him finally. "I think maybe I haven't taken enough action in the past."

David nodded sympathetically, and wished he hadn't. He concentrated on keeping his legs steady.

"Has Janet talked about me much?" Rob asked.

"I don't know," David said. "A little, I guess."

"Well, I think it was definitely the right thing, coming down here like this. I wasn't getting anywhere on the phone. Come on, let's go talk to Janet."

"She's still sleeping," David said. Rob jumped up, and David took both their cups, the cream tubs and empty sugar envelopes, and put them in the trash. The trash can had a swinging orange lid that said THANK YOU in yellow letters.

They cut across the parking lot. David wondered what he could do to stop Rob from reaching the house. Rob wouldn't have come if David hadn't told those lies; it was a disgusting habit. Yet this particular story seemed truer to him than the idea of Janet's marrying Rob. He wasn't at all the type of man she would marry. She was much more likely to marry a man similar to the one in David's head, somebody strong and tall who looked a little like David himself, an older David. She would go back to school and make up her classes and become a doctor and marry a good-hearted, gentle man who knew how to protect her if he had to.

The sun was high enough for the streets to look ordinary, unhaunted. Neither Rob nor David spoke, and Rob walked with such big strides that David had to trot every few paces to keep up. When they reached the house Rob started right across the lawn to the front door.

"Everybody's still sleeping," David said, running now at Rob's side.

"Then we'll wake them up," Rob said. "It's a beautiful morning, no one should miss a beautiful morning like this one."

The door was locked, and David didn't have a key. He dug in his pockets as if ordinarily he carried one but had forgotten it. Rob reached over his head and pressed the doorbell with a single businesslike stabbing motion. David saw that his fingernails were cut so short they looked painful.

Rob let a few seconds pass, then rang again. "They can *hear* you," David said. "They're just putting their robes on."

Rob stood scowling, with his long finger pointed over the doorbell and his other hand buried in his pocket. David thought, suddenly, that he had helped bring everything bad in the world right here to the front door. He should have done something to prevent it.

"Who's there?" Mom's voice came uncertainly from behind the door. David knew she must be frightened.

"It's Rob, Beverly," Rob said, and his deep voice slit the morning air. David thought it must be audible to the end of the block. "I happened to find your son wandering around out here, and I brought him home."

David felt like a hostage. To let him in, Mom would have to let Rob in too.

"Rob?" Mom said. "Schmidt? Janet's Rob?"

"The same. Rob and David, two lost boys."

"David? Are you out there?" Mom asked.

He paused, thinking of self-sacrifice. But he knew Rob would get in, one way or another. "Yes," he said quietly, and said, "Yes" again.

Mom opened the door. She had on her white robe, and held an unlit cigarette between two fingers. She looked first at David, blankly; then she looked at Rob. Her face worked a beat too slowly into an expression of cordial surprise.

"Rob," she said. She put the cigarette in her mouth and stared at Rob's black eye.

"How are you, Beverly?" Rob said, extending his hand.

"They still let me run around loose." Mom put out her hand and let it be shaken. Rob squeezed her hand with quick gentle pressure, assuring her there was no danger anywhere.

"Surprised to see me?" he asked.

"Oh no," Mom said. "First I'm going to pour us both a cup of coffee and I'm going to light this cigarette, and then you can tell me how a man who lives five hundred miles away happens to show up at daybreak on my doorstep with my son."

"David and I already had our first cup," Rob said.

"Sure. He's been drinking coffee ever since he turned twenty-one. Come in."

The three of them walked through the dusky hallway to the kitchen, which was full of new light. "Janet's still sleeping," Mom said, "and Lizzie's deciding on today's outfit."

"The house looks good," Rob said.

"Still standing," Mom said. She took the steaming kettle from the stove, took cups from the shelf.

"I don't drink coffee anymore, Beverly," Rob said. "You wouldn't have any herb tea, would you?"

"I think the best I've got is Lipton's."

"That's fine."

Rob walked a slow circle around the kitchen, hands in his pockets. He paused before the refrigerator, and frowned over the cartoon held there by the plum-shaped magnet (an old man sitting dejectedly in a room full of balls, thirty or more of them, while his wife says, "Maybe you're trying to juggle too many at once").

"I hope you'll pardon my appearance," Rob said. "I didn't have time to wash up."

"What did you do, drive all night?" Mom said.

"Pretty much. I slept a couple of hours in my car out front, waiting until you all woke up."

"Were you lurking in my garden last night?"

"No," he said. "Why do you ask?"

"Never mind. Here." She handed him a steaming cup of tea, its string and paper tab dangling over into the saucer.

"Thank you, Beverly," Rob said. "You're all right, you know?"

"Sure, I'm the Fourth of July. Why don't you wait down here a minute and I'll go wake Janet up. Cream's in the refrigerator if you want it, and sugar's in the little canister that says 'Sugar.'"

"Thanks," Rob said.

Mom left the room, taking her unlit cigarette with her. On her way she brushed David's shoulder with her palm, tracing its shape, to remind him she remembered he was there.

"She's great," Rob said.

"I know," David said. He went to the stove, poured himself a cup of hot water, and scooped freeze-dried coffee into it.

Rob looked over at the table in the breakfast nook, and seemed to consider sitting there, but didn't. David leaned against the sink and sipped at his coffee, which was getting easier to do.

"How's the sixth grade?" Rob asked him.

"Okay," David said. Rob looked so strange there in the kitchen, in his suit and his bruise and his day-old whiskers, like an important man and a bum at the same time. David knew this was the moment for confessing. Soon Mom would come back, then Janet would come, and the world would go rolling lopsidedly along with his lie stuck in it. But one moment stretched into the next, in the liquid way they did when he had something to do and didn't want to do it; each idle moment was so silver and fine, even just standing there with a coffee cup in his hands and Rob bouncing slightly on his heels, working for something to say. David let another moment and another go by, and then Lizzie came into the kitchen, dressed for school.

"Well Lizzie," Rob said. His face lit up with more than ordinary polite good cheer. He looked as if he expected Lizzie to rescue him.

Lizzie, who had not spotted Rob right off, stopped short and stared at him. "Hi, Rob," she said, as if finding him here in the kitchen was just what she'd expected.

"Surprised to see me?" Rob asked.

"Yes," Lizzie said. David had slipped his coffee cup into the sink, to avoid stupid questions. Lizzie walked around Rob and opened the refrigerator door with a firm sense of destination, as though there were a staircase hidden inside. She brought out a carton of milk and put it on the table, where it was never put.

"How've you been?" Rob asked her.

"Okay," she said, watching the milk. "What happened to your eye?"

"Well, I had a little fight."

"Oh." She positioned herself a little differently inside her shirt, a fake leopard skin she'd gotten after two months' steady insistence. David considered insulting her; he could think of ten things off the top of his head. Instead he kept quiet, and watched Rob watching her.

"Have you heard the new Michael Jackson album?" Rob asked. At Christmas, he and Lizzie had based their relations on a shared love of Michael Jackson. They danced to "Don't Stop 'Til You Get Enough" over and over, Rob swinging his hips and arms in massive gestures that filled the living room.

"I've *got* it," Lizzie said. "I've had it for a month."

"What do you think?" Rob asked her.

She narrowed her eyes in her suspicious, finicky way. "I like it," she said tentatively, in case of a trick.

"Me too," Rob said. "I play it all the time."

Lizzie nodded, tight-lipped, pleased. David longed so to insult her that he had to hold his breath. He wouldn't do it with Rob there. It would be showing him too much of the family.

Mom came back, saying, "Janet will be down in a minute." She had lit her cigarette, and smoked it halfway down. "Good morning, Sparkle," she said to Lizzie.

"Don't call me that," Lizzie said.

Mom picked up the milk carton, glancing at it with accustomed surprise (things turned up in strange places with humanlike obstinacy; it was the way of the world), and put it back into the refrigerator.

"Rob, what about some breakfast?" she said.

David thought, Don't feed him, so hard he checked around to be sure he hadn't said it out loud.

"That'd be great," Rob said. "I haven't eaten since lunch yesterday." He smiled his proud smile, showing gums.

"I will make the toast," Lizzie said with gallant resignation.

"You've never made toast in your life," David said. He couldn't contain himself.

"Yes I have," Lizzie said.

"She never makes toast," he told Rob, helpless in his frustration over Lizzie's conceit, her *wrong*ness. "She never does anything. I'll bet she doesn't even know where the toaster is."

"I've been hearing about Lizzie's toast ever since we first met, David, my friend," Rob said. "I'm told she only makes it on special occasions."

David had blundered. Now it was Lizzie and Rob against him.

Lizzie took bread from the breadbox and said, "David sticks his boogers under the table. There's one there right now."

"More than enough, little darlings," Mom said.

Mom cooked the eggs and bacon, Lizzie made toast, and David set the table because he didn't want to do nothing. Rob leaned against the counter, drinking his tea, talking to Mom and calling her Beverly.

"Well, Beverly, even a bathrobe becomes you," he said while she turned the bacon. She didn't laugh.

"So how goes the practice?" she asked.

"All right. Fine. I seem to be passing for a real attorney. The suit and tie help."

"The first time I met you you were wearing overalls. I thought you were a farmer."

"Overalls and Birkenstocks," he said. "One uniform traded for another. I still meditate."

"Well. That's nice."

"If I have to work late I lock my office door and take the phone off the hook for half an hour," he said. "I never skip meditating. And I can tell you with absolute certainty, Beverly, that it's made me a better lawyer. So my hippie days paid off."

"Good," Mom said.

"How've you been?" he asked.

"Me? I'm always the same." She stirred the eggs and with her free hand held her robe closed over her chest.

"Maybe you'd like to try meditating someday," Rob said. "I'm always looking for converts."

"Do you think it would make me a better assistant administrator of schools?"

"It might make you a more relaxed one."

"If I was any more relaxed I couldn't stand up. Why don't you tell me to run away to Brazil? That's more what I have in mind."

Rob smiled and sipped his tea, his one eye shining.

They had just sat down to eat when Janet came downstairs. Her footsteps were audible on the treads, and a quick silence stitched the air before Mom resumed her story about Buzz Sorely, her boss, who in Mom's stories was a combination of menace and fool, dangerous in the way of a brontosaurus, which might crush you out of simple disorganized stupidity. She was still talking about him when Janet appeared in the kitchen doorway and stood there, as if waiting to be asked in.

She wore jeans and an old checkered shirt. Her hair was tied up in a knot. Rob had been watching the empty doorway and now he looked at Janet with only a small change in his face, a certain deepening of his eyes that reminded David of the remoteness that came into a dog's eyes when you scratched it in just the right place.

"Oh God," Janet said. "Did I do that?"

"Yes you did," Rob told her. "You did a very nice job."

"Did what?" Lizzie said.

"Shut up," said David.

"Gave him that eye," Janet told Lizzie. "I didn't think I hit him so hard." She made a fist, and looked at it with surprise and satisfaction.

"You *hit* him?" Lizzie said.

Janet nodded, looking at her fist. Then she looked up at Rob. "I just can't believe you," she said.

"Why did you hit him?" Lizzie asked.

"Aren't you happy to see me?" Rob said.

"What do you think? I thought you had more respect for me than this."

"Did you hit her back?" Lizzie asked Rob.

"How about some breakfast, Janny?" Mom said. "Lizzie's made her special holiday toast."

"No thanks. I'll just have some coffee." She went to the stove to pour it, but stopped halfway and planted her hands on her hips. "Were you the Peeping Tom last night?" she asked.

"No," Rob said. "What, did you have somebody out there?"

"What Peeping Tom? Where? Here?" Lizzie said.

"The police were here last night," David told her. "They walked all over the house with flashlights. They even went in your room. You slept right through it."

Lizzie's jaw quivered in disbelief. "Why didn't you wake me up?" she said to Mom. Her voice was quiet; she didn't have enough power in her lungs for a shout big enough to match the offense.

"David thought he saw someone," Mom said. "There was no point in having any more excitement than we had already."

Thinking of Rob as the man in the yard altered the quality

of last night's fear. The event itself changed: David had not been endangered but just comically put out over a silly character sneaking through the flower beds. It had a parallel cartoon version, with David a short, brave animal, a sort of beaver-bear, and Rob a goggle-eyed human with stork legs and a plumed hat, tiptoeing around on his oversize feet while ghostly hearts and exclamation points rose up out of his head.

"I told you to always wake me up," Lizzie said. She settled peevishly into herself.

Janet brought her coffee to the table. Rob half stood, and she motioned him to sit down again with a single, flat-handed command. David was impressed by the gesture. He would use it himself someday. Janet stood by the table, between David and Lizzie, across from Rob. She was wearing perfume.

"I still think it was you," she said. "The minute I heard there was a man outside, I thought of you."

"It could have been any of your boyfriends." Rob smiled.

"Anyway, we all lived through it," Mom said. "Clear light of day, and we're all in one piece."

"I'm just trying to figure you out," Janet said to Rob. "I'm standing here trying to remember what I could have told you to make you think it would be a good idea to hop in the car and drive all the way down here and stand outside my window."

"I guess I didn't think about it at all," Rob said. He checked Lizzie, briefly, for sympathy.

"Oh, I can appreciate it in a movie sort of way," Janet said. "That's how you expect me to appreciate it, isn't it?"

Rob gave an elaborate shrug and crossed his eyes. Lizzie giggled.

"I'd just like to think you had more respect for my decisions," Janet said.

Rob turned serious, chin lowered, and said, "My being here doesn't have to affect your decision in any way, shape, or form. I'm just somebody having breakfast in your kitchen. If you tell me to, I'll get up after breakfast and drive right back to San Francisco."

"Good," Janet said. "Finish your breakfast, and go back to San Francisco."

He looked at her in his doting, doggish way. "Really?"

"Really."

"Well, all right."

"All right."

"Maybe you should sleep a couple of hours first," Mom said.

"No thank you, Beverly. I'll be all right."

"He could take a nap in my room," Lizzie said.

"No thanks, I'm fine," Rob said. "I'll stop somewhere on the way and meditate."

"It's a long drive," Mom said.

David could see that things were turning against Janet. She seemed to know it, too. She shook her head, and the smell of her perfume, still too fresh to have settled into her body, swelled in David's nose.

"I'm sorry, Rob," she said. "But it was a bad idea. Do you see that?"

"Yes," he said gravely, though he didn't sound convinced.

Janet kept on shaking her head. "It's just the worst possible time for me to see you. You know that. It isn't fair—shit, I don't even know what I'm saying. I'm going to go upstairs. Call me when you get back to the city, so I know you're safe, okay?"

"Okay," he said.

"Good-bye." She walked out of the kitchen. David thought he heard her whisper something, though the words were lost.

They all waited until her footsteps had sounded on the last stair. A floorboard creaked in the upstairs hall. Rob winced. "Well," he said, "thank you for breakfast."

"You haven't finished," Mom said.

"I'm not really hungry anymore. I think the sooner I get on the road again, the better it'll be."

"I'm sorry, Rob," Mom said. "But it's her decision."

"I know," he said. "I just thought—I don't know what I thought. I didn't think at all. I just left the office and got in my car and drove to Los Angeles. I'm probably as surprised as she is to find me here." He glanced around at the kitchen with such bewilderment that David felt a pang of sympathy despite himself. Everything about Rob's face had changed: the sharpness gone out of his eye, the thrust out of his jaw. With a shock, David could see how he had looked when he was twelve.

"Well," Mom said, "let me see if I can dig up a thermos. I'll give you some tea for the road."

"No thanks. I think I'll just pick up and go right now. Bye, kids. It's been nice seeing you." He took his napkin from his lap and dabbed his mouth with it, carefully.

"Good-bye," Lizzie said. When Rob stood up she jumped out of her chair, and followed him to the door. Mom and David came close behind.

"What's your favorite song on *Thriller?*" Lizzie asked him at the threshold.

"Oh, I don't know. I like all of them. What's yours?"

" 'Beat It,' " Lizzie said. "And 'Billie Jean.' "

"Those are my favorites too," Rob told her.

"Also, 'Thriller,' " Lizzie said.

"Right, that one's great too. They're all great. Thanks for breakfast, Beverly."

"I don't really like 'Baby Be Mine' all that much," Lizzie said.

"Do call when you get back, okay?" Mom said to Rob. "Just so we don't worry about you."

"Right. Take care, David my friend."

"Uh-huh," David said.

"Bye, Rob," Lizzie said. "Drive carefully."

"Bye, Lizzie."

"I *do* like 'Baby Be Mine,' " she said. "I just don't like it as much as the others."

"I know how you feel. Bye."

"*Bye.* Drive carefully."

Then he was gone, nimbly down the two concrete steps and along the white walk to the street. From the back he looked wholly respectable, a man in a suit, off to work. Lizzie waved to him, and when he got to the sidewalk he waved back.

"Come back soon," she called.

As Rob's suit and hair disappeared around the hedge, David said to her, "That was a stupid thing to say. He's never coming back."

"Shut up, you asshole," she said.

"Back in the house, both of you," Mom told them.

They returned to the breakfast nook and ate the last of their eggs. "Well, it's too bad he came all the way down here like that," Mom said.

"Why wouldn't Janet talk to him?" Lizzie said.

"Because she didn't want to," David said. "She thinks Rob's a shit."

"You're a shit."

"Because she needs more time alone," Mom said. "You have to trust Janet. She knows what's best for herself."

"But Rob wants to marry her," Lizzie said.

"Well, Sparkle, she just doesn't want to be married," Mom said. "She wants to try again to get into medical school."

"She could get married *and* go to medical school," Lizzie said.

"She doesn't seem to think she could. That's her choice."

Lizzie paused, thinking. "Don't call me Sparkle anymore," she said.

"Sorry," Mom said. "It's an old habit."

Mom took the dishes to the sink, and David and Lizzie hung around the kitchen, uncertain about how to reenter the normal day. David thought maybe Janet had been a little too hard on Rob. He drove five hundred miles, and all he got was a few bites of scrambled egg. Then again, he hadn't been allowed to stay around long enough for anyone to uncover David's new story.

They heard the sound of Janet's movements upstairs. Although no one said anything about it the air in the kitchen tightened, and David sidestepped a few paces closer to the door, so he'd be the first person she saw.

Her perfume entered, and then she did. Her eyes were dry. "Having devoured her mate," she said, "the spider went back to her ordinary business of picking up stray flies."

"You did what you had to do," Mom said, keeping busy at the sink.

"I know I did. That doesn't make me feel any better."

Lizzie squinted at Janet as if she was far away. "I would have let him stay," she said.

"That's because you're a pinhead," David told her.

"And you're a faggot."

"Where do you both learn words like that?" Mom asked. "Who are you people, anyway?"

"Rob is more persistent than you think, Lizzie," Janet said. "He's not a *bad* guy but, well, he's just very determined to have his own way. A gentle no doesn't work very well with him."

"I would have let him stay," Lizzie said.

"Let's send Lizzie to San Francisco to live with Rob," David said.

"Let's get you both off to school," Mom said. "I can't tell you what a thrill it's going to be not to hear your voices for the next eight hours."

"Maybe I could stay home today," David said. He was thinking of keeping an eye on Janet, and of staying out of the sights of Billy's gun for a while longer.

"Maybe you could run upstairs right now," Mom said, "put your school clothes on, and scrape the moss off your teeth."

"If David gets to stay home from school I do too," Lizzie said.

"Nobody's staying home from school," Mom said.

"Why don't they?" Janet said. "Just this one time. I'll take them to the beach or something. It'd be good to have company today."

"Do you want to write the notes explaining how they got suntans while they were sick?"

"Sure. We'll put powder on them or something. Come on, Mother, be a sport."

"Yeah, be a sport," David said.

"We're not doing anything today," Lizzie said. "There are no tests."

Mom poured soap into the dishwasher. "Tell you what," she said. "As of today, you kids make all the decisions. I'll just go to work and come home and do whatever you say. For every day you get older I'll get a day younger, and before you know it we'll be right back here again with me asking you if I can skip work for a day. How would that be?"

"Great," David said.

While Mom got dressed for work, David, Lizzie, and Janet put on their bathing suits and gathered towels, suntan oil, the transistor radio. Janet filled a sack with fruit from the refrigerator. The house was charged with the sweet strangeness of going, made all the better by the unexpectedness of the trip. A spur-of-the-moment journey improved the house in David's eyes; it widened its circle of possibility.

When Mom came downstairs in her cocoa-colored skirt and jacket, carrying her purse, Janet drove her to work. Before they left Mom kissed David and Lizzie on the forehead and said, "Be sure you have dinner ready on time tonight. And the electric bill's due by Friday."

"Okay," David said. He was taken with the fact that Mom when she dressed for work looked like anybody. Strangers had no way of knowing she was peculiar and kind. He thought with satisfaction of how Lizzie hadn't realized that yet.

He and Lizzie stood in the living room in their bathing suits, watching Janet and Mom pull out in Mom's car, a light blue Camaro with blue upholstery. Everybody called it the Blue

Baby. Out in the neighborhood, at this moment, Billy was calculating David's progress toward school; he might even be waiting in a tree or behind a parked car, his weapon cocked, thinking, Any minute now. Rob was driving back to San Francisco and Dad was in Spokane with Marie. David and Lizzie stood right here in the living room, surrounded by walls. They both looked out the window, not speaking. When they were alone together they didn't fight much. They hardly talked at all. Lizzie lifted one skinny leg behind her and held her ankle with her hand. Of all the people in the world Lizzie was the only one who had no smell, or if she had a smell it was enough like David's own that he could barely detect it. She just smelled like a person. David glanced down at her bare legs, the one folded up like a stork's and the other knob-kneed, dusted with freckles, the unfreckled parts so white they were almost blue. Standing with all her weight on that one thin leg she looked so fragile that David reached over and pushed her off balance, to put her back on two feet. She stumbled sideways and came at him so fast her body might have been attached to his by an elastic band. She punched his shoulder, hard as she could. He said, "That's too hard, you fucker," and walked into the kitchen, because he didn't want to fight. He just didn't like her looking so delicate, so close to falling over.

Janet came back in the Blue Baby fifteen minutes later, and they loaded their beach things into the trunk. David and Lizzie had some trouble working out the question of who would sit in front, which Janet resolved by flipping a coin. Lizzie had the front seat on the way to the beach, David would have it on the way back.

They drove through the neighborhood, heading for the freeway. Janet steered with one hand, and in that hand she kept a cigarette pinched between her index and middle fingers. She was not a careful driver. She paid only marginal attention to the road, as if it were not quite interesting enough to hold her attention.

"What's the name of the company Rob works for?" Lizzie asked as the houses ticked by.

"Thorson and Lee," Janet told her. "It's called a firm. The companies lawyers work for are called firms."

"Why does he want to be a lawyer?" David said. "It's a stupid thing to do."

"He likes it. He likes making all that money. He even likes wearing a suit. He didn't like those things quite so much when I first met him."

"Why not?" Lizzie asked.

"Oh, he just had different ideas then, Lizzie. A lot of people did. He thought he was going to be a lawyer for poor people. You know, keep them out of jail when they get arrested for things they didn't do."

"Why do they get arrested, then?" Lizzie asked.

"Sheesh," David said.

"For a lot of reasons. Anyway, it's no concern of Rob's, because he changed his mind. He works for rich people instead."

"Why?" Lizzie asked.

Janet took a drag from her cigarette, and the car drifted toward the center line. She brought it smoothly back on course. "Because law school is a lot of hard work, and he decided he should be paid back for it. And because his drugs are very expensive. Whoops, don't tell Mom about that part. Anyway, you think all kinds of wonderful things about the future until you see how much you're going to have to pay for it."

"Do you still want to be a doctor for poor people?" David asked.

"At this point I just want to be a doctor, period," she laughed. "No, that isn't true. I still want to work in clinics for people who don't have any money, yes. But I haven't spent one day in medical school yet. Who knows how much I might be corrupted."

"You wouldn't be," David said.

"Yes she would," Lizzie said.

David started to tell her she didn't know what *corrupted* meant, but decided not to chance it. Instead he propped his arm over the back of the seat, in the style of Baretta, and looked out the rear window with the expression of superior boredom he'd been working on. It was then that he saw Rob's car, the brown Celica, following them one car behind.

At first David was too surprised to speak at all. Then he gave what originated deep inside him as a shout but thinned in his windpipe and came out as a squeak instead, which he managed to pull down a notch or two so it ended as a high-pitched groan.

"Are you all right?" Janet called from the driver's seat. The car swerved gracefully into the next lane as she looked over her shoulder at him.

"He's following us," David said.

"Who?" Lizzie said.

"Him," was all David could think of. The man's name was suddenly nowhere in his head.

"Shit, I knew it," Janet said. She steered the car back into its rightful lane.

"I don't see anything," Lizzie said. She craned her head up over the sausage-shaped headrest on the back of her seat and said, "Oh, there he is."

"I thought he was going back to San Francisco," David said.

"I knew he wouldn't," Lizzie said.

"Let's go to the police."

"Shut up, you crazy pinhead."

"We're just going to go to the beach as planned," Janet said, "and forget there's a lunatic driving behind us. Okay?"

"We could try and lose him," David suggested.

"Not in the Blue Baby."

"Do you want me to drive?"

"You can't," Janet said. "You're twelve."

"I can drive, though," he said. Though he'd never tried it, he felt certain he knew how from years of observation. It looked like a simple process.

Janet checked the rearview mirror and took a quick, nervous hit of her cigarette. "Let's just relax, hmm?" she said. "Lizzie, turn around and face the front, okay?"

Lizzie kept on watching Rob's car, her chin pressed into the headrest.

"He must be crazy," David said.

"How about if we sing?" Janet said. "What songs do you both know?"

"I don't want to sing," Lizzie said.

"David? Come on."

"I don't think I want to sing either," he said. He glanced back at Rob, whose face behind the wheel looked no different from that of any other grim, businesslike driver.

"Then I'll do a solo number," Janet said, and she began singing "Nowhere Man," in a loud, off-key voice. David joined in midway, when it became apparent that she wasn't going to get embarrassed and stop. The two of them sang.

David had been listening to Janet's Beatles records since he was a baby. He knew them better than he'd ever known nursery rhymes. After "Nowhere Man" they sang "Yellow Submarine," "Eleanor Rigby," "Taxman" and "Norwegian Wood." "Norwegian Wood" was such a sad, elegant song that David sang it in a sort of English accent which was, to him, the voice of true feeling.

They sang some Neil Young songs they both knew, and

some Grateful Dead. Then they switched over to television songs. Lizzie joined them on "Mr. Ed," because they couldn't remember all the words and she was proud of the fact that she could. They sang all the way to the beach, and Rob held steady on their tail.

When they got off the freeway and onto city streets, and the broad blue band of the ocean appeared before them, shimmering above the silvery glare of traffic, David felt as if they'd traveled through dangerous country and reached home. They were by then singing "The Star-Spangled Banner," having nearly run out of songs. Janet pulled into the parking lot they always parked in, and gave two dollars to the old man who sat on a folding metal chair in front of his gray wooden booth. The man's eyes bugged out and pointed in slightly different directions. Ever since he was a kid David had been afraid of the man and had discreetly avoided looking at him. Now he seemed like an old friend, a protector. Rob waited behind them, and after they'd driven onto the lot David watched Rob pay the man, who took his money and let him in.

Janet parked at the far end of the lot, at the edge of a chalky red bluff that dropped down to the beach. The bluff had been pitted and tunneled by rain, and David knew that from below it looked like a gigantic ant farm. Janet pulled up close to the edge, so the front of the car appeared to be hanging out over the ocean. The dark blue water met the paler sky just along the tops of the fenders. Janet turned off the ignition. "Just sit here a minute and don't say anything, okay?" she said. "Let me talk to him."

Rob parked alongside, got out of his car, and ambled over, smiling, his teeth very white. Lizzie called, "Hi, Rob," and he said, "Hello, Lizzie" as though he were surprised to see her. He put his fingertips lightly on the sill of Janet's open window.

"Beautiful day," he said.

Janet maintained her driving posture. "Rob," she said, "what I want you to do is get back in your car, pull out of here even though it just cost you two dollars to get in, and drive back home. I know you think it's a good idea, keeping after me like this, but it's not. It makes me think some of my worst thoughts about you are true."

"We haven't talked enough," he said.

"How much should we talk?"

"We should talk until I understand why we were planning our wedding exactly five days ago and now today you won't give me twenty minutes after I drove five hundred miles. We should talk that much."

"That'll be hard," Janet said, "if you don't understand already." She looked straight ahead and gripped the wheel as if she expected the car to run out of control into the ocean.

"Well maybe I should ask questions, and you try to answer them. How would that be?" Rob said. The wind worried his shirt collar and his hair, which was cut into short, overlapping shreds like a television hero's.

"Please just go, Rob."

"Question number one: Was anything you ever said to me about love true, to the best of your knowledge?"

"Don't turn into F. Lee Bailey or I'll drive right over this cliff."

"Are you going to answer the question?"

"No."

"All right. Try this: What have I done that's ever made you anything but happy?"

"You're asking the wrong questions."

"Tell me the ones to ask."

"See, I can't seem to make you understand that it's not your *fault*. It's me, it isn't you. If I stay with you I'll give in to all my cowardly urges to just be protected by you. I won't do the work to get into medical school. I know just what kind of asshole I am."

"So what should I do?"

"Let me go."

"I can't."

"Well, I've gone."

"And I'm following you. If you come back to San Francisco I promise not to protect you."

"That's not something you can offer. That's like offering to remove your head."

"Maybe you and I could talk privately for ten minutes. Maybe the kids could go down to the beach."

"I won't go to the beach with just David," Lizzie shrieked.

"Well, that settles that," Janet said.

"Have you thought about me for one minute in the last five days?" Rob said. "Has the fact that I'm suffering been of any concern to you?"

"You know it has."

"I don't know it from the way you're acting, no. No, I don't know it at all."

Janet nodded. She held onto the steering wheel. "Listen, kids," she said. "How would it be if we all walked down to the beach, and Rob and I can talk while you two go swimming. How would that be?"

"Rob is in a *suit,*" Lizzie said.

"I'll be the best-dressed man on the beach," Rob said. "Come on, Lizzie, let's you and me head on down, and if the others want to come along, they can."

"Okay," Lizzie said, and she was out of the car. She scurried around to the other side. Rob offered her his hand, which she took hesitantly.

"Come on, David," Janet said. "I promise this won't last long."

"Okay." He was pleased with the fact that, Rob and Lizzie having paired off, he and Janet were made into a couple. They gathered the towels and the sack of fruit.

A gently sloping trail started at the far corner of the parking lot and traversed the cliff face, strewn with candy wrappers and shards of amber glass. They had to go single file on the trail. Rob went first, followed by Lizzie and Janet; David brought up the rear, holding a stack of towels. He tasted the talcumy dust the others raised. He had on his plaid trunks and his Stevie Wonder T-shirt, and a pair of tennis shoes which struck him as ridiculous. They made a joke of his skinny legs. Walking ahead of him, carrying the grocery bag, Janet looked far more dignified. She wore sandals and a man's white shirt (Rob's?), which fell below the bottom of her swimsuit. She wore the sleeves rolled to her elbows in fat cuffs that emphasized her thinness in a complimentary way.

The beach was sparsely populated. People lay on towels here and there, and a few surfers bobbed in the water, watching for good waves, as docilely expectant as commuters at a bus stop. When he reached the base of the trail David immediately stopped to take his shoes off, hopping first on one foot and then on the other. Rob, Lizzie, and Janet walked down to the boundary line where the sand turned wet, and David loped to catch up, the shoes gratifyingly heavy in his hands. Rob stood against the water in his gray suit, hands in his pockets.

"Kids, Janet and I are just going to take a little walk up the beach," he said. "We'll be back soon."

"I want to come too," Lizzie said. She had on blue rubber thongs, her green one-piece bathing suit, and her leopard-skin shirt.

"We'll be back in ten minutes," Rob said, and David thought he saw something tighten in his smile.

"How about if you two set up camp?" Janet said. "Pick out a good spot and sort of get things organized."

"Yuck," Lizzie said. She was working into tantrum position, shoulders hunched up and head bent as if she was about to batter down a door.

"Give us just a little break, will you, Lizzie?" Rob said, and his smile went that much tighter.

Lizzie paused in her tensed, trembling way, and David waited with mixed dread and glee for the first screech. Rob would see what she was really like. Instead of screaming, though, she held steady a second longer than usual, then began to deflate. Her shoulders inched back down.

"Okay," she said. "But come back in ten minutes."

David had never seen her headed off like that. Her tantrums were like thunderstorms—you could protect yourself from them but you couldn't lessen their force. He would not have been much more surprised if Rob had commanded rain from the clear sky. He had to admit to a certain respect for anyone who could deal with Lizzie.

"Right," Rob said. "Ten minutes."

"Don't go in the water before we get back, okay?" Janet said.

"I'm going to," Lizzie said, though David knew she had no intention of going in any deeper than her knees, for fear of getting her hair wet.

Janet and Rob walked off along the water's edge, just shy of the point to which the waves washed, hesitated, and withdrew, leaving lines of dead brown foam and small living bubbles boiling up out of the sand. David watched people noticing Rob in his suit. A fleshy blond woman who sat hugging her big knees on a candy-striped towel stared after him, as did a skinny old man who jogged by, coming in David and Lizzie's direction. When he passed David and Lizzie he smiled, showing uneven yellow teeth, and said, "You see something new every day."

David and Lizzie could not quite think of what to do with themselves. David spread out the towels in a spot he decided was too close to the water and moved them farther up. He brushed off the stray grains of sand and straightened the corners. Lizzie stepped out of her thongs and drew her initials in the wet sand with her toes. Janet and Rob grew smaller and smaller. Janet, who was closer to the water, walked slightly bent against the wind, the hem of the shirt flapping up to show how her turquoise swimsuit cut in twin diagonals across her bottom.

In front of Lizzie a gull dipped down low over the water, skimming at an angle, its lower wing tracing the heaving surface. Lizzie had drawn her initials several times and was now working on her full name, longhand, in the big loopy lettering she'd invented for herself. As David glanced back and forth between Janet and Lizzie he was suddenly appalled by the ocean's size. It had always seemed friendly to him, a broad wet playground, but now he saw how it pushed up onto the sand, taking a little more with each wave, eating already into the farthest of Lizzie's initials. It could rear up at any moment, a foaming wall ten feet high, and crush them all against the cliff, hungrily sucking their bodies back out with it, leaving only smooth glossy sand behind. Down the beach, Rob and Janet stood facing each other. Though they were far away, David thought he saw Rob lean forward and kiss the air close to Janet's mouth, and Janet brush the kiss away as if shooing a bee. Lizzie finished writing her name and walked a few paces into the water, letting it break in plumes over her shins. David had an urge to grab her and drag her back up onto the dry sand.

Janet and Rob came back. When they got close enough to be heard Rob looked at his wrist and called, "Nine and a half minutes."

David nodded, with no idea of what to say. Lizzie trotted up from the water and said to Rob, "You look funny in that suit."

"I know I do," he said. "I'm a funny kind of man."

"Ha ha," Janet said.

David wondered if his second lie about the boyfriend had been uncovered. He believed for an instant that what they would do was sit him down and tell him they'd compared notes and realized he was the source of all their troubles.

"I wrote my name in the sand," Lizzie said, in a wide-open little-girl voice David hadn't heard from her since she was six or so.

"Whoopee-do," he said.

"Looks nice," Rob told her. "You do good work."

"My real name is Elizabeth," she said. "Can you read it?"

"Give us a break, huh Lizzie?" David said. "You sound like a total fool."

"Be quiet, you stupid pinhead," she said, and David was gratified at least to have her returned to her normal, unpleasant self.

"I'm going to go get the sand out of my shoes," Rob said. "I'll see you kids tonight."

"Tonight?" David asked.

"He's coming over for dinner," Janet said. She spoke to a point in midair, to the left of David's face, her eyes unfocused.

"Yay," Lizzie said.

David was so surprised that, although a good line about Lizzie making up a fresh batch of toast came into his head, he didn't use it.

"So I'll see you tonight," Rob said.

"See you tonight," Lizzie said.

"See you." Rob reached for Janet's shoulder and patted the air an inch above it, as if she wore an invisible shield. Then he started across the beach toward the trail.

"Okay, everybody," Janet said. "Sorry for the interruption. The day at the beach can now officially begin."

"Did you really ask him over for dinner?" David asked.

"Yes," Janet said casually. "Don't worry, it'll be over soon enough. I just couldn't—well, I want to be fair to him." She hugged her elbows and watched Rob, laboring up the trail.

"You didn't *ask* him to come to L. A.," David said.

"Well, maybe I did, in a way."

"Oh," David said uncertainly.

"Come on, let's go for a swim. Come on, Lizzie."

Lizzie had been watching Rob's progress along the cliff, hugging her elbows. "Okay," she said, and didn't move.

They spent several hours at the beach, swimming and lying in the sun. Janet didn't talk much. She would run out into the water, swim until she looked no bigger than the bobbing gulls, and come back in again to lie heavily on the sand, her skin goose-pimply, a scrap of scalloped yellow kelp caught in her hair. David and Lizzie played haphazardly by themselves. The day would not settle into itself; would not descend from its feeling of suspension, as if the real day was still to begin. Lizzie paraded up and down along the wet sand, practicing different walks, and David gathered shells, gull feathers, pretty stones which, as they dried, turned to disappointing grays and browns, their intricate veinings erased. He didn't see why she had asked him to dinner.

By one o'clock Janet suggested they had probably all had enough sun and ought to think about getting home. Then to head off Lizzie's tantrum she agreed to a movie instead. They picked up their things, loaded themselves back into the car, and drove to Santa Monica in a logy, sun-dazzled silence.

They found a matinee showing of a Clint Eastwood movie and sat together in the cool, stale darkness that smelled of mildew and old velvet. They were three of no more than a dozen people and it was exciting to be in a place so entirely forbidden—even if they weren't cutting school, no decent person was supposed to be at the movies on a sunny afternoon. David checked out the other people in the theater and found them to be mostly ordinary old people who sat watching the screen without expression. Only one man, sitting two rows behind and several seats over, acted like he was seeing the movie, and he apparently saw a different movie from the one on the screen. During the tense parts, when Clint was fighting three men at once or dodging bullets on his motorcycle, the man giggled like it was a comedy. Once he said, "Death to the commie faggot," just when Clint was in the worst trouble. David strained to look at him without being noticed. The man had a big shapeless body, and he seemed to be wearing three shirts. His head was too small for the baseball cap that rode down over his eyebrows. When David felt the man's attention sense his own, and thought that in another half-second the man's shaded eyes would swing around and lock with his, he snapped his head back toward the screen so fast his neck popped.

Janet slipped her arm over the back of his seat. He leaned in toward her, letting his shoulder brush her ribs. He forced himself not to look at her, for fear she'd take her arm away. On screen, Clint flew his motorcycle over mountainous terrain most men couldn't have walked across. His girlfriend clung to his back, wide-eyed and mute, while he tricked the helicopter that was chasing them into a high tension wire, where it flowered into flame. David glanced back at the man, who was tittering, and glanced at Janet. The last of the explosion colored her face. Her skin paled and cooled as the helicopter dissolved into black twisted worms. She smiled at David and took her arm away. The man in the baseball cap said, "Better luck next time, buckaroos."

Mom told Janet there wasn't anything in the kitchen but a few old bones and some hanks of hair.

"I'll go to the store after I've dropped you off," Janet said. They had picked Mom up at work and were now driving through the grid of streets to the house. When they'd pulled into the district building's parking lot Mom had been standing out front, waiting for them, holding her purse in front of her with both hands. They were late. Seeing her in her cocoa-colored suit, backed by the squat, square salmon-tan of the building she worked in, clutching her purse like it was all she owned, David had felt a shock of nonrecognition. She looked so old and abandoned. She might have been anyone.

"What time is he coming?" she asked, sitting in the back seat with Lizzie, her purse fat on her lap.

"I don't know. After seven." Janet drove loosely, with one hand, and the car drifted from one side of its lane to the other.

"Well, I guess we can pull something together for him," Mom said. "It won't be anything fancy."

"Actually, I think dinner is the last thing he cares about," Janet said.

"Oh, I know that," Mom said.

Janet let them out in the driveway and went off to buy groceries. Mom hustled David and Lizzie inside. "If anybody from school drives by and sees you out here in swimsuits, they'll get me for an accessory," she said.

"Don't you want Rob to come over for dinner?" Lizzie asked.

"I want your sister to be happy, is what I want," Mom said. "Come on now, inside."

"But Rob is nice," Lizzie protested as she was urged through the front door by the pressure of Mom's fingertips on her thin shoulders.

"Sure he's nice," Mom said. "Nice has nothing to do with it. I want you both to run upstairs and change into your real clothes right now. *Macht schnell.*" She slapped them both lightly on their rumps, and Lizzie hollered, "Ow," as a general declaration of unhappiness.

Up in his room, David changed into underpants and worked his legs halfway into his jeans before he lay down on his bed. Overhead the paper galaxy taped to the ceiling shone on unchanged. Dad had stood on the bed in his socks, right where David lay, to tape it up. He remembered dinners with Dad, who sat enormous in his rolled shirtsleeves, chewing. Dad chewed each mouthful with hungry distaste, as if everything served to him had tiny bones in it. Once Lizzie, who was hardly big enough then to reach the table but refused to sit in a highchair, spilled a glass of milk and Dad slapped her across the face with a hand big and flat as a board. Everybody sucked in a quiet breath. Lizzie, in the shaved second of rising shock and astonishment that would peak and then drop off into tears, glared at Dad with such piercing hatred that David started to cry at the same moment she did, from his own helplessness and from his conviction that Dad's only response to such a look would be murder. He'd howl the house down, he'd fall on them like God gone crazy. Instead he stuck his fork deep into his potato, while Mom gathered David and Lizzie and took them to finish their dinners in the kitchen.

David pulled up his T-shirt to look at his narrow, prominent rib cage, stained pink by the sun. Sometimes he was amazed to find himself in such a small body. The single hair, which had grown with its own insane life, stood up from the hard circle of flesh that covered his heart. He pulled at it but found it as it always was, firmly planted, as if it had roots sunk deep inside. He would get bigger. He would grow more hairs. It was like a werewolf movie, this change happening all by itself. You could fight it until your brain burst but the monster took over anyway and suddenly there it was, right where it wanted to be, nestled in the warm soft heart of things.

When he heard Janet come back, David finished dressing. He left his room and walked downstairs, past the blare of "Beat It" that came from behind Lizzie's door. Janet's and Mom's voices came from the kitchen, hushed in a way that made him go quietly, not exactly planning to listen but uncertain of how to approach, afraid of snapping a delicate thread he imagined stretched across the kitchen door.

As he drew closer he could hear Mom saying, "—handled it right the first time, is all."

David paused, not really to listen.

"That's the kind of thing it's always easy for other people to say," Janet said.

"Just be careful. This is how it starts."

"Nothing is starting. I am having the man I lived with for three years over for dinner, after which he'll sleep on the sofa. After which he'll drive home."

A numbness sank to the bottom of David's throat. No one had said anything about Rob sleeping over.

"It just has a familiar ring to it, is all," Mom said.

"Well, it's different this time. Do you want to know why?"

"Yes. Tell me."

"Because I realized I'm not in love with Rob. I'm just not. At bottom it has nothing to do with my becoming a doctor or not becoming one. The main point is, when I got turned down by the med schools and we started talking about marriage and yes, by the way I do know about the connection between the two, anyway when we started talking *wedding* and maybe even *children* I looked over at him, I can remember the particular moment even, we were standing in the bathroom together, he'd just gotten out of the tub and I was brushing my teeth and he sort of brushed against me with his hip and I thought to myself, This is not the man. Automatically, like a button had been pushed. Does that make any sense?"

"Well, I guess so," Mom said.

"It's not that I'm holding out for somebody handsomer or more charming or anything. God knows, it's more like the opposite. I've always been sort of astonished that he was interested in me at all, he could have gotten somebody so much— well, he just could have. He was so damn good he made me mad. So I punched him. Do you know what I mean?"

"I don't have the foggiest notion."

David's heart rose. Janet didn't love Rob; there was no danger. Rather than walk into the kitchen he tiptoed back upstairs, to feed on the fact that Rob had no claim here. He was not loved, he had no rights. As David passed through the curtain of Lizzie's music he thought he would be more careful, starting now, to treat her more kindly, to work on becoming the sort of man who deserves to be loved, who doesn't need to be driven out of the house.

Rob arrived a little after seven, carrying daisies in a cone of green paper and wine in a pale green bottle. David greeted him at the door.

"Hi, Rob," he said. He liked Rob better now. Rob was changed; shrunken.

"Hello, my man," Rob said. "Look here, I brought flowers for the women and wine for you and me."

"Oh," David said. Rob had shaved, and his shirt looked like it had been washed. In the cartoon version, Rob would have been a rabbit that slipped under a bear rug and crept along, scaring everybody, until the rug caught on a nail and the rabbit walked on, growling and snarling, with no idea he'd been exposed.

Lizzie called from upstairs, "Is that Rob?"

"Hello, Lizzie," Rob called.

They both heard her footsteps pounding down the hall from the bathroom to her own room.

"She's been trying to make herself beautiful for an hour," David said. "She put on Mom's lipstick and Mom made her take it off and then she put it back on again. They had a big fight."

"I happen to like my women natural anyway," Rob said. "How about if I drop these things in the kitchen?" He gestured with the flowers and the wine, a shrugging motion, like an international sign of harmless intentions.

"Come on," David said, and Rob followed him obediently to the kitchen.

Mom and Janet were there, working on the dinner. Mom stood at the oven with a huge flowered mitt over her hand, and Janet was mixing something with a whisk in one of the blue bowls.

"Here he is," David said, and thought it a peculiar statement.

"Evening, ladies," Rob said.

Janet and Mom seemed connected, like a single unit, although they were standing at opposite ends of the room. David would not have been surprised to hear them speak in unison.

Janet said, "Hi," and Mom said, "Evening, Rob," a moment

later. Mom had on maroon pants and a blouse with ruffles which looked too big for her; Janet wore a flimsy pink shirt with no sleeves and a pair of tan pants tied high up on her waist with a thin cloth belt. She put the whisk down and accepted the wine and flowers out of Rob's hands. She said, "Thank you, these are nice," in an uninflected way, as if they were no more than expected. For a dizzying moment, David felt more connected to Rob than he did to Janet or Mom.

"Smells great in here," Rob said. He inhaled extravagantly to show it.

"Just baked pork chops," Mom said. "No big deal." She finished the adjustments she'd been making in the pan and closed the oven door with the firm, commanding touch she had for familiar objects.

"It's a big enough deal to a starving man," Rob said.

Janet checked the cupboards for a vase to put the daisies in. She found one, an old studded white vase on a single heavy foot, and filled it at the sink. Watching her do that, so calm and efficient, a part of David met up with a part of Rob and knew how a simple thing, a girl knowing where the vases are kept, could make you feel awkward and in the wrong.

"What did you do with yourself all day?" Janet asked.

"I bought a disposable razor and shaved in a Texaco station," he said. "And I went to a Laundromat and washed my shirt. You have to picture me sitting there, two in the afternoon, in just pants and a jacket. If you start seeing men go around wearing suit jackets with no shirt underneath, it was me that started the trend."

Mom and Janet laughed appreciatively, and Rob offered the big smile that showed his gums.

"Would you like a drink?" Mom asked. "I don't know exactly what there is. I keep a little brandy in, and after that there's just whatever anyone's left here over the years."

"I drink anything," Rob said.

Janet, having arranged the daisies in the vase, went to the farthest cabinet, where the liquor was kept. 'Brandy, crème de menthe," she announced. "Sweet sherry, something in a bottle shaped like a fish, some Drambuie, Jesus, Mother, I think I remember this bottle from when I was a *kid,* and look here, a bottle of Old Bushmill's."

"The Bushmill's, please," Rob grinned, in such an unsurprised way that David wondered whether something was going on. He checked the liquor every now and then, and didn't remember seeing anything called Old Bushmill's. The bottle Janet brought out looked like it was brand new.

"Can I do anything to help?" Rob asked.

"You can stay out of the way," Mom told him.

Janet gave him a glass full of amber-colored liquor and ice, which he accepted with a knowing smile. Janet didn't smile. She went back to her bowl and whisk.

"To the whole Stark family," Rob said, raising his glass. "Good people."

A silence passed. Rob looked at the cartoon on the refrigerator and chuckled, as if he'd never seen it before. When Lizzie came in all four people turned to her gratefully.

"Here she is," Rob said.

Lizzie had settled finally on her old best dress, which was slightly too small for her. The sleeves bunched in tight sausagy gatherings at her armpits. David could imagine the agony of indecision she'd gone through. She had a new dress that fit her better but this older one, purple flecked with little blue specks like confetti, she considered a magic dress, the single most perfect thing she had ever owned. She'd decided to chance it. All around her lips the skin looked smudged and bruised, where she had put Mom's lipstick on one more time and then, thinking better of it, rubbed it off with a Kleenex.

Lizzie didn't speak to Rob. Instead she walked over to

where Janet was working and said, "What's that you're making?"

"Just salad dressing, hon," Janet told her.

Lizzie watched a moment and said, "You shouldn't put so much salt in it."

Janet tapped the whisk on the rim of the bowl, three measured beats. "Tell you what, sweetie," she said. "You finish up the dressing, in your own special way, and I'll entertain our guest. How would that be?" She handed the whisk to Lizzie.

"I don't want to," Lizzie said.

"Come on. You make it so much better than I do." She pressed the whisk into Lizzie's hand. Lizzie, trapped, said, "Well okay," and set about pretending that she knew how to make salad dressing.

Janet came over to where Rob and David stood, brushing her hands against her thighs. "Come on into the parlor, men," she said. "I've just been relieved of duty."

The three of them went into the living room, Janet in the lead and Rob and David following. *Men.* David tried the word out in his mind. Come on, men. He and Rob.

Janet passed up the sofa and sat in the orange chair, where no one could sit beside her. The chair had been there nearly as long as David could remember—it dated back to the time when all the furniture in the house looked like that, its arms and legs made of coffee-colored wood and its joints held together by six-sided black nailheads big as quarters. After Dad left, Mom had started buying new furniture, but she regretted her choices once they'd been made and for years now the house had stood frozen, half one style and half another. The sofa was a pair of slender gray burlap pads that floated on four spindle legs. Mom said one day when her ship came in she was going to throw it all out and start over from scratch.

Rob sat on the sofa and David did too. "So here I am, bouquet and everything, just like a suitor," Rob said.

Janet sat holding the armrests of the chair with both hands, and she kept her feet on the floor. "A suitor is the last thing I want," she said.

"You hear that from a lot of women these days," Rob said. "How's your other boyfriend?"

David's blood went cold. A high, thin ringing seeped into his ears.

Janet paused, smiled, and said, "Fine. All my other boyfriends are just fine, thank you."

"Good," Rob said. "I'm glad to hear it."

"How are your other girlfriends?" Janet asked him. "How's the stripper's dissertation coming along?"

"Getting tired of her," Rob said, sipping his drink. "I'm thinking of getting rid of her."

None of this made any sense. Was it possible Janet actually *had* another boyfriend? Had David stumbled blindly onto the truth?

"Don't get rid of her," Janet said. "You may need her."

"I don't think I will. I know exactly what I need."

"I think maybe you just feel guilty," she said.

"What have I got to feel guilty about?"

"There's the telling statement, right there." Janet stood up, as she had been waiting to do. "Excuse me," she said in a stage whisper. "I'm going to go check on the state of the salad dressing."

"Be kind," Rob whispered back. Although David believed Lizzie should be called on her tricks, he didn't like the idea that Rob and Janet shared a secret image of her that differed from her own. Janet walked out of the room and left David and Rob sitting together on the sofa.

Rob stretched his long arm out along the backrest. His fingers brushed the knobby bone of David's nearer shoulder, and David automatically pulled his shoulder away.

"Do I make you nervous, my man?" Rob asked.

"No," David told him.

"Good. I'm your friend, I shouldn't make you nervous. Tell me, David. Did you make that up about Janet having a boyfriend?"

Here it was. David's face burned, and he heard himself say, "Uh-huh."

Rob's expression did not change, his tight smile held steady. "Did you really?" he asked.

David nodded. He was afraid his eyes would begin to tear if he spoke. He tensed as for a blow.

"Well, it's all right," Rob said, and laughed like it was a good joke, a normal funny thing to have done. "I won't tell."

"Oh," David said.

"I've told a few myself," Rob said. "Matter of fact, that's one of the things lawyers are paid to do."

"Uh-huh," David said. For a sharp, thrilling moment he loved Rob. He looked at Rob's shirtfront with moist eyes, wishing more than anything to butt his head gently into the snowy cotton. After a moment he asked, "Can I have a sip of your drink?"

"I guess a sip won't hurt you," Rob said. "Don't tell."

"I won't." David took the glass from Rob's hand and drew a practiced draught, nowhere near big enough to be risky.

"Glad to see you can appreciate the right stuff, David my man," he said, and David loved him all the more even though he knew there was mockery in his voice. How could he have been so wrong about Rob?

Janet came back, and David handed the whiskey glass to Rob. "Don't let him con you into getting him drunk," she said.

"David's not conning me about anything," Rob smiled. "How are things in the kitchen?"

"Fine, if you like ketchup on your salad. Pretend you like it, or there'll be a scene that'll curl your hair."

"She gets away with an awful lot, doesn't she?" Rob said. David thought gratefully, *At last.* Someone besides him realized the truth about Lizzie.

"Please don't draw conclusions about what you don't understand," Janet said. "Let's just say she was dealt with a little harshly when she was a baby. She and some other people too. Are you ready for dinner?"

"Starving," Rob said, and he gave her the smile. David imagined Rob smiling at him that way.

Everybody seemed to have a good time at dinner. Mom began to relax, and by dessert she was telling jokes, including a long one David lost track of halfway through. Something about Moses and a talking dog. David laughed along with the others, for appearance sake, and then Rob told a simpler one about two Polacks who go skydiving. He looked at David as he told it, and David could hardly hold still from nervousness and laughter. He thought the joke was really funny.

Janet didn't laugh much. She sat smiling with her head cocked, and when the others quit laughing she said, "Did one of the men at the firm tell you that one?"

"I guess so," Rob said. "Why do you ask?"

"Because it just doesn't sound like the kind of joke you'd tell, is all. You used to tell a different kind of joke."

"People change," he told her.

"You're telling me."

"Anybody want more coffee?" Mom said. "Rob? More tea?"

"Please," Rob said.

"No thanks," Janet said. She rested her palm on her coffee cup and looked at Rob.

"Something funny about my face?" he asked.

"I'm just trying to remember you," she said.

"I'm sitting right here."

Lizzie said, "Rob, do you know how to play crazy eights?"

"No, but I bet I could learn."

"Don't let Lizzie teach you," David said, "She'll leave out half the rules until you start playing. I'll teach you how."

"I will," Lizzie said.

"I will."

"I will."

"I'm going to put gags on both of you in about two minutes," Mom said. She went into the kitchen for the tea.

"Maybe you can both teach me," Rob said.

"I'll tell you all the things Lizzie leaves out," David said.

Lizzie thrust her lower lip at him and he turned away, cringing, as if she was too ugly to look at. When he turned his head he noticed that Janet was watching Rob with a sad smile on her face, her hand still covering her empty cup.

They all played crazy eights at the dinner table. David, remembering his promise to himself, managed not to fight with Lizzie even though he knew she was cheating. As they played David noticed Rob's wrists, which were thinner than you'd expect, covered with fine reddish hairs that curled slightly in a uniform sickle shape. Rob's fingers picking up the cards were long and graceful, with tufts of paler hair at the knuckles. David's own hands were pink and stubby. Whenever anybody said something funny David smiled hugely, with his upper lip raised, showing his gums.

Once, after losing three hands in a row, Lizzie said to him, "Why are you smiling like a monkey?"

"Why do you smell like a fish?" he asked her, and decided the truce had been a stupid idea. You couldn't be nice to someone like Lizzie.

After they got tired of playing cards they went into the living room to watch TV. Lizzie was told she could stay up until the end of "Dynasty" and no longer. She plopped poutily down on the sofa next to Rob, not daring to press the issue because "Dynasty" already ran a half hour later than her usual bedtime. David slotted himself in quickly on Rob's other side, and noticed for the first time a deeper smell of Rob's, under his cologne, something like pencil shavings when you empty the sharpener.

Janet and Mom sat in the two orange chairs. Janet had brought out the last of her dinner wine, and Rob was drinking another Old Bushmill's. Occasionally he passed it over to David in silence, as if they had a private understanding, and David took big, chancy sips. Everything felt so solid and fine; he was so happy just to be sitting on the sofa taking swallows of Rob's drink.

After the program ended, Lizzie was maneuvered upstairs into bed. David thought she would kiss Rob good-night but she was humiliated at being the first to go and didn't speak to him at all. She just trudged noisily upstairs. David knew so well the regret she felt afterward he could almost feel it, dripping through the ceiling like a leak.

He himself didn't have to go to bed for another hour, and he sat luxuriating in his one undeniable, irrevokable privilege. He was older than Lizzie, and always would be. There was nothing she could do to catch up. He accepted another sip of Rob's drink as the newswoman, the one whose hair came to a single perfect hook on one side of her head, appeared on the screen and said in her urgent, honest voice, "Good evening. President Reagan announced at a press conference today that he would seek to increase the defense department budget by ten billion dollars in 1985. More on this and other stories at eleven."

"Asshole," Janet said.

"You mean Reagan, or that woman?" Mom asked.

"Oh, both of them. I don't think the world has ever had so many assholes in it as it does right now."

The newswoman had been replaced by a commercial, the old ladies who liked to squeeze the toilet paper. Rob said, "There have always been plenty of assholes. You're just learning to spot them better."

"I've always known how to spot them," Janet said.

"I don't know," Mom said. "It seems like the older you get,

the harder it is. I've voted for a new asshole every four years since, oh, Kennedy. But he was one too, in a way."

"Everybody has their reasons," Rob said.

The toilet paper commercial dissolved into another one, for coffee, with a husband wrinkling his nose over his cup as if it had a rat turd floating in it. This struck David as funny. He tried to hold it in, though, because the talk around him was turning serious.

"But when did we all get so damn reasonable?" Janet said. "At what point exactly did we sort of shrug our shoulders and say, 'What the hell, you can't fight it, everybody's got their reasons?' "

"It's always been like that," Rob said.

David took Rob's glass from his hand and helped himself to another sip, and another. The husband liked the new coffee better. He closed his eyes and smacked his lips like it was the most delicious thing he'd ever tasted. A sputtering laugh escaped from the side of David's clamped mouth like air from a balloon. He had an alternate version of the commercial in his mind: the wife says, "Honey, what's wrong with my coffee?" and the husband says, "Well, it's got a rat turd in it." He couldn't not think about it.

"That sounds like revised history to me," Janet said. David looked at her with bug-eyed seriousness, thinking, *Hmmm*, like a professor. This was funny too. A glow had come over him, a good warm haziness that started in his blood and tingled his skin from the inside. Everything was so fine, and so completely itself. As the others talked David sat appreciating the sofa, the comforting familiar scratch of its stiff gray fabric. It was a perfect version of a sofa, and it was his. His sofa, the one out of all possible sofas.

Rob was saying something about Indian reservations, how the Indians never wanted a lot of white kids there helping them in the first place, it was all a big joke to the Indians. David looked over at Mom, who was following the conversation with her eyes like she was watching a tennis match but a more serious kind of tennis match, one in which the ball might blow up at any second and kill whoever had it on his side of the net. She was so fine. And she was his. His own perfect mother. He thought hard about the fact so he wouldn't forget it.

"That sounds like asshole talk to me," Janet said.

Here, honey, try this coffee. Mmm, that's the way I like it, with no rat turds.

David held the laugh until he thought his head would explode. Then in a moment of blissful giving-in it shot out his nose. He snorted, and the sound of his own snorting was funny. He laughed so hard he lost his breath, and Rob's drink, which he was still holding, splashed onto his shirt.

"Hey, what's so funny?" Rob asked.

"Wait a minute, he's drunk," Mom said.

"David?" Janet looked at him questioningly. "Shit, you are, aren't you?"

The idea appealed to him. Drunk, he was drunk. He had crossed over into another country, one he'd been wanting to visit for a long time. This was it. A warm floating feeling like your whole being is in your head, and everything around you small and funny. Funny. He just couldn't stop laughing.

"Whoa," Rob said, pulling the glass from his hand. "God, I had no idea."

David wanted to say to them, "Wait, I'm still here," because they were treating him like he'd been completely transformed when in fact all he was was himself pushed up a little bit higher, better able to see the hilarity of things. But he was giggling too hard to speak.

"Bed," Mom said. "Somebody get on the other side, he's too heavy for me."

Rob hoisted him up with difficulty (Rob wasn't so strong!) and though David felt sure he could walk perfectly well on his own, he gave in to the occasion of his drunkenness and let himself be half carried, half dragged between Mom and Rob. His laughter was solidifying into something else, a hard ball that stuck in the back of his throat, but he kept laughing for fear of having to know what to say if he stopped. As Mom and Rob guided him upstairs he laughed until the laughter took on its own unraveling force, until it became a thing that lived outside him and hung in the air over all their heads, a ghost. By the time they reached the top step (the stairs were both impossibly long and brief, a huge journey over in an instant), the hard ball had slithered down into his stomach, which bucked and trembled. The first heave came so fast he had only a moment to stop laughing, poised silent at the top of the stairs, held by firm hands—he had that one clear moment in which he saw himself, his own exact size and shape, his position in the world—and then he bent forward and vomited, a flecked brown streak that flashed raggedly across the carpet. He heard Mom say, "Bathroom," in her dead-calm voice.

He was carried to the bathroom and managed to hold down the second wave of vomiting until they reached it. A thick thread of saliva dangled from his chin. Mom held his shoulders as he bent over the white, gleaming toilet bowl. He retched and retched but the ball wouldn't dislodge itself from his belly. Faintly, he heard Rob's voice from above, saying, "I'm sorry, God, I had no idea." Mom's voice replied, "It's all right, he's been trying to get drunk since he was nine. Now he knows what it's like."

When he was finished throwing up, when the sickness had settled into a solid immovable thing in his gut, Mom stripped his shirt off and washed his face and chest at the sink. He saw his face in the mirror and was surprised by it. His eyes looked back at him like somebody else's. He saw that they were brown with spots of gold in them. His skin in the hard white light seemed to have turned gray. After Mom had rubbed him clean with a washcloth, which left red blossomings on his bare chest, she steered him out into the hallway toward his room. Janet and Rob were in the hall, standing close together, and when David negotiated the first few uncertain steps in their direction Janet came and smoothed his hair, saying, "Well, I guess tonight you're a man."

He smiled weakly and glanced at Rob, who stood with his hands in his pockets, looking apologetic. David's mind leaped up out of his body and he thought with a pang of Rob turned away, sent home to San Francisco. He had to go. Janet didn't love him enough. But it was all so sad. As David was led down the hall he said in a voice that came out deeper than his voice ever had before, "I'm sorry, Rob," and Rob said, "Forget it. It was my fault."

David slept without dreaming and woke in the dark, his mouth parched and his stomach queasy. He wanted water but lay still for a long while, thinking vaguely that sickness inhabited the air of his room, and if he moved it would sense him and attack.

The coyotes were far away tonight, their howls faint as bird calls in the hills. At a good enough distance they sounded like loons. David listened to them and thought with wonder of how he had been drunk. Drunk. He had thrown up in front of everybody, too, and had had to be washed afterward by Mom. He could not decide whether he was a good interesting criminal or a fool, or both. At least Lizzie hadn't seen him.

He heard footsteps on the stairs. Whoever it was stepped soundly onto the fifth tread, which squeaked. David sat up into a renewed wave of nausea. When his head cleared the footsteps had topped the stairs. He jumped out of bed and ran to the door.

Rob was walking slowly down the dark hall, his shoulders tensed against the blackness, his right hand raised before him to ward off obstacles. He had on his pants but no shirt. If he saw David he made no sign and for a long second David stood in his own doorway with the big dark man coming toward him, hair and broad shoulders edged in the weak, icy light that shone in through the single window at the far end. David thought Rob saw him and would come make a joke or two about getting drunk. He and Rob would sit in the dark together, telling drunk jokes. He tried to think of one in advance.

Rob stopped at Janet's door and waited there, ready to knock but not knocking. David said Rob's name, softly, to tell him he had the wrong room. Rob turned his large indistinguishable face in David's direction. His voice hissed, "Get back in your room."

David obeyed instantly, unthinking as a mouse popping down its hole. He stood inside his room, behind the closed door, the pulse jumping in his neck. He heard Rob open Janet's door.

After a silence the murmur of their voices came through the wall. First Rob's, then Janet's—low and high, an alternating current of sounds too different to be like music. Rob's growl stretched on, Janet's answering whispers were shorter. David moved from the door to the common wall and walked back and forth in front of it, seeking the spot at which the sound was strongest. He could not make out a single word. His blood raced, and he circled before the wall like a penned animal, searching and searching for a way out, unable to imagine that there might be none at all, checking the same places over and over again.

The rhythm of the voices picked up, though they didn't get any louder. They took on a faster, more urgent pace. David, having decided that the most audible point was toward the far corner, between his dresser and the outside wall, wedged himself into the narrow space and put his ear to the wallpaper. He worried they would sense his presence. It didn't seem possible that he could be so aware of them and they completely ignorant of him. Their voices alternated rapidly now, Rob Janet Rob Janet Rob. David thought they must be fighting. He couldn't imagine what to do. He worked himself against the wall as if he hoped to squeeze through it.

The voices stopped. The noise on the other side of the wall went dead, and after a moment David heard the sound of Janet's door opening and closing. He feared they might have gone out together, but no, the bedsprings creaked in Janet's room, she was still there. Rob had gone alone. David went to his door and listened there, holding his breath. The fifth tread squeaked. Rob was back downstairs.

It had never occurred to him that Rob would invade the house like that. Upstairs was where the Starks' most private lives went on, where Mom walked in her bra and girdle. David lay down on his bed and the bed, full of its warmth and its unmistakable odor, seemed to have been touched by Rob. He waited, ready, for the sound of Rob's return. If Rob came upstairs again David would be ready. He wouldn't let himself be flicked out of the way.

He didn't fall asleep for over an hour and when he did, it was against his will. He fought to keep his eyes open but his mind kept drifting into vivid realms of its own, until even the simple thought, Stay awake, flowered into a giddy sensation of flight, of wind and gray sky and a stone building he thought he had seen once, with turrets and a spiked iron gate. His dreams deepened, and when he woke again all he knew was that he had had another monster dream, something about a blackness that dragged itself over the rotten leaves of a forest floor, all hungry attention, watching for lights.

In the morning all that remained of Rob was a pile of folded blankets and sheets and a pillow, neatly stacked on one end of the sofa. Mom made breakfast for David and Lizzie; Janet stayed in bed. "I don't know what time Rob left," Mom said as she scrambled the eggs. "I didn't hear him, did either of you?"

"No," David said. He and Lizzie were sitting at the table. Lizzie scraped the tines of her fork along the table's edge and did not speak.

"Well, he's probably halfway to Santa Barbara by now," Mom said. She beat the eggs with a gentle lap-lap-lap that sounded like Mom herself.

"I guess so," David said. "He was weird."

Lizzie skated her fork along the tabletop so hard a pair of thin curled shavings, like question marks, rose in its wake. "Hey," David said. "Lizzie's digging into the table."

"Shut up, you pinhead asshole," she said, She gripped the fork handle and looked at David with such hatred he thought she might jump across the table and stab him. He said, "Mom?" just to be sure she was keeping an eye on things.

"Please don't murder each other," she said. She prodded the eggs in the frying pan. "Lizzie, don't destroy the furniture, I just finished paying for it."

Lizzie's tightened face drooped in on itself, as if some of the air had been let out. She blinked and pressed a single tear from each eye. Then she got up and walked, slowly, out of the kitchen, still holding tightly to the fork. She could be heard walking slowly upstairs.

"What's the matter with her?" David said.

"Never mind," Mom said. "Just eat your breakfast and get off to school. I'll take care of Lizzie."

She put a plateful of eggs and toast in front of him, and went upstairs. David sat alone. He pushed the eggs around on his plate for a while, then dumped them in the trash and covered them with a few wadded-up paper towels. He took the milk carton from the refrigerator and stood there with the cold air falling down over his pants and shoes, downing the milk in big gulps that made his head ache. He put the carton back. He was surprised and a little disappointed at having no hangover.

David had a dull ache in his chest, a coldness, like a sack of old wet leaves hung heavily around his neck, and he wondered if that was what was meant by a hangover. It was subtler than he'd imagined it. On his way out of the kitchen he checked his reflection in the toaster, and found his face in order. He tried out a new smile, a close-lipped, crooked one like Gonzo's on "Trapper John."

He picked up his books and his lunch and the note Mom had written excusing yesterday's absence. Outside it was a regular morning, with a high pale sky and a flock of round, plump clouds that lay just above the rooftops. The horizon was just beginning to deepen with the day's smog.

David checked the street for Rob's car. It was not there; all he found was the usual string of Camaros, Mavericks, Gremlins. He must have been halfway to Santa Barbara. It was over. Janet could start studying for medical school and the worst David had to worry about was Billy. The sun was shining and he walked along the familiar tree-lined street with his arms (his own!) swinging, their tiny gold hairs catching the speckled sunlight that worked its way through the branches of the trees.

He thought that today he'd try talking to Billy. They had been best friends since second grade, they had seen each other naked—it wasn't possible for Billy to just turn into somebody else, a stranger. As David walked toward school he planned his approach. He'd walk right up to Billy, unafraid, and say something like, "Don't be crazy, Billy, you know what good friends we are." Something like that. He pictured Billy's face as he hesitated, adding it up. "Come on," David would say, and Billy would smile in that unwilling way of his. When Billy had to smile he couldn't stop himself, it came over him like a sickness. Remembering Billy, just like that, struggling to stay serious but giving in always, finally, to the power of friendship or a good joke, David felt cheerful about the possibility of everything.

He felt so good he started to sing. "Beat It" was the first song that came into his head and he sang it under his breath. He tried out a new walk, a bouncier one, more like a dancer, as though a cord tied around his chest kept lifting him slightly off his feet.

The blow hit him on his shoulder blades, so strong it carried him three gigantic steps before he pitched over onto his hands and knees. Rather than his dropping down, the sidewalk seemed to rear up and collide with him. For a moment the cement was a vertical surface, he smacking into it as if he'd flown into a wall. A weight flung itself onto his back, and he knew it by the smell. Billy. Hands scrabbled for his neck and though he squirmed like a weasel the fingers closed around his windpipe. He wriggled his way onto the grass but the hard squat fingers dug in and he knew instinctively that resistance was no way out; the only hope was to go limp. He collapsed onto the grass, his elbows squeaking over the slick waxy surface. The two hands lifted his head by the neck until he thought it would crack, then brought it down. He saw the patch of lawn like a miniature landscape, each grass blade throwing a shadow. He managed to tuck his chin so his forehead took the brunt of the blow, and when his head struck a dazzling white light erupted before his closed eyes. Billy's hands pulled his head up again and loosened a bit, uncertain of how much damage had been done. David was able to flip halfway around and get a purchase on Billy's shoulder. Billy lay diagonally across David's back and David pushed with the angle of Billy's position, forcing him off. He struggled to his knees and was met by Billy before he could stand. Their faces locked. They grappled one another, briefly fumbling and rearranging themselves like lovers. Billy dug his thumbs into David's shoulders and David grabbed hold of Billy's arms. They pushed, each trying to force the other over and to end up on top. Billy was stronger than David and as David felt himself start to falter he threw his weight to the side instead, to save himself. Billy went with him and they landed hard on their shoulders, still locked together. Billy's strong breath whistled into David's face. Billy tried to roll on top and David pitched him over and then David tried to do the same and Billy pitched him over. They rolled along this way. David felt the grass prickling under him. Blood flowed warmly from his nose, and he tasted the iron of it as it crept over his lips. It seemed to him that the fight was failing, its main fury used up in the clumsy jockeying for position. He was about to say, "Okay, Billy, that's enough, let's call it a tie," when Billy, on one of his swings to the superior, worked an arm free and punched David in the stomach. The wind rushed out of him and suddenly he was watching Billy from far away. He heard himself gasp, a thin squawk like no sound he had ever made before. It scared him and it scared Billy too, he saw it on Billy's face. That scared him worse. He could not pull air in and the harder he tried the louder and more insistent his squawking grew. Then the air caught in him, roundly. He drew a deep rapturous breath. Billy's face lost its worried look and with gleeful confidence he swung back and planted a good one on David's jaw.

The world turned blazing white. David's head rang hollow, and his vision when it returned came from the outside in. Though he could see sky and earth at the periphery, a pale fireball hung stubbornly at center, where Billy ought to have been. He tried blinking it away. He realized Billy had gotten off him and he began to make out, through the corona, Billy looking down at him with satisfied contempt. David tried to stand but when he moved the brightness flared hotter. He sank back down to rest his head on the grass. Faintly, he saw Billy point an index finger at him and shoot.

"That's it," Billy said. "You're really dead now." He blew the smoke from the tip of his finger, turned, and walked away.

David lay waiting for his vision to return. He dabbed at his nose and felt the gummy wetness of blood. It came to him that Billy had jumped out of the tree; he must have been waiting there, knowing David would pass underneath. He must have been there yesterday too, waiting. David wondered if a passerby would stop and take him to the hospital. His body had not yet quieted enough to feel much pain, and he didn't know how badly he was hurt. He thought probably he should not move, in case anything was broken. A couple of older boys walked by, smoking, on their way to school. One of them said, "Hey, kid, did you get hit by a car?" David said, "No." They paused, ground out their cigarette butts, and moved on.

After a while the pain gathered and centered itself in his head, a steady pulsing. The pain had roots in his jaw but they extended from a seed of pain buried deep inside his skull. His bones did not seem to be broken. Cautiously he sat up and looked around. His books were scattered. The geography book lay open on its spine, the breeze flipping its pages. His pale brown lunch sack lay fatly on its side. He got to his feet and gathered the books and the lunch. He also found Mom's note, vivid in its white envelope on the grass. He could not quite believe a fight like that would stir so little commotion in the neighborhood. On both sides of him houses similar to his own sat placidly unconcerned. This made neither more nor less sense than the fact that Billy hated him to the point of murder when David had done nothing. Nothing. You could edge so mysteriously into the wrong: for spilling milk at the table or scratching yourself in public or for nothing at all, for not doing something you were supposed to do but didn't know about.

He took Mom's note from its envelope and read it. "Please excuse David's absence, he was feeling a bit under the weather. Beverly Stark." The note would be just as good tomorrow as it was today. David started walking toward school but when he got to a particular corner he cut between two houses, after checking to be sure no one was watching him. He went around behind the row of houses that lined the street, straddling a poured-concrete gutter, with people's backyards bordered by chain-link fence on one side of him and, on the other, the steep embankment that led up to the freeway. Cars made their whizz-ing noises as they passed overhead, invisible as rockets. The embankment was covered with shiny green ice plant, touched here and there by a reddish blush; people said black widows made their nests in ice plant. On his right, through the dia-monds of the fence, were the things that were always there: a redwood picnic table, a swing set, a dry plaster birdbath done up like the stump of a tree, an empty plastic wading pool covered with pictures of goggle-eyed fish.

He scrambled along this passageway until he reached open country, the broad expanse of undeveloped earth he and Billy used to consider their own private terrain. The scraps of orange plastic hung limply on their stakes. At the far end of the raked plain was a shallow valley full of weeds, and in that valley, sunk down among the brush and foxtail, was the front seat of a car. It had been there for as long as David remembered, a brown tuck-and-roll that had faded gradually to the color of an old cigar. Gray stuffing puffed out of a sickle-shaped cut along its backrest though the stuffing was almost gone by now, having been picked at, David supposed, by birds building their nests. Here the great man-made mountain of the freeway swung around in a slow graceful curve like a dam. It marked the limit of the neighborhood. If you went farther than this you went in a car. David and Billy had pulled the seat around so it faced the freeway and sometimes, when they couldn't think of anything else to do, they had sat there watching the big supple arm of the green wall as if it were a movie screen.

David spent the day on the car seat, with his books stacked neatly on the powdery dirt. The blood dried around his mouth and he picked it off with his thumbnail. He knew he should be thinking of something but for a long while he sat thinking of nothing at all, the bearded heads of foxtails rattling softly around him. He could not seem to hold Billy in his mind for more than a second or two; Billy had become too strange to think about. Instead his mind kept settling, of its own accord, on Dad.

Dad used to drop down like a panther from a tree. He would come home mad from work and when he was like that you stepped carefully, hoping you wouldn't break a secret rule. A bomb was hidden somewhere in the house and you had to duplicate all your ordinary movements perfectly, to keep it from going off. Even Lizzie knew about it, and she was a baby then. On the angry nights she played quietly, without talking to herself, and when her dolls' arms and legs wouldn't go into their clothes right she treated them gently, like important but slightly retarded guests. When Dad wasn't around she bit them and knocked their heads against the floor. David, too, played cautiously, and didn't make a sound.

But try as you might, sooner or later someone would make a mistake. It could be anything. Once David scratched his crotch, though Dad had told him before never to scratch himself in front of people. The moment he did it an alarm sounded in the back of his head but it was too late. Dad snatched him up from behind, lifting him by his armpits, and David let out a shriek, which was a stupid mistake because noise made everything worse. Dad held him dangling in midair while Lizzie and Janet watched, sympathetic but helpless. The big hands would shake him the way a dog shakes a rag and then put him down so as to swat him on the butt and on the shoulders. It was important to keep quiet. If you kept your mouth shut it would end faster.

For a while he'd thought of himself as a girl, a tough girl who fought crime. He started acting out adventures with Lizzie's dolls, but Mom and Dad put a stop to that. So he went back to his own toys, his cars and soldiers. He picked out one of the soldiers, a small khaki-colored man with a helmet and bayonet, and made up stories in which the man was really a girl, who cut her hair short and joined the army. Her name was Donna but she called herself Don. She was such a good soldier that even when they found out she was a girl they let her stay in the army, leading the troops. David carried that one soldier around in his pocket for years and he had it still, tucked into the top drawer of his bureau.

In a few weeks, when school was out, he and Lizzie would go to Spokane. Dad was different now. He didn't hit you, he seemed to be having a better time. Marie, his new wife, was all right too, but she carried a silence with her. She was so thin

David could see the ribs that started under her collarbone; you could tell she had a skeleton inside, and looking at her sometimes made him lose his appetite. She cooked thin stews with big chunks of squash and eggplant and baked loaves of dry brown bread.

Dad wore plaid shirts now and smoked hash from a green stone pipe he bought in Mexico. He laughed his sudden laugh that was like a spring popping out of a box. He called David and Lizzie "the only good energy I put out in my old life." He hoisted Lizzie up onto his lap and pinched her bottom. Lizzie didn't like it but neither she nor David ever worked up the courage to say anything. They were all alone in a strange city with Dad. Quiet Marie, who smoked hash and went hours at a time without speaking, did not seem as if she'd be any help if things started getting dangerous.

David spent the whole day hiding out in the little valley, thinking alternately of Dad and of nothing at all. When he grew tired of sitting he'd walk around, pitching stones and practicing his dancing. He worried about growing up to be a bad dancer. Then he'd go back and sit on the car seat some more. By afternoon the seat had come to seem like his rightful home, the only place he had ever lived.

He estimated when it was time to go back. He forced himself to wait until the sunlight had turned golden and his shadow stretched out long and thin, for fear of leaving too early and getting caught walking around the neighborhood. He realized when he climbed up out of the valley and started across the bare field that he'd probably waited too long; school might have been out for an hour by now. As he walked through the concrete gutter a kid in one of the backyards, a kid from third or fourth grade, stared at him. The kid sat cross-legged on a redwood picnic table, squeezing a yellow tennis ball. He was foreign-looking, with big astonished eyes and thin purplish lips. David had seen him around. It occurred to him that he hated this kid; this kid was everything weak and stupid in the world.

David hollered, "Stop staring at me or I'll climb over this fence and pound you." To his surprised satisfaction the kid jumped up, terrified, and ran inside through the sliding glass door. David hurried on.

He got to the house forty-five minutes late, but Mom still wasn't home. He remembered she had a doctor's appointment today. The heavy afternoon stillness hung in the house, squares of yellow sunlight stalled on the living room carpet. Time always stood like this until Mom came in. She tipped the balance and things tumbled with increasing speed toward evening, dinner, TV, bed. David had for a long while been afraid that if Mom ever failed to come home the house would stay frozen, with nothing connecting one minute to the next. The enormousness of her importance made her seem correspondingly prone to accident. Last year he had had a habit of phoning the office if she was so much as ten minutes late, but she made him stop doing it.

Janet didn't seem to be home. He walked upstairs, avoiding the fifth tread, to clean himself in the bathroom. He had decided not to tell anyone about the fight with Billy, at least not until he understood it better. At the moment it struck him as embarrassing, his not knowing why Billy jumped on him. What if the reason was obvious to everybody else?

When he passed Lizzie's room he heard her inside, talking to Pia Rogovsky, her current friend, who David called Pee-U Rogovsky because she smelled like a combination of Vicks and old cooking. Lizzie fought with all her friends and had to find new ones every couple of months. Pia Rogovsky had pierced ears with little gold hoops in them, and she lived in a world of blissful puzzlement that put her beyond insult.

David went into the bathroom and got a look at himself in the mirror. A thin circle of dry brown blood clung to one nostril, and he had a little bruise on his forehead, no more prominent than a brown spot on an apple. It was less than he'd expected. He took off his dirty jeans and shirt and stuffed them in the clothes hamper, then went to his room in just his under-pants, hoping Pia Rogovsky would choose that moment to step out of Lizzie's room and see him. She didn't. He put on his old jeans and the Stevie Wonder T-shirt and lay down on his bed to look at the stars.

The first of the phone calls came about half an hour later, just before Mom was due home. David ran for it and beat Lizzie by four or five feet. When he said "Hello," though, the caller hung up. David kept the receiver to his ear for a second before putting it back.

"Who was it?" Lizzie asked.

"Nobody," he said. "They hung up."

Lizzie looked at him like he had answered the phone wrong and scared off a call that might have brought good fortune. She turned back to her room where dark little Pia stood in the doorway, smiling with happy confusion.

The phone rang again half an hour later. Lizzie caught it this time, with David two paces shy. The caller hung up again. After the first surprise had faded from her face Lizzie looked at David this time as if he had offended whoever it was so com-pletely that things had gone beyond even her powers of rescue. David sneered at her and returned to the normalcy of his own room, where he was not guilty and where time passed in a more manageable way.

He knew the moment he heard Mom come in that some-thing was wrong. Something in her walk, a heaviness. Instead of going into the kitchen to wash her hands, she came upstairs and went into her room, which was a violation of ordinary procedure. David listened and heard nothing after the soft closing of Mom's door. Lizzie's music put a pulse in the air. Janet was out somewhere, and no one moved around in the kitchen, starting dinner, tapping pans with a spoon. Something was wrong.

He ventured out into the hallway, and walked through Lizzie's music, past the stairwell to Mom's door. He stood outside it for a while, in the silence. Then he knocked.

"What is it?" Mom's voice sounded startled, as if she'd been caught at something embarrassing.

"It's me," David said.

"Just a minute," she said. David thought she must be hiding whatever he'd surprised her with, slipping something back into a drawer. In a panic he opened the door and walked in.

"Hi," he said, groping for something to do with his hands. His neck craned forward. Mom was standing by her bureau, taking a ring off her finger. She smiled guiltily.

"What's doing?" she said.

"Nothing, What are *you* doing?"

"I was trying on my old ring." She held it up for him to see, a silver band with a tiny diamond set in prongs. "This was my wedding ring from Ray."

"Uh-huh."

She slipped it onto her finger, held her hand before her face. "It doesn't fit anymore," she said. "It's too big."

"Oh," he said, and pulled his neck back in.

Mom twisted the ring on her finger.

"Did you go to the doctor's?" David asked.

"Yes."

"What's wrong with you?"

She shook her head. "Nothing," she said. "Everything is fine."

"Then why did you go?"

"You get to be my age, you have to have your tires rotated every so often. What do you think you'd like for dinner?"

"You're not sick?" he asked.

"Nope. Everything's fine." She turned the ring on her finger as if she were tuning in a distant radio station.

"Oh," David said.

"Do me a favor, would you?" she said.

"Okay."

"Leave me alone in here for five minutes, and then I'll go down and start dinner. We can have fish sticks tonight, how's that?"

"Good."

"David?"

"What?"

"You love Lizzie, don't you?"

"I don't know," he said.

"Would you help take care of her if she needed it? You have to remember, she's only ten."

"But I'm only *twelve,*" he said, too loud.

Mom laughed. "I know," she said. "You're the one that guards the house, though, aren't you?"

He could not at that moment have said whether he was more flattered or terrified. "I'm only twelve," he said again, this time at the right volume.

Mom looked down at her ring and the two of them stood in awkward silence, like old friends who have met at a party and should have everything to say to one another.

"Fish sticks sounds good," he said, to break the silence.

"Good," she said. "I'll be right down."

"Okay."

He waited a moment, and let himself out the door. In the hall, he heard the final notes of Lizzie's record, followed by the click of the needle.

I t was Friday, and if David could manage to stay out of school this one last day he wouldn't have to see Billy until Monday. Cutting school again would be too risky—by today they'd surely call the house to make certain he wasn't seriously ill or moved away. That was what they did. He went downstairs and told Mom he felt sick but she didn't buy it. She could see through his lies with a piercing clarity that unnerved him; when weighing a statement of his she always scrutinized him with her chin lifted and her neck arched, as if he had a tiny window in the top of his head only she knew about. The trick with Mom was to try and keep from mentioning the lie at all, and even when he carried a lie around inside him she regarded him in her suspicious, high-chinned way, the way she would look at the refrigerator if she could smell something going bad inside.

So he went to school. Although he wished he was braver he couldn't make himself pass under the avenue of trees and instead went the long way around, an elaborate route that involved cutting through several yards. He climbed the fences in a casual sort of way, with a little smile and a shrug for the benefit of no one in particular, as if the fences were a silly joke, another of life's funny inconveniences.

He waited until the last possible minute to walk into class. Billy was already in his seat at the rear, and David had a hard time getting from the door to his own desk. He lost the knack of walking. When he got within range of his seat he took too large a step, then had to take a second, mincing step to get close enough to the chair to sit in it. He spent the whole period concentrating fiercely on Miss Mullin.

When the period ended he rushed off to art. In art they were making planets, with balloons and papier-mâché. Mrs. Pilegi had assembled paste and paint and crepe paper and glitter, and told the class to let itself go. David was assigned the planet Mars. He took his balloon and his shredded newspaper and a jar of red paint to the farthest corner. He knew Mrs. Pilegi was an asshole, and he knew why everybody but nerds hated coming to art. He himself was a nerd. But even stupid work like pasting newspaper onto a balloon held his attention, and freed him from the unending stream of events and decisions that made up the days. There were so many possible mistakes, so many hidden rules. In obeying one you were usually breaking another. Laying strips of newspaper over the taut blue skin of a balloon was a safe, sure action and he wished sometimes he could live forever in that moment, seated by a window making a simple, useless thing. He hoped Mrs. Pilegi wouldn't come badgering him to express himself more, and he tried to keep his tongue from wandering outside his pursed lips.

He was able to stay out of Billy's way until lunchtime. They met in the yard, among the kids who were eating lunch. David was crossing to the old spot by the fence, his lunch sack in his hand, and Billy walked in front of him, on his way somewhere else. David froze. He was especially aware of the furry feel of the bag's rolled top curled around his fingertips. Billy turned and did not so much look at him as through him, as though he didn't exist. Billy had a faint, untroubled smile on his face and he kept walking in his own direction, looking more at peace than David could remember seeing him.

Whenever they passed each other through the remainder of the day, Billy looked at David with the same contented remoteness, as if David were a memory too distant to be either good or bad. David was relieved at first, but as time passed it troubled him more and more. It gave him no way to act. If Billy had apologized, which was David's wildest hope, or if he'd attacked again, there would have been an obvious next thing for David to do. This way, he felt invisible; invisible and small. After fifth period, when they saw each other for the third time, Billy had drifted beyond his half-smile into an expression of calm, complete nonrecognition, so that David would no more have considered talking to him than he would a stranger at the Plaza. With a click of pleasure, he began to hate Billy. It wasn't fair, whatever he'd done, to erase him like this. He was in the right. With his hand in his pocket, he straightened his thumb and index finger into a pistol. The next time he saw Billy he'd shoot him cleanly through the head. After school let out he walked home without hesitation by the usual route. The trees were empty. No one shot at him. No one remarked his passage at all. As he walked he counted up the various possible ways of murdering Billy. He could drop a trash can onto his head from the second floor. He could trap a rattlesnake and put it in his locker. He could string piano wire across the street, stand on one side of it, and shout insults at him until he came running, right into the wire.

Later, after Mom got home, he told her he definitely wasn't going to Spokane this summer. He sat at the kitchen table with a glass of grape juice which he told himself was wine. He dipped his finger into it and drew invisible pictures on the tabletop.

"I'm not," he repeated, with as much finality as he could put into his voice.

Mom had set her purse down on the counter and was washing her hands with dish soap at the sink. "Well, I can't send Lizzie alone," she said.

David hesitated and drew a series of mountain peaks with his moistened finger. "She doesn't want to go either," he said.

Mom dried her hands with a dish towel, and didn't put the towel back on its hook. She twisted it between her fingers. "You just have to go, honey," she said. "It's not my decision, it's the court. You know that. When you're a little older, you can decide for yourself."

David drew a long jagged streak, lightning, across the table. "Dad pinches Lizzie too hard," he said.

"He pinches her?" Mom said in that low, collected voice.

"Uh-huh," David said, his courage suddenly reduced by half. He drew some little circles with his finger.

"Where does he pinch her?" Mom asked.

"Huh?"

"I mean, where on her body?"

"I don't know," David said. "All over."

Mom stepped forward, as if tracing the low sound of her own voice to its source, which was somewhere in David's vicinity. "And what does Lizzie do?" she said.

"Well, she laughs," David said. "He tickles her too. But she said the pinches hurt." He was so nervous now his eyes were clouding. If he started trouble, Dad would find out. He also had another secret, a secret within the secret: when they were in Spokane, a part of him wished that he was the one to be tickled and mauled. It didn't seem fair that Lizzie was the center of everything. More than once, more than a few times, he had walked past Dad with the focus of his being switched from his head to his butt, hoping Dad would snatch him up and pinch him. He was terrified of the possibility that Mom would see that through the window in his head.

"Did she have bruises after?" Mom said. "Did you see red marks on her skin?"

"No," David said. He could feel himself passing over into the wrong. Mom was by this time standing close beside him and he shifted his weight over a bit, away from her.

She shook her head. "I'll call Mr. Blochman," she said, "but I don't know if there's anything he can do. David, if you really have to go to Spokane this summer I want you to keep a close eye on your sister, because she's very little. You sometimes forget how young she is. If either one of you gets hurt, if your father hits you just once, I want you to call me right away. Do you understand?"

"Uh-huh." A thick ooze worked itself up from the pit of his stomach into his throat and he realized, remotely, that he was about to cry. He wouldn't do it in front of Mom. He got up and walked out of the kitchen. Mom let him go with only a single rough pat to his shoulder, for which he would always be grateful.

"I called Blochman," she said at dinnner. "He said he thinks you should probably go visit your father. He's going to look into it, but he said he thought you should probably go."

David and Lizzie said, "Oh," at the same time.

"Why don't you get another lawyer?" Janet said. "All this character ever seems to do is throw up his hands and say he'll look into it."

"He can't change the law," Mom said. "If I could find a lawyer who could do that, I'd go to him in a minute."

"Frank's lawyer seems to have gotten him exactly what he wanted," Janet said.

"Frank's lawyer got him much less than he wanted. Three weeks in the summertime, that's it. It really isn't much."

"Three weeks with Frank Stark is a *very* long time," Janet said.

"Maybe you and I should talk some more about this later."

"Okay. Maybe you're right."

"What did they tell you at UCLA?" Mom asked.

"I have to enroll as an undergraduate again. It seems the adult extension courses run more along the lines of creative writing and modern dance than they do organic chemistry. So I'll be right in there with the eighteen-year-olds."

"You're not that much older yourself," Mom said.

"I feel that much older. I don't know, it just sounded less . . . *humiliating* from a distance. When I actually got to the campus and saw all those bright, optimistic eighteen-year-old faces, I felt very old and stupid."

"That's ridiculous."

"Oh, I know it is," Janet said.

"You're going after what you want. It's what you've wanted since you were in high school."

"I know that. I really do. But haven't you ever had a dream where all the progress you've made, and all the changes you tell yourself you've gone through, are just sort of undone and there you are back where you started from years ago? Haven't you ever had a dream like that?"

"Oh, I don't know," Mom said. "Maybe I would if I thought I'd made all that much progress."

When she swallowed, David saw how her thin neck struggled the food down. Her skin didn't look right; just under the pink of the surface was a sooty grayness. He glanced at Janet, to see if she noticed anything wrong.

"You've made progress," Janet said. "You divorced that maniac, for one thing."

"Right, and got myself right back to zero."

"That's exactly where I feel like I am now."

"Oh no you're not," Mom said. "Not with a good mind and a pretty face."

"Everybody around here always pretends that I'm smart and pretty. I thank you all."

"You *are,*" David said.

She blew him a kiss.

They finished dinner and settled themselves in the living room. Friday was a good night for television. They sat in their usual places: Mom and Lizzie together on the sofa, Janet in one of the orange chairs, and David stretched out on the floor, because it seemed a more masculine position.

The telephone rang during "Dukes of Hazzard." Janet, closest to the doorway, got up for it.

She stayed away for quite some time, through a chase and a string of commercials and the escape that lay on the commercials' other side. The television drowned out her voice, and there was no way David could think of to discreetly overhear. She came back with a lit cigarette and stood in the doorway, smoking.

"You'll never guess who that was," she said.

"Rob?" David said quickly, to get himself into the conversation right from the start.

"Bingo," Janet said. "Now you'll really never guess where he is." She took a deep drag and exhaled a large disorganized cloud of smoke. Her exhalations were usually more directed. "He's at the Galaxy Motel in North Hollywood, where he's been since the day before yesterday, sitting in a room with the blinds drawn."

"What does he want?" Mom said.

"He wants me to meet him for coffee in Glendale, to discuss a whole new, revamped format for our union, is what he wants."

"You're not going to go, are you?" David asked.

"Yes she is," Lizzie said. "You are, aren't you?"

"Well, I guess I am," Janet said. "I mean, I told him I would."

"No," David said, and at the same time Lizzie hollered, "Yay."

"It's awfully late," Mom said.

Janet glanced at her wrist, which had no watch on it. "Must be almost nine-thirty," she said.

"Why don't you see him in the morning?" Mom said.

"Because by morning I may be reading about him in the newspaper. You don't know how he sounded."

"Oh, I know how they can sound."

"Pardon me. I forgot you know everything there is to know about men."

"How *who* can sound?" Lizzie asked.

David told her to shut up, and she kicked him. He didn't kick her back, out of respect for Janet.

"Well, if you're going, you're going," Mom said.

"For coffee, honey. To sit in a little Formica booth in Glendale and drink coffee and talk and then come back home."

"Do me a favor, okay?" Mom said. "Don't start calling me 'honey.'"

"Sorry," Janet said. "I'll see you all later."

"Tell Rob I said hi," Lizzie said.

David said, "Yuck, what a moron," but his heart wasn't in it. Lizzie, as if sensing this, kept quiet and settled her head onto Mom's lap.

"I can't believe that guy didn't leave town," David said after Janet had gone.

"He loves your sister." Mom sighed. "People act crazy when they're in love."

"But she doesn't love him, right?" David said.

"She says she doesn't. No, I don't think she does. I think more than anything she's just scared right now."

"What of?" Lizzie asked from Mom's lap.

"Well, she's afraid she's not good enough to do what she wants to do," Mom said.

"She's good enough," David said.

"I think so too," Mom said.

Lizzie said, "I think she should marry Rob."

Janet stayed out through "Dukes of Hazzard" and "Lottery!" Lizzie was sent to bed and an hour later David had to go too. He begged to stay up until Janet got home, but Mom shooed him upstairs where he got into his pajamas and lay rigidly awake until he heard Janet come in. It was almost midnight, according to the clock on his dresser, an old clock with Popeye pointing to the minutes and hours. He realized he had gotten too old for a clock like that.

He went out into the hallway. Mom was still in the living room with the television on, and Janet said, "Hi," and went in too. David positioned himself three steps down on the staircase, just above the point at which he could have been seen from the living room. Lizzie lay behind her closed door, sleeping her drugged, frowning sleep. He had to listen hard to separate Mom's and Janet's voices from the voices on the television, Johnny Carson talking to a woman with a foreign accent and a sharp, painful-sounding laugh.

"How did it go?" Mom was saying.

"Oh God, I don't know," Janet said. "You should see him, he looks like a wreck. He hasn't shaved, his eyes are bloodshot. I didn't think people really got like that, I thought it was just the movies."

"What did he say to you?"

"A lot of things. Basically he just doesn't understand what he did wrong. I mean, one minute we were getting married and the next minute I'd picked a fight and moved back home to start a career in medicine. I'm not sure if I understand it anymore, either."

"Well, the way I understand—"

The rest of Mom's sentence was overridden by the foreign woman, who said in a great braying voice, "But darhlink, *I'm* still here and where is *she?*" followed by an avalanche of laughter and applause.

"—oldest trick in the book," Mom was saying.

"It's no trick," Janet said. "You didn't see him."

"I don't have to. I saw Frank Stark with three days' growth on his face, begging me for a seventh chance."

"Well, Rob isn't Frank Stark, is he?"

"Of course he's not. But they all—"

A new guest entered to applause and whistles, which ate into Janet's next sentence.

"—you *stop* about that?" she said. "My father wasn't the last good man on earth."

"I never said he was."

"It's what you think."

"No I don't. I know your father had his faults."

"Name me one."

"Well, he was probably the worst dancer in the United States."

Janet laughed. "Shocking," she said. "I'd just like to know one thing, actually. Why do you hate Rob so much? What has he ever done that's made me anything but happy?"

"What are you talking about? I don't hate Rob."

"Yes you do, you've hated every boy I've gone out with since I was fifteen."

"Calm down. Just calm down, now."

Neither of them spoke for a minute. A man on Johnny Carson was talking about stunt driving. "—and at a hundred forty-five miles an hour, Johnny, with your clothes on fire, a jammed harness can be a very nasty thing." David automatically pictured Johnny's look of lockjawed amazement, then the small earnest bobbing of his head when he found a person both impressive and foolish.

Janet said, "I get so tired of you pushing men away from me. They're never good enough. Are you really that anxious for me to end up alone?"

"You're only twenty-three years old, honey."

"Don't call me 'honey.' "

"I beg your pardon."

"And don't try to make some spinster doctor out of me. This is my life, not yours."

"Of course it is."

Another silence stretched between them, full of television noise. Janet said, in a voice so quiet David could hardly hear her, "Of course it is. I'm losing my mind, aren't I?"

"No you're not."

"Yes I am. I can feel it slipping." Her voice quivered. She didn't cry. "I'm just so confused," she said. "I mean, ever since my father died and you married that, well that *man,* I've just, I haven't really known how to relax with anybody, I mean, I can't seem to really *be* with men, like sexually, and I keep thinking well maybe if I met someone else and oh, God, it just isn't *fair—*"

David couldn't sit apart any longer. He got up and strode downstairs, thinking that if questioned he'd tell them he just woke up or something. Something. He found the two of them sitting together on the sofa, holding hands. They ignored him, or didn't notice him. They kept their faces turned to each other. The knuckles of their clasped hands were white, from holding so hard. David lingered a moment in the doorway and then went timidly back upstairs, as abashed as if he'd interrupted two lovers. He went back to bed and lay curled into a tight ball in the middle of the mattress.

Rob was not back in San Francisco. Rob was right here, with whiskers and bloodshot eyes. Janet might think he'd gone back to his motel in Hollywood but David knew he hadn't; he was creeping around the backyard or sitting in his car at the curb, watching. The house felt twice as endangered now, being watched by somebody who knew it on the inside, who'd eaten and slept in it. David bit down on his own knuckle. He gave it a good long bite, the way Lizzie used to bite the plump pink rubber arms of her dolls.

His dreams that night were a swamp he fought to slog

out of. He must have awakened a dozen times, into a dull dazed awareness of his true surroundings, then he would sink back into the sucking mud of sleep. The dreams resided an inch below the surface of his conscious mind, so that when he woke he could determine the shape and size of his dream just as he could have made out a large dark body in murky water, a rough form without details. Always there was a monster or rather the suggestion of a monster, something that searched and snuffled just beyond the range of vision. He would hide from it but never in a safe place. Doors had no locks, trees were never high enough. Once when he woke up he thought a sound from outside had roused him. Though he wanted to go to the window he couldn't; he was paralyzed in bed. He imagined a giant waiting just to one side, knowing which window was his, so that when he appeared there a huge face would loom before him, grinning, eyes alight, lolling an enormous brown speckled tongue. He rolled himself into a tighter ball and squeezed his way back into sleep.

That morning at breakfast Lizzie was crazy to know what had happened between Janet and Rob. Janet was still sleeping, and Mom told Lizzie, "They had a good long talk, honey, and I think Janet's decided it would be better for her to stay here."

Lizzie's face drooped with disappointment—lightened, David suspected, by the small hope that now she might someday marry Rob herself.

"Now will he go back to San Francisco?" she asked.

"Yes," Mom said. "He has to get back to his job."

"Is he going to make it so we don't have to go to Spokane?" she asked.

"I don't think he can, honey. Remember what I told you about Spokane?"

Lizzie nodded sullenly, staring at her plate.

"What did I tell you?" Mom said.

"To be quiet when we're there, and if Dad starts bothering me, call you."

"That's right. And I'll jump on the next plane and pick you up. Okay?"

"Okay."

Lizzie glanced at David. They both knew the hole in the plan. If they called Mom, Dad would hear them doing it. Then they'd be alone with him for hours, him and quiet, stoned Marie.

It was Saturday, which meant that Lizzie would spend the day in her room with Pia Rogovsky, playing Michael Jackson and talking about herself. Pia was what Lizzie had always wanted, an interested, unquestioning audience. This was a friendship that could last for years.

David would ordinarily have gone to meet Billy and hang around the Plaza. Now he would have to think of something else to do. He spent the next hour sitting in the living room with the television on, checking the window every couple of minutes to find nothing there.

Janet came downstairs in her nightgown and got a cup of coffee from the kitchen. She brought it into the living room, holding it up at chest level with both hands. In the long white nightgown, with the cup steaming before her, she looked churchly, or what David remembered as churchly, since the Starks hadn't gone in years.

"Morning," she said. "What's on TV?"

"I don't know," he told her. It was a Bugs Bunny cartoon, which he was embarrassed to have been caught watching.

She sat beside him on the sofa and pulled her legs up so that her chin rested on her knees. It made her seem smaller than she was, small as Lizzie. She sipped tentatively at her coffee.

"Did you have a good time last night?" David asked, because it was the only way he could think of to phrase the question.

"No, I don't think you could say I had a really good time. But it was definitely the right thing, going to talk to him."

"Is he still at the motel?" David asked.

She nodded. "I'm supposed to be thinking. He's going to call here tonight."

"Oh."

"What are you doing today?" she asked.

"I don't know. Nothing."

"That sounds good."

"Do you want to go to the movies or something?"

"Thanks. But I guess I'd better stay home and, well, and think."

David drew in a good breath. "You shouldn't go back to San Francisco with Rob," he said.

"You don't think so either, huh?"

"Well, not really."

"Maybe you're right. I don't know." She sipped her coffee and looked at the screen. Bugs tied a knot in Elmer's gun so it blew up *pow* in his face. David saw the colors reflected in Janet's eyes.

"You could meet somebody you love more," he said. "I mean, you're really pretty."

"That's nice," she said, still watching the television. "Thank you."

"You are," he said, as if she had contradicted him.

"Everybody wants me to be a doctor, huh?"

"Yes," he said, though the moment he'd said it he had a feeling it was not what she wanted to hear. Something about the way her eyes narrowed. On television Bugs was dancing a little ballet while Elmer's shotgun blasts puffed up all around him like popcorn.

"What if I couldn't become a doctor, though?" she said. "What if I never got into school? You'd be disappointed, wouldn't you?"

"No," he lied. It occurred to him that he would be disappointed; he wanted Janet to be smart. He said "No," again, for emphasis.

"Would you support me in my old age? Me and Mom and Lizzie too, this whole houseful of women you've got here?"

"Uh-huh."

"You're a good man, David. Maybe if I don't go back with Rob I'll get lucky and meet somebody like you."

"Uh-huh," he said.

The day would not pass. Every time David looked at a clock it was impossibly early. Lizzie and Pia Rogovsky thumped and bumped on the ceiling in time to Michael Jackson; Mom vacuumed and drank coffee and cleaned the windows with short, squeaking strokes. Janet took a fresh cup of coffee and a pack of cigarettes and disappeared into her room.

After two hours of watching television, David went up and tapped on Janet's door. "Who is it?" she called in a slightly annoyed voice, as if he should have known better than to interrupt her.

"David."

"What is it, honey?"

"I don't know. Can I come in?"

"Okay. Sure."

He opened the door and went inside. Janet sat on her bed with an ashtray bracketed between her feet. She was still in her nightgown, smoking.

"Hi," she said.

"Hi." David waited at the door, uncertain of his next move. "Um, please don't call me 'honey,'" he said.

"Okay. Sorry."

"No. It's all right. I mean, well, it's all right." Actually, he wanted her to call him "honey." He didn't know why he said about two-thirds of what came out of his mouth. It was like having the tongue of another person.

Janet laughed, and he smiled in a way he hoped wasn't too stupid-looking. Mom had started making over Janet's room as a guest room a year ago, but never got around to finishing it. It had for now the feeling of a motel room, sparsely furnished in anticipation of thieving guests. The walls were bare, as was the bureau top under its framed mirror. Janet's narrow bed had been covered with a flowered spread, yellow daisies on an orange field, meant to be cheerful but actually sinister in a room that had no other decoration. As if in keeping with the spirit of the room Janet kept her empty suitcase propped by the door.

"What's up?" she asked David.

"I don't *know,*" he said. He ran his fingertips over the crackled gray flank of her suitcase, an old American Tourister. "What have you been doing?" he asked.

"Thinking. Just like I promised I would."

"Oh." He went and sat on the edge of her bed. His weight on the mattress tipped two cigarette butts out of the brimming ashtray. He picked them up and saw that fine gray ashes had sifted out to make a dark circle on the flowery field.

"Are you sure you don't want to go to the movies?" he said.

"No, I don't think so."

"Okay."

"You know what I've been thinking about, David? I've been thinking about how lucky we are. I mean, look at all this. A big solid house, and we all love one another, at least more often than not. Really, this is heaven."

"It is?"

"So I've decided we should all worry less," she said. "I mean, we may not find the perfect lover, and we may not grow up to be doctors like we thought we would, but we'll still be the same people. We'll still be ourselves. Isn't that a comforting thought?"

"Uh-huh." The idea struck him with a chill. To always stay

yourself, no matter what you did? To be always small and uncertain about everything?

"Good. That is my entire accumulated wisdom and I pass it along to you gladly."

"Are you sure you don't want to go to the movies?" he said.

"Mmm." She stretched her arms straight up over her head. David could hear the stitches in her elbow joints. "I've been toying with the idea of getting dressed."

"Do you want to go for a swim?"

"Nope. What I'm going to do is take a bath for about an hour, and mess with my hair, and I don't know, pluck things and trim things. I'm going to fix myself up."

"Well, I'm going to go downstairs," he said.

"Okay."

"Do you want anything? he asked. "Do you want a cookie?"

She laughed. He was becoming ridiculous. "No thank you," she said.

"Okay. See you."

"See you."

He got up and walked to the door, where he stood for a moment, working for one more thing to say. There was plenty he wanted to tell her but nothing would form itself into a sentence. He said, "See you later," closed the door, and went downstairs.

In the kitchen he took a few Oreos from the breadbox. He ate one and went back upstairs with the others. Janet had already gone into the bathroom. He could hear water running in the tub, and heard the creak and click of the medicine cabinet. He nearly knocked on the door before he realized, with a familiar swoop of vertigo, that he was behaving like a fool. Taking cookies to someone in a bathroom. Wait, before you step into that tub, have a cookie. He ran back downstairs. "We're always still the same people," Janet had said. In a way part of him would always be standing outside the bathroom door, bringing cookies to somebody who needed anything but cookies. He took up his position on the floor in front of the television, and ate the cookies himself.

The hours crept by. Janet spent two hours in the bathroom making herself beautiful ("Making myself bee-*yoo*tiful" is what she said, posing a moment with both hands linked behind her head and her hips wriggling like a belly dancer's); she smoked cigarettes with Mom in the kitchen and helped make dinner. David could hear the two of them laughing over the sound of the television. He wondered when Rob would call.

Pia Rogovsky was allowed to stay for dinner, after a long pleading call to her parents, two shadowy figures who rarely let her out after four-thirty and whose house, David imagined, smelled like Pia herself. She was not someone you could hate but she was a darkness inside the Starks' house, a small invasion. When her parents gave in she clapped her pink-nailed hands together and said "Oooooh." Mom went over the menu with her, asking if she liked this and liked that, and though Pia agreed to everything David noticed her, at the dinner table, mournfully picking the green pepper out of her spaghetti sauce.

Janet was cheerful at dinner and took care of asking Pia the polite questions. When Janet asked, "Where did you live before you moved here?" Pia hesitated, smiled and said, "Pittsburgh?" as if she wasn't certain whether it was the right answer.

"I was born in London," Lizzie said, and no one bothered to contradict her.

The telephone rang while they were eating dessert. Janet jumped up, saying, "Excuse me," and ran upstairs to answer it. David thought that if Pia wasn't there, she'd have picked it up in the kitchen, where she could be overheard. Pia sat spooning ice cream with moronic joy.

"Are you getting along all right in school here, Pia?" Mom asked. David could tell from the tilt of her chin that her main attention was slanted upstairs.

"Oh, yes," Pia said, as agreeable to that as she was to everything else.

"Pia hates this school," Lizzie said. "She thinks everybody in it is an asshole."

Pia's face darkened and she smiled, caught between two agreements. You couldn't really hate her, David thought. He wondered what Janet was saying.

"Let Pia answer for herself, please, Lizzie," Mom said.

"Well she told me she hates it," Lizzie said. "Didn't you, Pia?"

Pia smiled so hard David thought her face would split. "Sometimes I do," she said.

"A big fat girl named Roxanne Sexauer pushed Pia into a pile of dog shit yesterday," Lizzie said. "She stunk all day."

Pia smiled and smiled. David thought he could see beads of sweat pop out along her upper lip.

"That's terrible," Mom said, her mind elsewhere.

"I'm going to get some dog shit and dump it on Roxanne's head on Monday," Lizzie said proudly.

"You are not," Mom told her. "And please think of something else to call it."

"Dog doodle," Lizzie said, which sent her and Pia off into a spasm of giggling.

"I don't think I can eat any more," David said. "Lizzie makes me sick." After he'd said it, he decided he didn't like sounding so delicate in front of Pia.

"Just grit your teeth and be brave," Mom said.

Janet came down and took her seat again. She nodded to an invisible signal of Mom's.

"What did you tell him?" Mom asked.

"Everything's all worked out," Janet said. She smiled cheerfully at Pia and said, "So Pia, how are you liking the school here?"

"I hate it," Pia said politely. Lizzie fell into a renewed burst of giggling, followed by Pia. David would have taken his ice cream into the living room to finish it, but he didn't want to miss anything further Janet might say about Rob.

She didn't say anything about him for the rest of the evening. Pia had to be taken home right after dinner, and the Starks watched television together as usual. David was itching to ask Janet questions but hung back, for fear of violating the mysterious rules that held sway. He took his cues from Mom, who went along as if everything was normal. She smoked cigarette after cigarette, sitting beside Janet on the sofa. Once he saw her reach over and pat Janet's knee, without taking her eyes from the television. Janet stroked the back of Mom's blue-veined hand.

Bedtimes came, first Lizzie's and then David's. Before going up he reached for Janet in a movement that started as an embrace but halted halfway, from uncertainty. He stood a moment before her with his arms out, frozen, and she finished the gesture for him by taking both of his hands in hers, pulling him forward, and planting a smacking, exaggerated kiss on his forehead.

"Good night, handsome," she said.

"Night. Night, Mom."

"Good night. See you in the morning."

Up in his room he lay with his eyes wide, straining to stay awake. The house sounded only like itself, the steady drone of the television moving through the walls like the pulse of an engine. Mom's voice, Janet's voice, the minute ring of a dropped glass. Laughter. A car horn, a dog barking. Sleep took him against his will, opening slowly inside his head. With a final effort to be in the world a moment longer he speculated over a distant, muffled bang, knew it to be nothing more than a truck backfiring, and tipped over into dreams.

He woke knowing something was wrong. Something. He hesitated a moment, between his fading dream and his awakening. A door had opened and closed. He hadn't dreamed it; it was what woke him up. He got up and went, automatically, to the window. Nothing in the backyard. He stood still, holding his breath, weighing the darkness. Nothing. But he had the same odd feeling, the moth fluttering at his forehead.

He went downstairs, into the deeper dark of the stairwell, across the entry hall which was lit by streetlight that seeped in through the three small windows in the front door. They made three pale stepping stones on the carpet. The silent living room looked weighted, like a stateroom in a sunken ship. David walked into the kitchen.

The blue gaslights of the stove sent up their glow. Against the tiled wall, the blender and the crock of wooden spoons threw faint gray shadows surrounded by blue shadows. David paused by the window over the sink, checking the pool. The night sky was a mottled no-color, low clouds sending back the city lights, the elusive green-gray-yellow of a bruise. Behind him the refrigerator ticked.

He saw the white envelope standing on the table in the breakfast nook and knew immediately it was something. He approached it warily. It bore no address but sat propped against the salt and pepper shakers which, when he picked up the envelope, were revealed. A king for pepper and a queen for salt, with twice as many holes in her head as the king had.

The envelope was not empty. David took it over to the stovetop and switched on the light in the scalloped copper hood. Inside the envelope was a single piece of paper. It said:

Morning, everybody,
This is the chickenshit of the year, up to her old tricks again. I'm doing a shameful thing—sneaking out under cover of darkness, and going back to San Francisco with Rob. This is like something out of the movies—with everything but a ladder made of sheets—I hope you all can forgive me. The truth is I feel so shaky about this I just couldn't face telling you what I decided—I knew you'd all be disappointed in me. I guess I did too good a

job convincing everybody that staying with Rob would be some kind of grisly death—I guess I was trying to convince myself of that. The truth is he loves me very much and I think I really love him too—I just had a walloping case of cold feet, so I had to make up a reason for not getting married that would sound more convincing than plain old garden variety terror. I think I'm doing the right thing now, I really do. I'll call you tomorrow, from the city. Until then I offer my cowardly love, and my thanks for taking me in and putting up with me.

Love,
Janet

David put the letter down on the counter and raced up to Janet's room. It was empty, the bed neatly made, the suitcase gone. He went back downstairs and read the letter again. Gone. She had gone with Rob. He read the letter a third time. Maybe it was true, what she said about loving Rob and having had cold feet. He tried switching over into an alternate version of the truth, in which Janet never really cared much about becoming a doctor; what she really cared about was Rob. It felt hollow and wrong. He sat down with the letter at the kitchen table and thought about it. A week ago, she'd told him, "The bride has flown the coop." Now he imagined her in a white doctor's smock, flying out of control, floating up and up and out of sight. If he'd taken better care of her, if he hadn't told lies—he searched his memory for the moment at which Janet had made her decision to leave. What had he said to make her do it?

He stood and went out the front door, as if he expected some vestige of her still to be there, getting into Rob's car, stoppable. The street was empty, tinted with yellow light from the street lamps. The sky was the same bruised color. She had gone.

He sat down on the stoop, unconcerned about whether

anyone might drive by and see him in his pajamas. He bent over and held his head between his knees, looking down at the shadowed concrete step where a ragged weed, wiry as a stray dog, grew lopsidedly out of a meandering crack. She had gone without saying a real good-bye, without worrying about whether anyone else would be all right. Somewhere out on the highway she and Rob were speeding along in Rob's trim little car, unworried over anything except their own private future. David raised his head. Rob's car skidded on a curve somewhere in the desert. It shot over a cliff's edge and bloomed with flame, dwindling in the blackness. Janet was thrown out onto the rocks. She'd live but she'd never walk again, she'd come home in a wheelchair. Rob's car blazed on, spiraling down into a canyon that had no bottom. Coyotes howled in the mountains. Across the street, a gray cat skittered along a fence, keeping close to the shadow. Everyone in the houses on this street had been smothered by the night and lay now, tangled up in bed-sheets, silent as the furniture. Darkness gathered around the streetlights and hung low to the ground. David drew a breath that was like breathing fine, cold soot. Darkness lay in his own house, thickly on the rugs and tables, and on the stairs. Darkness had slipped under the door to Lizzie's room, dusting her as she slept her fierce sleep, and it found Mom alone in her room down the hall. It settled on her, filling her mouth and nose, sifting through her throat to her belly, into her blood to her heart. She had let Dad go, and she had let Janet go. She deserved to die.

David jumped up in a panic. He was trembling. He took back what he'd thought, hoping the curse was removable. He bit his hand. He could never do anything that mattered, he could only think thoughts that came crookedly true. A black sportscar shot by, materializing out of its own rumble. The idea came to him in the wake of the car.

He and Billy could go to San Francisco and bring Janet back. It was exactly the kind of thing Billy liked. They could hitchhike north together, have adventures along the way, and then knock on Janet's door where David would say, "Janet, I know you don't really love Rob. I've come to take you home." He could even kidnap her, a kindly kidnapping. In his mind it started turning into a movie. The actors who played Billy and David had had a fight, the way normal friends do, but when their old archenemy came around again they jumped straight into action together, their differences forgotten. They talked an easy, joking sort of talk. That made it possible for them to be friends and rivals at the same time. The actress who played Janet was the girl they were both in love with. At that point the story got too complicated. David figured he'd just get moving and let things work themselves into a conclusion. He told himself you couldn't plan too far ahead. Nothing ever turned out the way you expected it to, anyway.

He went up to his room and put his clothes on. The clock on his bedside table said 3:25. He couldn't decide whether to go now or to wait until it started getting light. He thought he'd rather wait for a little light. He sat on the bed, and before he knew it he was lying down, chewing on the corner of his pillowcase. He jumped back up again. He went to his dresser and opened the top drawer, with no idea of what he expected to find. Here in the drawer were socks, shorts, the green tin box marked STASH.

He took the box to his bed, sat down, and spilled the money out on the sheet. There were fifteen dollar bills and another dollar seventy-seven in change. He thought that should be enough.

He pictured himself, or his actor self, going to Billy's house, throwing gravel at the window and saying, "Psst, old friend, sorry to drop in unannounced like this but there's a spot of trouble and I think I may need your help." The Billy-actor would lean irritably against the windowpane, because he was the skeptical one, the one who never believed there was a plot and who always needed to be rescued from traps he refused to notice. He'd say, "What trouble?" and David would answer casually, "Well, Nixon's back. Seems we didn't finish him off last time after all." He tried it the first time saying, "Rob's back," but the name Rob sounded too usual and small.

Billy would say, "Where?" in an impressed voice. "San Francisco," David would reply. "We leave immediately." "I'll be right down," Billy would say, "Do you have the—?"

The gun. David knew suddenly what he had to take along to give the journey its proper weight. That way Billy, the real Billy, would know how serious he was. He could see himself standing on Billy's lawn with one hip cocked, holding the gun. Just thinking about it got him jiggling his legs in a nervous ecstasy.

He stood up and walked, carefully setting one foot after the other, down the hall to Mom's room. The darkness there was infused with her breathing and her sleepy smell. He held himself steady through a rush of fear. Slowly, moving on the balls of his feet, he walked inside and went to the nightstand. He pulled out the drawer. It creaked, and Mom muttered in a dream. David waited, expectant, but she settled herself and her breathing stayed regular. Moving by inches, holding his breath, he worked his hand in and touched the gun. It scraped softly against the wood as he withdrew it. It was much heavier than he'd expected it to be. Holding it against his thigh, away from Mom's vague form under the blankets, he sneaked out of the room. He realized with horror that he had made it.

David took a towel from the bathroom and wrapped it around the gun. He went into his room and got his backpack from the closet, a slick empty blue nylon bag with padded black shoulder straps. When the gun and towel were stuffed inside it was like carrying a heavy pillow. He couldn't feel the gun at all when he squeezed. Hefting the backpack in one hand he went downstairs to the kitchen, coins jingling in his pocket. He ate a banana and drank milk from the carton. He left the kitchen, then went back and took Janet's note from the table. He chose a pen from among the bouquet of pens and pencils that sprouted from the square flowered canister by the telephone, and wrote at the bottom of the letter, "Have gone to get her. XXXXX, David." He regretted the X's, but since he'd written in ink he couldn't rub them out. He slid the letter back into its envelope, propped it back up against the salt and pepper shakers, and walked outside into the spotlit night.

The pack bumped against his thigh as he walked to Billy's. He worried that the gun might go off and shoot him in the leg, and he walked as long as he was able holding the pack stiff-armed, away from his body. Once he heard rustlings in the shadows to one side of a house like his own. He thought he could make out a shape there, something small that stood watching him with invisible eyes. Experimentally, he waved his free arm. The thing disappeared. He walked on, full of happiness.

Billy's house lay in the shadow of its lemon grove, sheltered from the light. Lemons shone among the silent, waxy black leaves. The leaf-littered yard was spotted with lemons, the newly fallen ones gray on the ground and the rotten ones black. He went around to the side were Billy's room was. The walls of the house were covered with shingles, made of something brown and pebbly, each one outlined in black tar.

David stood under Billy's dark window. The prow of the roof cut into the sky. He just stood for a while, unable to move. It all seemed suddenly like a bad idea. When Billy came to the window David would have to say something interesting, and say it fast. He thought it over and settled finally on, "It's time to stop playing games and be serious." Then he'd show the gun. He hoped Billy wouldn't come down, take the gun away from him, and shoot him with it.

He started looking around for some gravel to throw. There wasn't any. He threw a rotten lemon instead, which struck Billy's window with a disappointing *plot* sound and left a smear, like a bug on a windshield. Billy didn't come to the window.

David threw another lemon, a riper one. It bounced off the window with a much more dignified sound, but it still didn't rouse Billy. Somewhere, close by, a cricket chirped; it seemed to come from everywhere at once. David threw another lemon, and another. The glass shivered liquidly after the last one, and he waited. No one came to the window. He could see the corner of Billy's curtain, a flimsy blue-and-green material that was like woven plastic. He knew Billy's room almost as well as he knew his own: the fake wood paneling covered with pictures clipped from *Soldier of Fortune,* the nicked furniture, the old black-and-white photo of Billy's father, in an army uniform, sitting on the dresser in a gold-colored frame. Billy's father looked a little like Ray. David had spent a thousand hours in that room, two thousand. Under the bed was a withered apple core he himself had tossed there the week before. It was like being shut out of his own home.

He searched the ground until he found a rock. It was much too big, almost the size of a tennis ball, but the yard was all grass and dead leaves, without a speck of gravel. The rock was cool and gritty. He threw it at the window underhanded, as lightly as he could.

It sailed through the glass with only a soft ping, a sound like crystal struck by a fingernail. It left a jagged hole of pure black on the glossy black of the window. David couldn't believe it. He had thrown so gently.

A light went on, and the hole disappeared. A rectangle of light fell at David's feet. Nothing else happened; Billy's face did not appear. David stood dumb for a minute, because he couldn't think of what to do. He stared up at the window and after a while Billy's mother's face appeared.

It had never occurred to David that Billy might get his mother. She was a sharp-nosed, small-chinned woman from someplace like Texas. She drilled him with her little eyes, and opened the window. David was out of the yard and halfway across the street before she could start screaming. He ran over the invisible line back into the ordinary neighborhood, got a block up the street, and crouched down behind a parked car, where he stayed for a few minutes in the hope that Billy would come running past, alone, and that he'd be able to get a sentence out before Billy cracked his head open. He unzipped his pack and worked the gun out of the towel, so he could show it to Billy right off. He was impressed all over again with how hefty it was, how comfortably it fit his hand.

After a minute a police cruiser passed in the street, going toward Billy's house. David froze half under the car, which he noticed was a Dodge Dart. He could see his nose reflected in the bumper. He thought sadly of how nothing ever happened the way you pictured it. The police car turned the corner and he sprinted across the street, with the pack in one hand and the gun in the other. He ran six blocks before he allowed himself to look back. Nothing.

Now he would have to go to San Francisco alone, or go home and sneak back into bed. He stuffed the gun into his pack. The idea of going home was so appealing that he walked two blocks in that direction before he remembered it was also possible not to. If he went home he could wake up in a few hours in his own bed, returned to his life with nothing worse than a broken window to worry about. Monday would come and the week would pass; Janet would stay in San Francisco with Rob, and David and Lizzie would go to Spokane. Mom would be lowered into the ground, hands crossed on her chest, her hair brittle with a permanent. Dad would hoist Lizzie high in the air and pinch her. Nixon would get reelected. David turned around and headed out of the neighborhood.

He thought he should take a map, but the only map he knew of back home was his own, the map of the universe. He decided to take a bus partway, and use the time on the bus to build his courage for hitchhiking. He wasn't sure how far eighteen-seventy would take him; he'd go somewhere close on the first ticket, and if he had money left over he could buy another ticket. His first problem would be finding the bus station.

He knew it was on the other side of the freeway, and that it would be much shorter to cross right over than it would be to double around to the underpass. The freeway could be heard from some distance away, its roar constant and penetrating as a river's. To reach it, David had to cut between two houses and cross the rough concrete gutter to the embankment. Overhead, the freeway threw a liquid shimmer of light into the sky, and as David climbed uphill, bracing himself with his free hand, he could smell the sharp green odor of crushed ice plant. He thought of black widows.

At the top of the hill he worked himself into a hedge of oleander, full of dust and the faint sweet smell of the leaves. On the other side of the freeway was an arctic brightness, a barren, floating landscape that bore no more relation to the streets below than an aircraft carrier does to a midnight ocean.

He crouched in the bushes, waiting for the traffic to break. Headlights came and came, if not from one direction then the other. They shone yellow in the white light of the high-intensity lamps. The lights appeared in the distance, grew brighter without appearing to grow larger, and then when they began to get larger they ceased gaining in brightness. There was a point, fifty yards or so down, at which they hovered, noiselessly, seemingly stopped, and then they shot forward, all noise. The black tires and gleaming body roared past, stirring up a gritty wind that fluttered the bits of trash at the road's edge. After each car had passed a small *whizz* hung in the air, like the reverberation of a plucked wire.

David gave up waiting for a clear field in both directions, and settled on a break in the westbound lanes. After a spate of heavy traffic no new headlights appeared, and he picked up his pack and ran. He crossed the hard dirt of the shoulder and made the asphalt just as another pair of lights appeared. Halfway into the closest lane he hesitated, wondering whether to turn back. The lights, though far away, were in the farthest lane and he would be running into their path, as if he were racing a train to a crossing. He decided to go. He sprinted over the first lane, and the second. Three more to go. Another pair of lights shone, in the lane he had just left. He had some trouble judging how near the first lights were; they seemed unnaturally bright. He kept running. The lanes were wider than he'd realized, and his strides felt short and slightly weighted, as if the approaching lights gave off a slow dull gravity of their own. He ran. When he reached the median the car was closer behind him than he'd thought possible. It might have been catapulted, so quickly did it shoot up from what had looked like a safe distance. He felt its wind on his back while he was still running.

The median was a wide strip of weedy ground. An oily wind worried it constantly. Traffic on the other side was thick. David waited, with nowhere to hide, hoping each car that loomed behind its lights was not a police cruiser. He wondered if people were staring at him. It was impossible to see faces behind the black windshields.

He began edging along in the direction of oncoming traffic, to give himself something to do. He saw a truck coming up, festooned with orange lights, and backed off a few feet out of respect for its bulk. The truck drew closer, its grumble rising. When the glare of the headlights struck David it blasted its horn, a gigantic sound that deafened him and nearly blew him over. The truck howled by, big as a freight train, its silver sides bearing letters that were too large to read, red A's and R's taller than David himself. The truck passed and after a half-second's calm a vacuum sucked him up and pulled him, stumbling, to the very edge of the asphalt. He beat his arms against the wall of air, to keep from being swept out into traffic.

Then David stepped on something in the weeds. A chill went through him, an ancient alarm. Something dead here. He looked down on the splayed hind leg of a dog, a little black-haired dog with the ears and muzzle of a fox. The dog lay twisted, its front end wrenched over at an impossible angle, the tongue lolling limp. David jumped back. He double-checked the freeway, thought it was empty, and took off.

The car was on him before he saw it. He felt the lights shine on his face like heat and when he turned they were right there, enormous. The hairs stood up on the back of his neck. He felt each one. He stood, just stood, greeting the car with an expression of bankrupt surprise while it swerved screeching around him, blowing his hair back off his face. The horn came a moment later, a diminishing bellow. Instantly the car was a hundred yards past, only its lozenge-shaped taillights visible.

Other cars bore down on him, and David was a moment appreciating the fact that he was unharmed and entitled to keep running. The next car's horn preceded it, a blossoming sound, widening and widening. He ran. When he reached the far shoulder he threw himself into the bushes there, dove into the darkness at their roots. The bushes were a cool, dusty, vegetable nowhere and he lay panting. He stayed a while in the sanctuary of the bushes, watching the cars whoosh past on the freeway. Now he could not go back. When he had regathered himself he crawled through the bushes and loped, at a sharp diagonal, down the embankment on the other side.

The far side of the freeway
was unknown territory. He passed through a neighborhood
of ragged little houses, bungalows with patchy lawns and
cracked, blistered paint. Music drifted from one, low horns
and a woman wailing, though all the windows were dark. David
hurried by.

The houses gave out eventually onto a street he knew, a
long strip with a McDonald's and a Taco Bell and a Winchell's
Donuts, which were like old friends. He had been driven here
before and gone to the Winchell's. Everything was closed now.
As he walked the street he noticed stores that had been invisible whenever he drove through with Mom. There was a dry
cleaner's with a picture of a faded, green-skinned woman in a
flowered dress, and an insurance agency with its name on the
window in gold letters and a gold trophy displayed inside, on
the sill, along with two dead flies. There was a beauty parlor
and a travel agency and a gift shop, all sad-looking and subtly
wrong.

The street rambled on, and David began to worry about his
direction. He knew the freeway ran to his left, and so the bus

station should be ahead and to the right. It was so different, though, on foot. The sky was low and opaque, without stars, and the street went on and on without turning into anything other than what it was, a flat broad boulevard lined with strange stores. He wondered if he had in fact been down this street before, or on another one like it. All the stores resembled one another. He had a sickening conviction that he was walking in circles.

Several blocks later, just as he was beginning to give up hope, the bus station announced itself like a full moon. The circle of brilliant blue, across which the graceful white dog flamed frozen in midleap, rose over the roof of a car wash. He ran the remaining three blocks.

The plate-glass windows and door of the bus terminal held in a heavy green aquarium light, and David stopped short, suddenly nervous. What if they wouldn't sell him a ticket? He reached into his pocket to touch the money. If he didn't have enough money to get to San Francisco, they'd be suspicious. He hung around the door, unable to move, until the man at the ticket counter looked up and noticed him. He walked in because he had no choice, and as he crossed the cloudy, dark green floor a part of him lingered behind, floating a foot back of his own head, monitoring the progress of his body. He saw himself go up to the ticket man and heard himself say, "Can I have a ticket to Santa Barbara?" Santa Barbara was the closest distant place he could think of.

The man, who was old and brown-spotted, with a loose mouth, dipped his chin and looked over David's head. "Traveling alone?" he asked.

"Yes," David said, and a vein in his neck throbbed so hard he feared the man would see it. "I'm going up to see my sister," he added.

"Your parents drop you off outside?" he asked.

"There's only my mom," David said. "And she works at night. I walked over. We live down the street." He was astonished to hear himself say it, and to find that he imagined the lie with fluid ease. He lived in one of the scrubby houses; his mother swept floors at insurance companies.

The man scrutinized David's face. He settled his mouth with a juicy suckling sound and said challengingly, "Thirteen fifty."

David dug into his pocket and pulled out the money. He had played it right. Proudly, he laid the bills and change on the counter. The man gave him his ticket, and told him the bus left in forty-five minutes.

David went and sat in one of a line of molded blue chairs. He put his pack on the seat beside him. Only two other people were in the waiting room, an old man and an old woman, their faces furrowed in thought as if they were straining to remember, and they paid David no attention. He had never been so entirely disregarded by adults before. The sensation thrilled him. Indifference was a sign of respect. These old quivering people (the woman's lips formed silent words) thought he could take care of himself.

He forced himself to stay in his seat, though he ached to walk around and check things over. A row of vending machines stood against the opposite wall, and he worked hard to appear as if he was not trying to determine what was for sale. Candy, Cold Drinks, Cigarettes, and an especially interesting one called Traveler's Aids. It sounded both musical and dirty, and try as he might he could not identify a single item behind any of the illuminated windows. He sat still, remembering not to jiggle his legs. He would get to Santa Barbara and hitchhike from there. He and Billy had hitched rides around the neighborhood, and David believed he had a certain power to make cars stop for him. It had to do with the way you held your face and your thumb. Friendly but not too eager, happily above it all, ready for a ride but just as ready to stay there on the curb, enjoying the sunlight. He had had to be especially charming to make up for Billy's scowl and his jabbing, dangerous-looking thumb. David always knew that when people stopped, they were stopping for him and not Billy. A spasm of joy came over him. His life would rise and rise, because he was smart and quick to give a right answer and able to do what needed doing regardless of the risk. Because he was *him.* He noticed he had started to jiggle his legs, and stopped. The old woman murmured on, soundlessly, telling herself the same thing over and over.

When the bus arrived, the dark had taken on the charged thinness that comes before the light. Only David rose for the bus; the old people remained seated. As he passed the Traveler's Aids machine he saw with disappointment that it contained Kleenex, a black plastic comb, a rain bonnet, a shoe horn, and two magnets in the shape of Scotties, a black and a white.

The bus smelled of rubber and disinfectant. Several people sat scattered around. There might have been a rule requiring everybody to sit at least two rows away from everybody else. David took a seat toward the rear, two rows down from a man with a crew cut and a dragon tattoo. The man was chewing gum, and as David passed him he blew a small mean pink bubble.

David settled himself with his pack on the floor between his feet, then changed his mind and hefted it up onto his lap. The bus pulled out, grumbling, full of its own weighty, swaying power. It cruised down the strip, and the first gray light gathered in the sky. David sank into the bus's movement, relieved to be without power of choice. Stores slid by, restored to their proper size and unimportance, and a phrase of Janet's drifted into his head. She'd said that being stoned made things funny and remote. Travel was like being stoned. The bus stopped at half a dozen stations, all of them both odd and familiar. Sometimes a few people struggled on, carrying suitcases or parcels, looking winded and beaten even this early in the day. At one stop no one got on at all. The bus's pneumatic doors whooshed open, hung, and closed again. It moved on. By the time it got to the open highway, hilly country covered in high yellow grass, dotted with gas stations and restaurants, the sun was throwing long shadows that raised the detail of every swell and rivet on the gas pumps. He saw a passing truck turn off its headlights and declare the beginning of day proper.

He did not start getting anxious until he saw the first sign for Santa Barbara. It hit him like a revelation: he was going to be alone in a strange city, with less than four dollars in his pocket and hundreds of miles to cross. Up until that moment he had imagined a transformed self getting off the bus and setting out to hitchhike; himself turned into a character on a TV show, canny and capable, moving with brisk certainty from one action to the next. Now he saw that he was rattling headlong into his own future, and that he remained unchanged, a disorganized bundle of vague impulses, likely at any moment to just sit down and stay. As the bus rolled along he dug his fingernails into his palms, to keep himself alert and ready for action. Since no one could see him clearly, he allowed himself to jiggle his legs.

The bus reached the Santa Barbara station the same way cars approached on the freeway—first too slowly and then too fast. It seemed to ride endlessly through the outskirts, motels and gas stations and chain restaurants, with sign after sign saying SANTA BARBARA; then the city popped up and they were there, pulling into a berth at the station, where the bus shuddered and stopped with a gassy sigh.

He shouldered his pack and meekly disembarked. The sun was strong by now and the morning heated up, full of the smell of gasoline and burned coffee. David walked into the station and fought an impulse to sit down, as if he was waiting for somebody to pick him up. He stood in line at the ticket counter, and when he reached the woman (middle-aged, aloofly annoyed, with a string of red, white, and blue plastic beads hung around her neck), he asked how to get to the highway.

"Coast Highway?" she asked, and he could not tell whether she was suspicious or just confused.

"The one that goes to San Francisco," he said.

He saw her sizing him up, and saw in her eyes the decision she made. There were people stacked up behind, it looked to be a long, bad morning, so just give the kid directions and get him out of the way.

"Out the door," she said, "and left. Eight blocks down." She looked with sour anticipation over his head at the next person waiting to be dealt with.

He found the highway with no trouble, after walking eight blocks along a street just like the one at home. The highway ran through town rather than skirting it, lined with restaurants and gas stations, thick with traffic. Alongside the highway was a wide dusty shoulder, where gravel and bits of broken glass caught the sun. He hesitated on the shoulder. A Sambo's stood behind him, cool and kindly under its red-and-yellow sign. He went in and had a glazed doughnut and a glass of grape juice at the counter, and thought they were the most delicious things he had ever tasted. Then he walked to the side of the road, arranged a careless smile on his face, and offered his thumb to the passing cars.

There were other hitchhikers arrayed by the road, all much older. The man closest had a pyramid of frizzy black hair and a gold front tooth that sent out a shiver of light when he smiled to acknowledge David's stare. David turned away.

Cars sped by. He realized that Mom had discovered his absence by now, but her life had slipped into a suspended state and he could not quite imagine that time moved for her as quickly as it did for him. He thought that if he got in a car and raced home he could almost catch up with himself, jump back into his bed like a spirit returned to its body, the journey wiped clean.

Cars shot by, and David kept a watch on the horizon for

police cruisers. He wondered if the gold-toothed man was looking at him. He felt a ticklish heat on the back of his neck. As the cars passed he tried to read the faces of the drivers for kindness or cruelty, since he was not quite sure whether he hoped somebody would stop or feared somebody would. Many of the drivers were serious-faced men in coats and ties who drove on without glancing at him, not even in curiosity. There were younger men as well, and some women; they tended to notice him, but all roared on. David felt a warm sting of shame on his face, for asking something of strangers who had no idea he was unique and privileged, with a whole universe inside his head. To their eyes he was not different in substance from the man with the gold tooth. It occurred to him that the man might believe himself to be just as real and worthy of attention as David was, though he imagined the man was more used to disregard. He moved farther away, regretted the blatancy of it, and bent over to retie his shoe, as if he'd had to walk twenty paces for that purpose. When he straightened up he could not stop himself from glancing back at the man and there it was, the tooth, shining. David adjusted the straps of his pack and sang "Beat It." to himself.

The first black man to pass stopped for him as if they were both members of the same club. The man drove a brown Chevy, dull with dirt, and pulled onto the shoulder just past the spot where David stood. He was a moment in registering the fact that this was a ride. For him. The car waited, its brake lights glowing through the storm of dust it raised. He could not think of what to do. He imagined bolting back to the Sambo's, but feared the humiliation even more than he feared the man. He trudged to the car, hoping the man might lose patience and drive on. When the man motioned for him to hurry up and come inside, he obeyed.

The man had short woolly hair and bloodshot eyes sunk deep in slack gray-black pouches of flesh. He wore a sport shirt covered with orange jungle flowers, and his big chocolate-colored arms looked taut as sausages.

"Shut the door," he said. "You letting the flies in."

"Sorry," David said, and shut the door. The man accelerated, and pulled back into traffic. David sat hugging his pack.

"What're you," the man said. "Eight, nine year old?"

"Thirteen," David said indignantly. The red eyes shifted suspiciously in their crepy pockets and David added, "Almost thirteen. August the third."

"And where you going, Almost Thirteen?"

David could not think of a lie. This man was too foreign to lie to. Who knew what he might or might not believe?

"San Francisco," he said. "I ran out of money for the bus."

"You ran out of money for the bus. Your momma know where you are?"

After a moment, David said, "No."

The man nodded, pleased to have been right. "I thought she didn't. What you going to do in San Francisco?"

Here it got complicated. He was willing to tell the truth, but couldn't think how. For a moment he wasn't certain himself why he was going to San Francisco. He disliked the man for confusing him so. "Nothing," he said, and was appalled to hear himself giggle.

"Nothing. Well now. You don't have to go all the way to San Fran to do nothing."

"No," David said, and looked out the window at the passing scenery.

The man said he was only going as far as Buellton and David said fine, though he wasn't quite sure where Buellton was. The man turned on the radio, to a station that played a screechy sort of jazz. He tapped the steering wheel in time to the beat. David swayed his legs with the music, which was good once he got used to it.

"You know, Almost Thirteen, I'm going to take you to the sheriff in Buellton," the man said.

"Oh."

"Just to keep you safe now. It's a long way to San Fran. How much money you got?"

"Ten dollars," David said.

"Now for what you want to go to San Fran? To do nothing, you say?"

"Well," David said, "not really nothing."

"I thought not."

"My girlfriend lives there," he said, and his cheeks flushed.

"Oh, your *girlfriend*." The man found this funny. "What, you girlfriend move out on you?"

"Well, yes," David said.

The man laughed, a deep dark sound with three descending levels. He slapped the steering wheel with the flat of his hand. "And you going to bring her back, huh?"

"Uh-huh," David said, uncertain about what was so funny but sure that the laughter was at his expense.

"The world is full of love now, ain't it?" the man laughed. "Every little traveler by the side of the road has got his heart full of love."

"Uh-huh," David said, and laughed a little, in hopes of entering the joke.

"Tell me, traveler, what you going to say to you girlfriend if you get to San Fran?"

David hesitated. "I don't know," he said. He was unable to cover the bafflement in his voice, which set the man off in renewed laughter. David thought with irritation that black people laughed too much.

"You don't know," the man said, rubbing under his eyes. "You just going to ring her bell and take it from there."

David looked out the window, holding his pack.

"Tell you what, traveler," the man said. "We get to Buellton,

I going to put you on a bus. Do my part for the lovers in this world."

"No thank you," David said, without looking back from the window. "Just drop me off in Buel Town."

"No sir. I will put you on a bus or I will take you to the sheriff. You fussy about charity, I give you my name and address. You can send me the money back."

"No thanks," David said.

The man laughed, and said nothing more. David thought with pride that you had to be firm with some people. He hoped the man would buy him the ticket anyway, no matter how staunchly he turned it down.

They reached Buellton, and drove its streets without speaking. The town appeared to be made up of nothing but motels and restaurants, strung along either side of a broad avenue that set the air shimmering with early heat. David was relieved when the man pulled over in front of a Greyhound station.

"I don't want a bus ticket," he said.

"Yes you do. Come on in." The man got out of the car and David, after what he considered a suitable pause, followed him inside. The station was so much like the one back home that he felt once again, with a swell of nausea, that he'd been traveling in circles. While the man went to the counter for his ticket, David studied a poster that depicted a smiling silver-haired couple, holding hands, seeing America by bus.

The man brought the ticket over. "We hit it right," he said. "Bus leaves in fifteen minutes. Here." He thrust the ticket at David, who accepted it and said, "Give me your address, please, and I'll send you the money tomorrow."

"Right, right," the man said. "Come over here to the snack bar, we'll have a cup of coffee."

He went with the man to the snack bar, which was nothing more than a folding table with a coffee urn, stacks of Styrofoam cups and a gray grease-stained box half full of doughnuts. A fat young woman with blotchy arms stood smoking behind the table, looking idly around as if she, too, were waiting for a bus.

"Two coffees," David said in a loud voice before the man had a chance to speak. He took the last dollar bill out of his pocket and laid it on the tabletop. He was hungry, and would have bought a doughnut, but all he had left was change. The man said, "What about a doughnut, too?"

"If you want one," David said.

"Two doughnuts," the man said, and laid another dollar on the table.

"Help yourself," the woman said. She filled two cups from the urn grudgingly, like a bystander who'd been asked a favor.

David dumped three packets of sugar and two of powdered cream into his coffee. The cream lingered at the top, a granulated crust, which he stirred away with one of the Popsicle sticks piled next to the sugar. The man asked him if he wanted glazed or powdered sugar. He said he didn't care, and the man knew somehow to give him glazed.

They took their coffee and doughnuts and sat in two blue chairs. The man carried David's pack for him, since he couldn't manage it with the coffee and doughnut.

"To love," the man said, raising his cup. David, suspecting a hidden joke, just drank his coffee. For the first time, it didn't taste bad.

"Just what is this girlfriend like?" the man asked. "She pretty?"

David nodded, and started on his doughnut.

"My boy, now," the man said, "has got a girl six foot tall. No fat. But I mean, *tall.*"

"How old is your boy?" he asked suspiciously.

"Eighteen in August. He joined the merchant marine."

"Oh."

"He lived with his momma back in Chicago. Your girl six foot tall?"

"No," David said.

The man laughed. "My boy's girl is pretty too. You sure your girl is pretty?"

"Uh-huh," David said.

"Love, love." The man shook his head. "Look here, here comes that bus."

David got up and put his full coffee on the seat. He hoisted his pack. He told the man thank you, and the man nodded. David took a bite of his doughnut and was embarrassed again.

"You do me one favor," the man said. "You get to San Fran, call your momma and tell her you all right. Call her collect. Even if it make her mad. Understand?"

"Yes," he said impatiently.

"You don't do it, I going to come get you."

"I'll *do* it," he said.

"Okay. Now go get the girl."

"Okay. Bye."

The man laughed, a last falling triple chord, and David turned and got on the bus with the half-eaten doughnut in one hand and the pack dangling from the other. Through the window he could see the man's broad flowered back as he left the terminal. To have an eighteen-year-old son, the man must have been older than Dad. It was then he remembered he hadn't gotten the black man's address, or even his name.

He fell asleep on the ride to San Francisco and when he woke the landscape had changed as completely as if the bus had crossed over into another country. They were riding through farmland; pale green leafy something (lettuce?) stretched in shining rows on either side of the highway, and a single spoke of black earth followed the bus along between the rows. Green hills rose on one side. The highway ran parallel to a railroad track, and in a thrilling parody of collision the bus passed a train going the other way. Through the windows of the train David could see the hills beyond, flickering like an old movie.

He stretched his arms and legs, without thinking, and it struck him as a good manly thing to have done. In front of him the top of an old man's pink, bald head rose over the next seat. It amazed him to think that all this went on every day, while he was living his life in Rosemead. The thought came as a surprise: he could live somewhere else. He had always known that, but never quite believed in it. Suddenly he saw how he could go and live in another country, where the soil was dark and the hills unearthly green. He could go to a new place and get a house there, with light coming in the windows at unfamiliar angles and strange plants growing in the yard. If you went to a new place like that you could learn everything about it; it wouldn't have the hard unknowable center that home did. If you moved far away you could stand outside of things long enough to get a good look and to thoroughly understand before you started getting all snarled up in them. Content with this thought, he propped his legs on the empty seat beside him and fell back into a deep sleep.

Several times he roused to see that the bus had pulled into a station. Dull and disoriented, he made sure they weren't in San Francisco yet. When the bus started up again its rocking would lull him back to sleep.

He woke finally to find that the bus had pulled into a big station where everybody seemed to be getting off. People were crowded in the aisle. He jumped up so fast he nearly left his pack behind. As he stood in line with the others, waiting to be let out, he looked through the window but all he could see was the smoky aluminum flank and leaping blue dog of the bus parked beside theirs. The bald man from the seat was gone. David stood behind a fat woman in a dark blue dress with white dots, which fit so tightly over her hips the dots were stretched into ovals.

He was sorry to have missed the approach to San Francisco. He wondered whether they'd gone over the Golden Gate Bridge. He had crossed it once before, a couple of years ago, when he, Mom, and Lizzie came up to visit Janet at Berkeley, but being with the family like that blunted it, made it less important than the house and yard in Rosemead. He'd been looking forward to seeing it fresh, by himself, on its own terms.

The driver, who stood outside the door, helped the fat woman down the bus's steps. He pantomimed helping David, without actually touching him. "Easy there," he said when David jumped down onto the concrete.

At the other terminals the buses had just pulled up outside

a numbered glass door, but at this one they parked under a great rippled aluminum canopy, thirty buses or more, some headed according to the signs for places as remote and unknown as Tampa or Calgary. David held his pack at arm's length, dangling, so it bumped against his leg. The place was full of people, most striding along with purpose but some loitering, leaning against posts or squatting on the floor. He saw an old man with a belly like a basketball, wearing a paisley shirt and a pair of green plaid pants held up with a rope, the frayed ends of which dangled from beneath the shadow of his belly. David giggled and looked nervously at the people around him, who hurried along as if nothing unusual was happening. The man in the paisley shirt ambled in a circle, belly out and head reared back, smiling. David hurried along too, and almost bumped into a black man in a trench coat. The man stood with his hands buried in the pockets of his coat, whispering to someone, and David was a moment in realizing that no one else was there. He was still another moment absorbing the fact that the man was a woman, with enormous breasts that strained against the buttoned face of the coat and a tuft of curly black hairs growing down from her chin. Her eyes put out invisible rays, which David crossed into. She registered him with the oiled, automatic click of a machine switching functions. Her eyes squinted and she said in a loud clear voice, "King of the Jews, thinks he's King of the Jews, but he's not long for this world, I can tell you. What's he think he's got in that pack? Bread for the millions? He'd got nothing in that pack I can tell you but worldly goods, goddamned worldly goods—"

David stood rooted for a minute, then walked carefully and quickly away, waiting several paces before looking back. The woman had turned to watch him, and when his eyes met hers she hollered, "Worldly goods and a ticket on the next train to hell. You laugh, you think the devil's just a baby story, but he nail your ass quick enough, yes he will."

David ran. He didn't stop until he reached the ticket

counters, where the presence of men in official Greyhound jackets promised protection and sanity. The woman did not follow him.

He got in line at one of the counters, to ask directions to Janet's street. There were three people ahead of him. Through the swinging glass doors he could see the street. It was just another street, with a Burger King and a men's store (20% OF AL HATHA SHIRT—that was all he could see from where he stood). The clock said five-thirty. He had not expected the trip to take so long. He wondered what Mom was doing right then. She had probably called the police. The police might even be looking for him, at that moment, in San Francisco. He wished he hadn't written anything at the bottom of Janet's letter.

When he reached the counter, he asked in a low voice, "Can you tell me how to get to Bush Street, please?"

The man at the counter, who was small and pumpkin-colored, with slicked-back gray hair and a thin gray mustache, looked wide-eyed at him and said, "Say what?"

"Bush Street," David repeated, slow and loud, as if speaking to a foreigner.

The man looked so intently at the ceiling that David glanced up there too. "Bush Street," the man said. "Don't know no Bush Street. Where's it at?"

"I don't know where it is," David said. He started to add, "If I knew where it was at I wouldn't have asked you, would I?" but he held it in. Still, he was pleased with himself for having thought of a comeback.

"I mean, what's it *near?*" the man said.

"I don't know," David said. "It's just in San Francisco somewhere."

"Oh." The man smiled up at the ceiling, sharing the joke with it. "San Francisco." He folded his hands on the countertop. He had long fingernails. "Do you know where you're at now, pal?"

David's knees went weak. What if he had slept through San

Francisco and ended up somewhere so far away he could never get back from it? "Yes," he said weakly.

"You're in *Oak*land," the man told the ceiling. "You come in on a bus?"

"Uh-huh," David said. "From Buel Town."

"And you're going to San Francisco."

"Uh-huh."

"You got off too soon, pal. San Francisco is the next stop. You better go see if that bus is still there."

"Oh," David said. If he went back he would have to pass by the man/woman in the trench coat again.

"Hurry up, now," the man said.

"Is Oakland very far from San Francisco?" David asked.

"No, but it's too far to walk. Go on, now. See if that bus is still there."

"Okay," David said. He started back the way he had come, and paused at the archway that opened onto the big metal-roofed hangar where the buses waited. He spotted the woman in the trench coat. She was pacing back and forth between a trash can and a pillar, as if they were goals she had to keep touching. At the trash can she stopped a moment, shouted something at it, and heeled around back to the pillar.

David checked the ticket counter. The pumpkin-colored man was writing out a ticket for a bearded man in a checkered cap. David caught his breath and ran across the wide linoleum floor, out the double glass doors, and into the street. The backpack bumped wildly against his legs.

He figured he could get from Oakland to San Francisco one way or another. When the man at the bus station said, "too far to walk," he meant too far for him, an old man, to walk. David could probably walk it. Or hitch a ride. He'd done pretty well so far.

A harsh late-afternoon whiteness hung in the air, sparking on the bumpers of cars. He could not decide which way to go, or who to ask about which way to go. People walked by: a skinny black man whose chin stuck out a foot beyond the cavity of his chest, two Mexican men in shiny shirts with landscapes printed on them, an old orange-haired woman in sweat socks and rubber beach sandals.

He went into the Burger King. Again he waited in line, this time with people who were ordering hamburgers. He got to the head of the line, where a young black girl was taking orders. She had her hair in corn rows, and wore a red badge that said HI, I'M YOLANDA on the breast of her striped apron.

"Hep you?" she said, her pencil poised over an order pad.

"Excuse me," David said. "Could you tell me how to get to San Francisco?"

The girl looked up from her pad and smiled. "Why sure, honey," she said. "Just click your heels three times and say, 'There's no place like home.' "

David giggled, a dumb high-pitched sound he sucked back in. "No, really," he said.

The girl shook her head. "That's like asking me how you get to France. I got some work to do here, these people are hungry."

"Oh," David said. "Sorry."

"Start out that way," the girl said, pointing right. Her fingernails were purple. "And ask somebody you see how to get to the Bay Bridge. Got that?"

"Uh-huh," David said. "Thank you."

As he left he heard her saying, "Must think this badge here says in-for-*ma*tion. Hep you?"

He got himself back on the street and headed to the right. The street stretched on and on, a daylit version of the one at home only wider, longer, more full of what looked like trouble. Nearly everyone he passed was black or old, or both. A man lay curled in a doorway, wearing a dirty orange Snoopy sweatshirt. In one store window a pair of swan-necked mannequins wore frothy bridal gowns; in another, old shoes were stacked like firewood. They were mostly men's shoes, big dusty brown or black oxfords. The words SHOE REPAIR floated across the window in reflecting gold letters, and as David passed by he could see his own face cut out in the shape of an *R*, hovering over the pile of shoes.

He hoped the Bay Bridge was ahead of him. He knew he should ask somebody but they were all so absorbed that he just kept walking, clutching the straps of his backpack, following the route pointed out by the glossy purple fingernail.

By the time the sun started to go down, he decided he'd better ask for directions. It wasn't sunset yet, but the light had dulled and the shadows gone long and blue. The street had curved around out of the region of stores and bars and coffee shops and become a neighborhood of motels. A skinny black woman wearing high heels and a dress as silver as a sardine kept pace with him for a minute, then got ahead, striding on her long brown legs. For the first time in his life, his legs were tired. He had always thought he could walk forever. That had seemed like his ace in the hole—he never got tired. He'd figured that if worse came to worst, he could always just outlast everybody else.

He stopped at a Mobil station, sandwiched between two motels. It was an old station, with a round sign featuring the winged red horse rather than the newer, square ones that just said MOBIL. Paint was peeling off the white canopy over the pumps, and as David looked at it a white chip fell off and fluttered to the concrete. It pleased him, to have been the only one in the world to see that little thing happen.

There were no cars at the pumps. He went into the glassed-in office, where a black man sat behind a gray metal desk. A pyramid of oil cans rose on the wall behind him. The man's face looked like it had been split with an ax. A deep healed-over cleft ran down the middle of his forehead, and one eye was half an inch lower than the other. David stood in the doorway, the knob slippery in his hand. The man looked at him with his off-center ivory-colored eyes, and said nothing.

"Um, could you tell me how to get to the Bay Bridge?" David asked.

"Bay Bridge is that way," the man said. He raised a salmon-palmed hand and waved, a single broad stroke, in the direction from which David had come.

"Is it, um, very far?" he said.

"Bout a mile," the man said.

"Oh. Well. Thank you." David went back out and closed the door behind him. He hurried back to the sidewalk and got around the corner of a motel, out of range of the man's vision.

A mile back. He had walked right past it. By the time he'd backtracked a mile the sun would be down behind the buildings. He didn't want to be here after dark. Up ahead, the immaculate aluminum and glass of a phone booth stood like a survival station planted by the civilized world. He could step into the booth, drop a dime in the slot, and call Janet, who would come pick him up. Having gotten to Oakland was almost as good as turning up at her front door; it was practically the same thing. He was halfway to the booth when he decided that no, it really wasn't the same thing at all. For it to mean anything he had to get all the way under his own power, from the front door at home to the door in San Francisco. But a mile back. A black man in a gigantic cap made of white yarn, which sat on his head like a prize chicken, walked by carrying a big radio. David stepped out between two parked cars and timidly presented his thumb to the traffic.

He was only there a minute when a car stopped in front of him, a white Honda Civic with a white man at the wheel. He couldn't believe his luck. The car behind the Honda honked, and David got in quickly and shut the door.

"Hi," the man at the wheel said, starting up again. His skin was pale and his hair was lighter than his skin, though he didn't look much older than thirty. He had a long, graceful neck and a hooked nose.

"Hi," David said. He cradled his pack in his lap. It was good to be sitting in a car, moving.

"And where are you going?" the man asked.

"To the Bay Bridge," David said. "I mean, to San Francisco."

"Your lucky day. San Francisco is where I'm going. Isn't life full of wonderful surprises?"

"Uh-huh," David said.

"Do you live in San Francisco?" the man asked.

"No."

"Where do you live?"

"Um, Buel Town."

"And what brings you to San Francisco? Business or pleasure?"

"I don't know," David said.

"Are you visiting friends here?"

"No," he said automatically. Then he realized there was no point in making up a story. Anyway, it was said; he'd let it stand.

"Just sightseeing," the man said. "My name is Warren."

"Hi. My name is David."

"Pleased to meet you, David."

"Uh-huh. Pleased to meet you too."

"David, would you care to smoke a joint?"

"Oh, sure," David said. The car was creeping through traffic. Overhead, a green sign said BAY BRIDGE in white letters. Round reflectors the size of dimes on the letters caught the sunlight. How could he have missed seeing the sign?

Warren took a joint thin as a wire out of his breast pocket, and lit it with the dashboard lighter. He wore a blue shirt with a tiny polo player stitched on the pocket in green. The twisted paper of the joint caught and flamed a moment, then Warren sucked in and held his breath. White-blond hairs stood up in the hollow of his throat. He passed the joint over to David.

"Thank you," David said, taking it between thumb and forefinger as Janet had done. He was grateful to her for teaching him how to smoke dope. He raised it to his lips and took a cautious hit, straight down into his lungs. It burned. His eyes watered a little, but he didn't choke it up. He gave the joint back to Warren.

"How old are you, David?" he asked.

David exhaled, a pitiful wisp of smoke, and said, "Fourteen."

Warren took a hit and nodded wisely, as if fourteen had been the right answer. He handed the joint back to David.

"Do you live in San Francisco?" David asked before taking his hit.

Warren nodded and expelled smoke. The car was filling with the hot sweet smell. "I can assure you I don't live in Oakland," he said. "I just come here on business."

"Oh." David forgot about having a hit of dope in his lungs. Smoke seeped out of his mouth when he opened it. He gave Warren back the joint.

"I work for the United States government, postal division," Warren said. "I sort mail. What exactly do you do for a living?"

"Well, nothing, really," David said.

"Do you live with your family?"

"No." He didn't want Warren taking him to a sheriff's office.

"When did you leave home?"

"About a year ago, I guess." David was surprised once again at how smoothly these alternate versions of the truth slid into his mind. He had a mother like Billy's, shrill, a horrible cook; his father went off to the Alaska pipeline years ago. He'd been hitching around on his own, having adventures.

"And what do you do for money?" Warren asked.

"Oh, you know," David said. Here the story fell short. He couldn't think of what a fourteen-year-old would do for money out on the road.

"I think I probably do know," Warren said. "Do I know?"

"Well, yes."

"I thought so." Warren smiled and winked, and David winked back. He wondered what sort of job Warren had imagined for him. Maybe if he found out he could go and get hired when he turned fourteen.

"Look there," Warren said. "The lady herself." They had turned onto the bridge. David nearly gasped at the suddenness of it. The car passed from behind a shadowed brick warehouse with the ghostly remnant of an ad painted on it, and San Francisco lay across a stretch of green-black water, ablaze with evening light. The buildings were bathed in gold, each window a square of orange flame. The pink sky deepened, behind the buildings, to purple.

"Pretty sight, isn't it?" Warren said.

David nodded. He felt grateful to Warren, as if Warren had given him a gift, and enamored of Warren as if the glory laid out ahead reflected partly on him. He *lived* there, in that golden city. David accepted the joint again and took a long, deep hit. It occurred to him that Warren was handsome, in a delicate, stemlike way. His eyes were milky blue, with a vivid black line running around the pupils. The sun caught his white eyelashes and turned them to gold.

"Gorgeous old thing," Warren said. "The dowager queen. Crazy old lady, absolutely haunted."

David was too absorbed in the distant city to speak. The girders of the bridge rolled by, pale gray X's, with the buildings shining behind them. Girders stretched up over the cars, throwing long lacy shadows that broke and broke over the windshield like filaments of spiderweb. He forgot to pass the joint back. Warren reached for it and brushed David's hand with his fingertips.

"Oh. Sorry," David said, giving him the joint. The air in the car was getting heavy, and he'd have liked to open a window. Opening a window seemed like a presumptuous thing to do, though. If the windows were supposed to be open, Warren would open one. David felt frozen in place, his head and eyes locked where they were. He wondered if he could be getting stoned.

"So you're here on a pleasure trip," Warren said. "That's wonderful. Did you hitchhike all the way up?"

"Well, no," David said. He was watching the city get closer, and his mouth talked by itself, independent of his brain. "I took a bus partway." He heard his voice as if someone else, a third person sitting between him and Warren, had spoken.

"Ah, a bus," Warren said. He made it sound significant. David wondered if there was something odd about his having taken a bus. A sea gull flew by, level with the car, so close he could see its glittering black eye.

"Yes," he said, and realized he was late in saying it.

"Where were you planning to stay?" Warren asked.

"I don't know," David said. The whole trip fluttered in his mind. Why had he come, exactly? For Janet. What if she wouldn't come back with him? Would he sleep tonight on her sofa? Would Rob let him stay? He had pictured himself getting to San Francisco in a speeded-up sort of way, like a movie, with one scene dissolving into the next: first he's in Santa Barbara, then he gets on a bus and (dissolve) he's on Bush Street in San Francisco. He had not figured every minute would be this long and this real.

"If you want to," Warren said, "you're welcome to stay at my place tonight."

David turned to him, through the heavy air. It took a long time to turn his head. "Thank you," he said. He wasn't going to stay at Warren's but he couldn't think of how to say no. Warren was kind, but strange. He was like an angel, impossible to judge by regular human standards. David saw that he had three silver rings on his fingers. His fingers were long and big-knuckled, the nails a bright, healthy-looking pink.

"You're very welcome," Warren said. "It will be my pleasure." He gave David the joint.

David took a hit and searched his mind for the right way of saying that what he'd meant to say was thank you but no, he didn't need a place to stay tonight. It was complicated, and he didn't want to offend. He gave back the joint and decided he'd work things out more clearly a little later.

The city drew closer; they were almost over the bridge. He could see the details of the buildings now, and though they were still gilded by the setting sun, their windows still molten, they were no longer so magical. They had water towers on their roofs, and balconies; cars moved through the streets. He looked back the way they had come and was surprised to see Oakland lit just the way San Francisco had been. The buildings were smaller but they, too, glowed, burnished gold with an edge of pink.

"Do you know where Bush Street is?" David asked.

"Yes I do," Warren told him. "Why?"

"I don't know," David said. "I have some friends on Bush Street, and I should go see them."

"I thought you didn't know anybody in the city."

"Well, I do know some people on Bush Street."

"I see. People on Bush Street." The joint was smoked down to a nub. Warren put it in the ashtray. David could not decide whether he was stoned or not. Time wasn't passing right. First it was one moment and then it was another. They were on the bridge and then they were off it, on a street again, buildings rising on either side.

"Tell you what, David," Warren said. "My apartment is on the way to Bush Street. Why don't we stop there, and we can both get cleaned up, and then I'll take you to see your friends on Bush Street. How would that be?"

David looked out the window; the moments ticked by. He was in San Francisco. This neighborhood was mostly warehouses, blank brick walls, and no one on the sidewalks. He was so hungry. He decided he was stoned. It was time to answer Warren. What he wanted most was to sit quiet for a while and watch the moments pass, without having to be in them. He was moving too slowly to keep up with them. "Okay," he said to Warren, because it was easier than trying to say anything else.

"Good," Warren said, and they drove on in a silence that was like sweet sleep. David watched the street changing and changing. Warehouses turned into liquor stores and closed-up luncheonettes. *Luncheonette* was a funny word. He giggled a little, and was glad that Warren said nothing. Warren was all right, another friend on the road. Without him, David would have had to cover this distance by himself, all this strange territory. The thought of trudging along this sidewalk, which was littered right here with broken glass and two piles of dog shit, made him feel all the more grateful to Warren. He was so hungry and thirsty too. He was so dry he could feel his tongue sticking to the roof of his mouth.

They turned onto a busy street, a regular city street with all kinds of stores, and with people walking along. A trolley car, not the ornate kind from the pictures but a solid-looking, serviceable one painted green and tan, rumbled past them and spit blue sparks at the intersection. The trolley was packed full of people. Up ahead a hill cut into the deepening sky, covered with houses, some of which had lights on that shone pale lemon yellow. At the top of the hill stood a titanic utility tower, a spindly four-legged thing painted orange and white, a robot insect from a Japanese movie, pumping power down through thin steel cables to the city. A yellow dog trotted along the sidewalk, threading his way among the pedestrians, with a blue bandana tied around his neck.

Warren's apartment was halfway up the hill. They turned off the busy street and into a steep neighborhood of three-story houses pressed close together. Some had diamond windows, some were painted bright colors. In one window, David saw a cactus with a single red flower sprouting from its top. Or thought he saw a cactus.

Warren parked on a level street at the top of the hill. David noticed that the street was called Mars, which struck him as right and logical. Warren swung his car expertly into a short space that left less than a foot on either end. "Ta-da," he said. "Home turf. Come with me, David."

David got slowly out of the car. He was definitely stoned, and getting worse. There was his one foot on the curb, there he was outside the car. There was Warren's face, very white, luminous in the dusk. Warren said, "Come, come," and started across the street. David remembered he was supposed to follow. He couldn't think of how not to follow—it would take too much explaining. As he started across the street he noticed he had his backpack in his hand.

Warren opened the door of a building. A blue door. He stood in the open doorway, waiting for David. He smiled. David realized that he was smiling too. How long had he been smiling? His upper lip snagged on a dry tooth when he tried to stop smiling. He had never been this thirsty. He told himself he would have a glass of water, then get moving again. When he passed Warren, Warren said, "Welcome to the House of Usher."

They walked up a flight of stairs. At the top of the stairs two doors faced one another. Warren put a key into one of the doors. A picture was pasted to the door, under the brass peephole. An angel, with wings and curly yellow hair, wearing sunglasses.

Warren held the door open, and David walked inside. The room was dimly lit through a single window. Warren flicked on a light switch by the door, and the light in the room turned yellower without becoming noticeably stronger. The light came from a brown paper umbrella sitting open on the floor with a light behind it. The umbrella had Japanese writing on it.

"The Copacabana," Warren said. "Go on in, put your things down."

David stepped, one foot and then the other, toward the middle of the room. He had never seen a room like it. The walls were painted dark green and the ceiling gray. The illuminated umbrella cast a halo of honey-colored light around itself. The furniture, a sofa and two chairs, was made of bamboo, covered with plump white cushions. Inside the fireplace sat a vase full of trumpet-shaped white flowers.

"You like?" Warren asked.

"Uh-huh," David said, though it was too strange for questions of "like" or "dislike" to apply. He realized he was smiling again and vowed to try and stop.

"Now," Warren said. "You're dusty and sweaty from the road, and you'd like more than anything to take a shower. Right?"

"Uh-huh. Um, could I have a glass of water?"

"Of course you can. There's mineral water, if you like. Or grapefruit juice."

"No thank you. Just regular water."

"A snap. Follow me."

David followed him through an arched opening, several paces down a short dark hallway to the kitchen. Warren turned on the light. The kitchen was so white, David blinked. Warren took a glass from a cupboard and filled it at the sink. The kitchen was not much bigger than a closet. David hung back in the doorway because he and Warren together in there would have been a crowd.

Warren dropped two ice cubes into the glass, from a miniature refrigerator that came only to his waist. "Here we go," he said, offering the glass to David. "Down the hatch."

David took the glass to his lips and drained it in several long, deep swallows. The ice cubes clunked up against his teeth. The water just seemed to disappear in him the way it would soak into a sponge. When he finished he was still dry.

"Oh, you do like that stuff, don't you?" Warren said.

David nodded, embarrassed.

"Would you like some more?"

"Please."

"No trouble, it just flows right out of the taps." Warren plucked the glass out of his hand and filled it again. On a shelf over the sink stood a line of chickens: a white glass chicken in a white glass basket, a yellow chicken and rooster that were salt and pepper shakers, a metal chicken on wheels, a white plastic chicken which, David knew, laid plastic eggs when you pushed down on its back. He drank the second glass more slowly. Although he was still thirsty he couldn't bring himself to ask for a third glass.

"Now what about that shower?" Warren said.

"I don't know."

"You can think about it. There's no rush."

"Okay."

Warren took the glass from him and filled it once again. David said, "I like that, um, umbrella in the other room," just to make conversation.

"Umbrella . . . oh, that." Warren gave him the filled glass. "That's just a stupid thing. I've been saving up for a real lamp."

"Oh." David drank his water. He should probably have picked something other than the umbrella to comment on, something Warren was prouder of. It was always hard to know.

"Have you been thinking about that shower?" Warren asked.

"Uh-huh."

"And what have you decided?"

"Well, I'd like to take one." He was anxious not to make any more mistakes. He noticed how Warren's chin had a raised white scar on it. He touched his own scar, up at his hairline.

"On down the hall." Warren pointed the way with a big-knuckled finger.

David took his pack, which he'd set on the floor, and walked down the dark hallway. Warren's voice, behind him, said. "That door there," and he turned through a half-open door into the bathroom and switched on the light.

"Plenty of clean towels," Warren said. "Shampoo, you name it. It's all completely self-explanatory, basic bathroom. Enjoy yourself."

"Thank you."

"Don't mention it." He went out and closed the door.

The bathroom was white, like the kitchen. David stood in the middle of it for a while, looking it over. Above the sink, a pair of sleek white hands, woman's hands, stuck out from the wall. One hand held two toothbrushes between its curled fingers, the other held soap in its cupped palm. There might have been a woman on the other side of the wall, sticking her hands through, except that both were left hands. David drank some more water from the sink, then looked at himself in the mirror. His eyes were red and it was only by seeing them in the mirror that he realized they burned. He blinked. They stayed red. He was supposed to take a shower. He settled his pack on the lid of the toilet seat and watched himself take his clothes off.

When he was naked he stood in front of the mirror for a minute or two. He was so skinny. He twisted around and looked at the bumps of his spine. Then he leaned over closer to the mirror, stretched his lips back off his teeth with his fingertips and, with his thumbs, pushed his nose up to see if he could detect his skull. He could. It was a bad idea. He turned on the water in the shower, which was actually a bathtub with a clear plastic curtain strung around it on a chrome rod. The tub had white lion's feet, clutching white balls. As he waited for the water to heat up he saw that a second dark curly hair had started growing out of his chest, right next to where the first one was.

Two of them now. He wondered why the second one had to come in right beside the first. He imagined himself grown up, with hair only on one side of his body. Then he wondered why it had happened here. Or when had it happened? How could he not notice a black hair growing on his own body? How could it suddenly just be there, a full-grown hair at least a quarter-inch long? The water beat against the shower curtain, and steam started fogging the plastic. Too hot. He turned the cold on harder and got in.

Water pounded against his thighs. Still too hot. He turned the cold faucet, and as he bent to do it water sprayed over his face. He hoped the shower would make him less stoned. Once he got the temperature right, he stood with the needles of water striking him on his face and chest, concentrating on what he would do next. He'd get out of the shower, get dressed, find Janet. He couldn't be stoned when he knocked on her door. What if Rob answered? He would have no idea what to say. Why did he let himself get stoned? He'd never expected it to have this kind of disorganizing effect.

Time passed, and he wondered how long he had been in the shower. It might have been a long time. He turned the water off. He did not seem to be any less stoned. If anything, he was more stoned. The two hairs lay pressed down on either side of his right nipple. The nipple was small and pink, made ridiculous by the dark doggish hairs. He thought no one would ever marry him.

The mirror was too foggy for him to see anything but his own shape, a pink haziness topped by a brown blur. He wiped a clear arc with his hand and saw his eyes. Still red. He wondered what time it could be. He dried himself with a white towel and started putting his clothes on, after puzzling over whether to start with his shirt or his jeans. Jeans first.

When he was dressed he took his pack and went back out into the hall. Warren had turned the hall light on. Warren was in the bedroom, smoking another joint.

"How do you feel?" he called to David. "Like a new man?"

The bedroom opened off the end of the hallway, just past the bathroom door. The light had been off before, but David had assumed it was a bedroom. Warren leaned back on the double bed, which was covered with a black spread. The walls here were painted gray, like the living-room ceiling. Warren extended the joint in David's direction, his brows raised questioningly.

"No thank you," David said. "I think I'd better go now."

"I'll drive you," Warren said. "Just let me jump in the shower first. I reek of the post office." He took another hit of the joint.

"Okay," David said.

"Come in here a minute. I want to show you something."

"What?" David asked.

"A six-foot anaconda that hasn't eaten in a week. Just come here, for God's sake. Are you always so jumpy?"

"No." David stood on the threshold, and his belly rose on a wave of feeling. Warren hit once more on the joint. Sinews shifted under the skin of his forearm; the swell of his bicep slipped lazily up under his shirtsleeve. He was stronger than David had thought. Watching Warren's arm, David walked into the room.

"Are you interested in whales and dolphins and things like that?" Warren said. "Sharks, octopi, moray eels?"

David considered the question, searching for a trick. "Well, I guess so," he said.

"Good. I happen to have a big fat book right here for you to entertain yourself with while I'm in the shower. Come here and have a look." He bent over and pulled a book the size of a welcome mat from the bedside table. He grunted at the weight. "Come here, look, look," he said, fanning the air with the hand that held the joint.

David came closer, into the circle of marijuana smoke. On the cover of the book was a picture of a shark swimming straight at the camera, jagged mouth agape, one round eye staring up, showing a crescent moon of white. The title of the book was *Underwater World,* written in yellow letters below the shark.

"This is a fascinating book, and well worth a few minutes of your attention," Warren said. He propped it on his lap and opened it to a picture of a bright-orange starfish prying open a clam. Then he flipped to a school of tiger-striped fish, thousands of them, swimming through bottomless blue water. "Do you think this could keep you entertained for a little while?" he said.

"Yes." David ventured closer until his knees bumped up against the bed; he jumped back as if he'd been shocked, then moved forward again. Warren smiled. David smiled back.

"Come, come," Warren said. He patted the mattress next to where he was sitting, then put the book down there and got up, the joint still smoldering between two fingers. He got off on the opposite side of the bed. "Make yourself comfortable," he said. "I'll be back in two shakes. Do you like music?"

He was always asking questions you couldn't say no to. "Yes," David said.

"Good. I can accommodate your every wish." A tape player sat on a low table on the far side of the bed. Warren picked up a cassette, held it close to his eyes and squinted. "Mozart," he said. *"The Magic Flute.* How do you feel about Mozart?"

"Fine," David said. He thought he had heard Mozart once. Warren picked up a pair of headphones, two blue foam disks connected by a white plastic arc.

"I have an arrangement with my neighbor," he said. "I promise to keep the noise down, and he promises not to burglarize my apartment. Come here, come here. Put these on."

He held them at arm's length, halfway across the bed. David put his pack down and knelt on the bed to reach them. A gray cord ran from one blue disk to the tape player. David held them, weighing them in his hands, and Warren pantomimed putting headphones on his own ears. David put them on his ears. Warren spoke, and he took them off again.

"—at the fish," Warren was saying, "and listen to Mozart, and I'll be right back. Okay?"

"Okay." David sat down on the bed, with his shoes hanging

over the side. He put the headphones back on. Warren pantomimed taking off his shoes, and he did it. His shoes dropped
heavily, noiselessly, to the floor.

Warren put the tape in. The headphones came to humming
life. There was a thin squeak, then a silence. Then music.

He watched Warren leave the room to a rising swell of
violins. The music was like a thread being pulled through his
ears. The violins grew louder, rounded a sort of curve, and got
softer again. His head filled so completely with music that he
saw the room as if he wasn't in it, as if it was a display behind
glass.

He picked up the book and settled it on his lap. There were
the thousands of tiger-striped fish and, on the next page, a
moray eel peering out of a black hole in a crusty brown rock,
with intelligent yellow eyes and a grinning lizard mouth. David
shuddered. The eel wasn't so bad, but there might be anything
on the next page. He turned the page and found, with disappointment, nothing but a school of tuna flashing silver through
a shaft of turquoise sunlight.

Music rose and fell in his head. Voices now, singing in a
foreign language. As he turned the pages he wondered if Mozart
had been thinking of fish. There were pictures of sharks and
one of an octopus and several of a seal eating a penguin, a
sequence in which the seal flipped the penguin off an iceberg
like a peanut off a spoon. David hurried past it, then went back
and looked again. It seemed to him that the music and the
pictures made perfect sense together; they were like a movie.
He began to see connections between the pictures themselves,
as if they were all episodes in a single story. Here a blue angel-
fish hovered like a gas flame; here a penguin stood (he went
back to the iceberg sequence one more time), hopeless in
black and white, just before the seal flicked it headfirst into its
jaws. Each picture caused the next with a logic that lay just
beneath David's intelligence. Though he could not say what

the next picture would be, the moment he turned the page it was always the perfect follow-up.

Warren appeared beside him on the bed. David didn't see or hear him come back from the shower. He felt a weight on the mattress and looked up into Warren's face. Warren had on a pair of jeans but no shirt. A medallion of white-blond hairs curled on his small, surprisingly muscular chest. He went with the music.

David smiled at him and he smiled back. Warren had bright, questioning eyes and a long nose. His face was so big. He had a thin, smiling mouth with dots of white whisker stubble above and below. David watched Warren's mouth until Warren's face came closer and kissed him on the lips. A woman sang a single high note. A sluggish bubble rose lazily from David's belly and filled his head. He looked straight into the pale blue disks of Warren's eyes. The woman's high note ended. David pulled his face away and jumped to his feet. The headphones stretched to the end of their cord and fell crookedly off his ears onto the bed. The silence was shocking.

Warren sat on the bed, smiling. David wiped his mouth with the palm of his hand and looked at his palm. It was wet. He wiped his mouth with his other hand.

"Why did you do that?" he asked Warren.

"Because you wanted me to," Warren said in a satisfied voice.

"No I didn't." He wiped his mouth again, this time with the back of his hand.

"I think you did."

David's eyes filled so suddenly with tears that they were running down his face before he realized he had started crying at all. "No I didn't," he said. He could feel the thickness in his voice.

"What's the matter?" Warren said. "You don't like kissing?"

"*No.*"

"Well honey, then what are you doing in—Wait a minute. You're not, are you?"

"Not what?" David said. Warren floated in front of him, a pink blur through the tears. He wiped his nose with his finger.

"How old are you really?" Warren said.

"I don't know. Twelve."

Warren whistled. "Twelve. I thought you were just under-developed."

"I'm not," David said, uncertain of what he was denying.

"Come on, stop crying," Warren said. "There's no harm done, kisses wipe off. Put your shoes on and I'll drive you to Bush Street."

"No." David could tell from Warren's silence that he had said it at the right volume.

"All right," Warren said softly. "Do you want some money?"

"No," David said again. His eyes cleared a little. He picked up his shoes and put them on, hopping first on one foot and then on the other. Warren got up off the bed.

"When you're a little older, this won't seem so bad," he said. "I have a feeling it may come to seem very usual. Please don't cry."

"I'm not crying," David said, and just that suddenly he wasn't. The tears dried up. He lifted his pack and walked out of the room, with Warren following.

"Look, it's starting to rain," Warren said when they got to the living room. David looked at the window and saw silver slashes of rain against the glass. The tears had left a ragged heaviness in his throat.

"Uh-huh." He went to the door.

"Wait," Warren said. "You liked this parasol, didn't you? Take it with you."

David hesitated, holding the doorknob. Warren jumped across the room and picked up the paper umbrella. When he lifted it the light behind was exposed, a glaring round bulb on three black metal legs. The light in the room changed from pale gold to white.

"Here," he said, offering David the umbrella. After a moment, David accepted it. The handle was a stick of bamboo, wrapped at the bottom with thick green cord.

"It won't do in a typhoon," Warren said. "But it's better than nothing."

"Thank you," David said. He looked up at the umbrella and saw the painted Japanese letters, backwards. Ordinarily he'd have asked what they said, in case it was something embarrassing that a Japanese person might laugh at.

"You're most welcome," Warren said. "Have a safe trip."

"Okay." David now had both hands full, and Warren opened the door for him.

"If you feel like coming back when you're older, you know where to find me. Drop in anytime."

"Uh-huh. Thank you. I mean . . ." David got the umbrella out the door and stood in the hallway with it over his head. It cast a patch of golden light around him.

Warren stood in the doorway with the door half closed. "Do you really like that umbrella?" he asked.

David shrugged, and nodded.

"See? Things aren't so bad. Night."

"Good night."

Warren shut the door. The paper angel came up close, her perfect red lips pressed together, her eyes indistinguishable behind the dark glasses.

He walked out into the street with the umbrella over his head. Rain thumped against it like gravel on a drum. David closed the umbrella and put it in his pack, so it wouldn't get ruined. The rain fell on his head and shoulders as he walked down the hill. He watched his white tennis shoes on the glistening concrete. He thought about nothing. His mind was as empty as it had ever been.

He came to the bottom of the hill, where the quiet street intersected a busy one. A group of people waited at a bus stop. He asked one of them, a woman in red overalls, how to get to Bush Street. She reeled off a series of buses. Bush Street was far away. David lost track after the second bus but nodded comprehendingly as the woman spoke. When the woman was finished he thanked her and went to wait at the stop across the street, where she'd directed him. He held his pack tightly to his belly.

The bus came in a few minutes, crackling with hard white light. David hung back and was the last one on. The driver was a thin black man with a pocked face and a goat beard that came to a grizzled point. He held the wheel straight-armed, as if he were driving a plow.

"How much is it?" David asked.

"Sixty cent," the man said without looking at him. He pulled a lever and the doors closed with a rubberized sigh.

David dug sixty cents out of his pocket. It was nearly the last of his money. "Could you tell me how to get to Bush Street?" he asked.

"Transfer at Van Ness," the driver said. He tore a slip of paper off a pad, flicked it in David's direction.

"Thank you," David said. He accepted the paper. As he started down the aisle the bus lurched forward. He nearly fell over into a Mexican woman's lap, knocking her big brown knee with his pack. He said, "Excuse me." It didn't help. He struggled into an empty seat. He was wet from the rain. Everybody on the bus knew there was something wrong with him.

When he got off at Van Ness, an old woman with her dress buttoned wrong walked up as if she'd been expecting him. She said, "Got a quarter?" in an impossibly deep, froggy voice. He gave her his last one because he didn't think in time that it was possible not to.

He stood at the corner of Van Ness, wet, waiting for his next bus. There were two other people. They were both women, both carrying umbrellas and big purses. The darkness was complete now. The utility tower at the top of Warren's hill, studded with red lights, blinked to warn low-flying aircraft. Lights had come on in the windows of houses on the hill; one of the lights was Warren's. He had wanted Warren to touch him. A part of him had known Warren would try to touch him when he first stepped into the car in Oakland. His clothes clung wetly to his body. For a moment he had no idea why he had come here, or what he would do next.

A police cruiser pulled up. There were two cops inside. The

one who was not driving got out. A black cop. He walked toward David. He was no more or less logical than the woman who wanted a quarter.

The cop said, "Your name David Stark?"

"No," David said. He heard his voice from far away, a fluttering thing, a scrap of paper.

"What is your name, please?"

"Um—" He hesitated, and knew he was lost. "It's David Stark," he said.

The cop nodded. His head grew directly out of his shoulders. "David Stark," he said. "Your family is worried about you."

"I know," David said. He wondered if he was trembling. He checked his hands. They were trembling.

"You come on with us, David Stark," the cop said, "and we'll put you together with your family again."

"Um, I was just coming to see my sister. Could you take me to her house? She lives on Bush Street."

"No sir. That we cannot do. We're going to take you to the station, and we'll call your sister from there. Come on into the car now, hmm?"

David speculated a moment over whether he could outrun the cop. The cop looked pretty old. As if he sensed what David was thinking the cop spread out a big pink hand and said, "Come on now. Hmm?"

David went. The two women were staring at him. The closer of the women wore a bandana around her head and gold hoops in her ears, though she wasn't a gypsy. David tried to walk proudly, like a good, interesting criminal.

The cop opened the back door for him. As David was getting in, the cop said, "I'm going to have to take the backpack up front."

"Oh," David said.

"It's the rules." Again the big pink hand appeared. David looped the pack's strap over the man's palm.

"Thank you," he said.

"You're welcome." David got in the back of the cruiser, and the cop closed the door after him. The back was separated from the front seat by thick wire mesh, just like you'd think.

"It's him," the black cop said to the other one at the wheel. "T-shirt with Stevie Wonder on it."

"Boy's got taste," the other cop said.

"Well, I wouldn't know," the black cop said. "Who's Stevie Wonder?"

They pulled out into traffic. "Stevie Wonder is the greatest pro ballplayer who ever lived," the other cop said.

David looked back and saw his bus coming. He sat with his arms folded over his chest. The black cop took up a microphone and said into it. "This is car nine-oh-six. We have apprehended a runaway at Market and Van Ness and are bringing him in. Stark. Right. Ten four."

They really said "ten four." David looked at the people in the car next to them, three Japanese men in a Pontiac, and wondered what they would think of a kid sitting in the back of a cruiser. They did not appear to think anything at all.

"I can't believe we found him," said the cop at the wheel.

"I told you it was him. I spotted the shirt."

"You got a sharp eye, man. Hey, you ever heard of Miles Davis?"

"Nope. Who's he?"

"He's a famous ballplayer too."

"I don't follow baseball." They both laughed. The black cop went "Haw haw haw."

They drove with traffic, and left their siren off. David was no emergency. He wondered if they would test him and find out he was stoned. He wondered what they would think about the gun. His legs started jiggling and he let them do it. He had almost gotten to Bush Street. He whispered, "Sorry, Janet," and liked himself for having done it, for saying something like that right out loud in a police car. For one fine soaring moment he imagined a movie he was the star of, about a kid who travels enormous distances through the north woods to rescue the girl he loves. He survives terrible dangers. He swims icy rivers and outruns packs of wolves, he battles criminals and murderers, and is falsely arrested just before he reaches the final shootout. He tried to picture what the ending would be. In the movie version he'd escape from jail and save his girl amid a swarm of bullets.

The police didn't find the gun in his pack until they were at the station, until David had checked in with a sergeant and been sent to sit alone in a room with a big blond table surrounded by chairs. The room had no windows, and three of its walls were covered by bulletin boards, scrabbly-looking white cork covered with pinholes. The only piece of paper was a pale green sheet with three telephone numbers written on it in blue ink. There was no telephone.

He sat in the room for a long while. He switched from chair to chair. The man who finally came in was not a cop at all. He wore green corduroy pants and a plaid shirt.

"Hi, David," the man said, with such cheerful recognition David wondered whether they'd met before.

"Hi," he said with a friendly smile, just in case.

"Mind if I sit down?" the man said. He had a wide round face and no hair on top of his head. The hair on the sides, spaniel-colored, drooped down over his ears.

"No," David said, still grinning uncertainly.

The man pulled out a chair next to the one David sat in. He was wearing Old Spice lime. "My name is Darrell," he said, extending his hand.

"Hi," David said. They shook hands. Darrell's was so dry it might have been talcumed.

"I just want to talk to you for a few minutes," Darrell said. "Would that be all right?"

"Uh-huh."

Darrell nodded, a series of short elastic bobs of the head. "How are things at home?" he asked.

"Okay."

"Have you been having some trouble there?"

This was difficult to answer. He was not sure what Darrell meant by "trouble," and not sure what the right answer would be. "I don't know," he said.

Darrell nodded and nodded. "How do you get along with everybody back there?" he asked.

"Okay." He wondered if he should mention Lizzie, and decided not to.

"Really okay? Everything at home is really just fine?"

"I guess." He was not holding up his end of the conversation. To be polite, he added, "Are you a psychiatrist?"

"I'm a counselor," Darrell smiled, nodding. "Does that bother you?"

"No," David said.

"Good. David, can you tell me why you left home?"

"Well, I was going to get my sister. She's my half-sister, really. Her name is Janet."

"I know her name is Janet. What exactly do you mean when you say you were going to 'get' her?"

"Well, she went off with this guy Rob, and she doesn't really love him."

"Did she tell you that?" Darrell asked.

"Uh-huh. Sort of."

"Then why do you think she went off with him?"

"I don't know." He searched his memory for a phrase. "I think she was afraid," he said.

"Afraid of what?"

"I don't know."

"What do you think?"

"Well, I think she's afraid she won't get to be a doctor."

"Does she want to be a doctor?"

"I don't know. I think so."

"What do you think about the man she went off with?"

"Rob. He's okay."

"Is he?"

"Well, my mother doesn't like him very much."

"Do you like him?"

"No. Not very much."

"David, what were you going to do with the gun?"

"Well, I just sort of thought I should take it."

Darrell nodded. "Did you ever think you might shoot anybody with it?"

"No," David said.

"Did you think you might shoot your sister's boyfriend with it?"

David thought for a moment. "No," he said.

"Are you sure?"

"Uh-huh."

"What if it had gone off accidentally? Would you have been sorry if it did?"

"Well, yes."

"Do you know how many bullets were in the gun?"

"Oh. There were bullets in it?"

"Actually no, there weren't any bullets in it. I wondered if you knew that."

"Oh."

"Did you know for sure that there were no bullets in it?"

"Yes," David said.

Darrell nodded and nodded. "David, if you left home again, would you take a gun? Do you think it's a good idea to take a gun with you?"

"No," David said. And he added, for good measure, "I wouldn't leave home again anyway."

"Would you be afraid to leave home again?"

"No," David said, and realized only after he'd said it that it was true.

Darrell sighed. "I guess that's enough for now, David," he said.

"What's going to happen?" David asked him.

"Your sister's out there arranging things. She's going to put you on a plane back home."

"Janet's here?"

"That's right."

"Is she going to come in here? I mean, in this room?"

"No, we'll send you out to her. It won't be long. Do you have to use the bathroom?"

"No," David lied. He could hold it.

"Okay. It's been nice talking to you, David." Darrell stood up and shook his hand again.

"Bye," David said.

"See you." As Darrell left the room, David wondered if he'd gotten his answers right.

A cop came for him some time later. He took David down a corridor, and instead of going back the way David had been brought in, the cop directed him down a second hallway and into a waiting room. As he went, David searched for a less pathetic way of being. He walked with a slight cowboy bend in his legs.

Janet was standing in the middle of the waiting room, smoking a cigarette. David stopped and stood, unable to negotiate the last few paces. She smiled at him, holding her cigarette between two fingers, and they stayed that way a moment. Janet wore jeans and a white shirt with the sleeves rolled up. Her hair hung loose around her shoulders.

"Are you okay?" she asked him.

He nodded. They both stepped forward. She took his hand rather than embrace him. "I can't believe you did this," she said.

"I know," David said. "I'm sorry."

"Don't be sorry. Nobody got hurt. Come on, I think we can go." She looked over his shoulder at the cop. "Can we go?"

"Yep," the cop said.

"I signed about a thousand forms," Janet told David, "and you're released to my care. I fooled them into thinking I was an adult."

"Oh."

They started out of the waiting room, and she rested her hand on the back of his neck. "There's going to be some court stuff in L.A.," she said. "I think you're going to have to see a shrink for a while. But don't worry. I've been to half a dozen of them and they've hardly done me any harm at all."

She guided him out of the room and down a wide hall with a speckled brown linoleum floor.

"What are we going to do?" David asked.

"Rob's waiting outside in the car," Janet said. "He helped me with the negotiations and everything, and then he couldn't stand to be here anymore. He's going to drive us straight to the airport. I've got you booked on an eleven o'clock flight home."

"Oh."

"They gave me your pack. It's out in the car. They're going to keep the gun for a while."

"Uh-huh."

She laughed. "I asked one of them if you'd set the record for gun-bearing, and he thought it was a big joke. He said they had a nine-year-old in last week, with a magnum."

They reached the front door. Through the glass panel, David could see the street, awash in yellow light. In a minute they'd be with Rob, in his car. He stopped walking and said, "Janet?"

"What?"

"Um, do you want to come back home with me? I mean, do you want to stay in San Francisco? You don't, do you?"

She sighed, and draped her wrist over his shoulder. "That's what you came all this way to ask me, huh?"

He nodded.

She shook her head. "You traveled five hundred miles to tell me in person how I should come back home and not marry Rob. Who had just traveled five hundred miles to tell me I *should* marry him."

"Uh-huh."

"What is it about you men? Why do you have to make everything into a quest? I mean, David, why didn't you just pick up the telephone?"

"I don't know," he said.

Janet held the door open for him and he walked outside and down a half dozen granite steps. They were on a quiet, brightly lit street. Across the street a building said GARAGE in pink letters.

"This way," she said. They crossed the street and went into the garage. Janet rang for the elevator, which opened its doors with a dangerous-sounding *skreak*. Inside, the elevator smelled of piss. White light glanced off the scabbed white walls.

He and Janet rode up in silence. This was his last chance to say something to her, something only she would hear, but he couldn't think of what. The passing moment cut through him. He had nothing for her but his presence.

The doors opened and they got out. Rob's car was parked two rows down. As they walked along the concrete, their footsteps ringing, Janet said, "Don't worry if Rob seems a little testy. He's sort of upset about all this."

"He is?"

"He thinks you were bringing the gun to shoot him. I told him you weren't." She paused. "Were you?"

"No," David said.

"Try to reassure him that you had no intention of killing him, okay? It would make him feel better."

"Okay."

Rob was sitting behind the wheel of his car. Janet opened the passenger door and said, "Here we are. Sprung."

She tripped the latch and pulled up the seat so David could get in back. As he crawled in he said, "Hi, Rob."

Rob looked at him over his shoulder, without turning in his direction. "Hi," he said in an empty voice.

Janet got into the front seat and closed the door. Rob started the car.

"We have to stop at the first phone booth," she said. "I promised Mother I would."

"Right," Rob said, pulling on the *R* like a zipper. *Rrrr-ight.*

David sat in the middle of the back seat. His pack was there, his towel folded neatly on top and the folded umbrella sitting on top of the towel.

"Are you hungry?" Janet asked him.

"Uh-huh," he said. His hunger had persisted so long it had become a steady state, something he thought no more of than breathing.

"We'll get you something at the airport. Can you hold out that long?"

"Sure."

She reached back over the seat and took his hand. "What I want to hear about now," she said, "is the last fifteen hours. How did you get up here, exactly?"

"Well, I took the bus partway," he said. "And I hitchhiked."

"You're much too young to hitchhike," she said.

"He had a weapon," Rob said. "That's why people don't pick hitchhikers up, because some of them have guns in their back-packs."

"An unloaded gun," Janet said.

"Yeah. Did he know that?"

Janet maintained her grip on his hand. "He said he knew. I believe him."

David was returning to his old smallness, sitting in the back of a car, being talked about. Rob piloted the car down a spiral ramp. He drove too fast, and the tires gave out a constant, pained squeal. Janet pressed David's hand. They all kept quiet until they were down off the ramp.

"So you hitchhiked," she said. "Did you have trouble getting rides?"

"No," David said. He thought of Warren. He'd decided not to tell anyone about Warren, at least not right away.

"Who picked you up? I mean, what kind of people?"

"Well, a black man picked me up," David said. "And a lady did."

"Just two rides? Oh, wait a minute, there's a phone booth. Rob, pull over."

Rob pulled over without saying anything. He had to switch lanes, and he cut off another car doing it. The car sounded its horn as it passed. Rob held tightly to the steering wheel.

He parked in a no-parking zone, beside a phone booth which stood before its reflection in the obsidian window of a dry cleaners. "Come on, David," Janet said. "We'll be right back."

The two of them got out of the car. Janet stepped into the booth and dialed. David propped the door open with his shoulder. The glass pan of the overhead light held the shadows of dead moths. Janet said, "Collect, please, from Janet," and then, after a few seconds, "Hi. I've got him.

"Yes, he's fine. Wait till you see the little striped suit he's wearing. No, I know it isn't funny. Sure. Just a minute."

She handed the receiver to David. They had a moment's trouble jockeying around one another, then David put the receiver to his ear.

"Hi, Mom," he said.

"David. Are you all right?" Her voice threaded itself through the static.

"Uh-huh."

"Good. When you get home I'm going to kill you."

"Oh."

"No, not really. I've just been crazy with worry, is all. Is Janet putting you on a plane?"

"I guess so."

"Okay. I'll pick you up at the airport. Oh, wait a minute, Lizzie wants to say hello."

The line went hissingly quiet, and Lizzie said, "Hello?"

"Hi, Lizzie." Her voice sounded so small and distant. It occurred to him that he shouldn't have left her and Mom alone.

"Where are you?" she asked.

"In San Francisco. Didn't Mom tell you I was in San Francisco?"

"Yes. Did the police let you out?"

"Uh-huh. I'm going to come home."

"Are you okay?"

"Yeah."

"Mom's going to kill you when you get back."

The line quieted again, and Mom came on. "Don't worry," she said. "You're safe here. Let me talk to Janet for a minute, okay? I'll see you at the airport."

"Okay."

"David?"

"What?"

"We're glad you're all right. We both love you."

"Oh. Well, I do too. I mean, I love you too."

"Now put Janet on. I need to get the flight number from her."

He passed the phone back to Janet, and they shuffled around each other again. While Janet gave Mom the information about the flight, David hung around outside the booth. He could see Rob's dark face inside the car, and one finger tapping on the steering wheel. He stuffed his hands into his pockets and leaned against the glass wall of the booth. Faintly, he could feel Janet's voice vibrating on the glass.

———

When they got to the airport Rob let them out in front of the terminal, and went to park the car. David took his backpack with him, the towel and the umbrella tucked inside.

He and Janet stood in line at the ticket counter. He was surprised to find that they didn't talk, not even with Rob out of the way. Janet smoothed his hair and rested her hand on his shoulder. Something in the way she kept touching him made him think she was anxious to see him go.

They moved up until only one person stood ahead of them, a woman with two blue plaid suitcases. David said to Janet, "Do you love Rob?"

"Stop that," she said. "You're only twelve, you won't know what love is until you're at least fourteen. Do you know that what you did was wrong?"

"Well, no," he said.

"It was. I love Rob, I'm going to marry him. I've made my decision. And David, to come after me with a gun—"

"I wasn't after you."

She sighed, a dry, papery sound. "Frankly, I'm a little worried about you," she said.

"You don't have to be," he told her. "I can take care of myself."

"What?"

"We're next," he said.

She turned and said, "Stark," to the blond, uniformed woman who was wearily smiling. "I made a reservation on the eleven o'clock flight to Los Angeles. For one."

By the time they got the ticket Rob had come back from the parking lot. He was waiting for them with his hands in his pockets, the fluorescent lights graying his face.

"All set," Janet said. "Now let's get you something to eat."

"Okay," David said. The pack, now light as a teddy bear, flopped against his leg as he walked.

They went to a fast-food stand, Rob several paces ahead, walking with his arms swinging out from his body and his shoulders canted forward. At the stand, Janet ordered David a hot dog, french fries, and a Coke, and coffee for herself. Rob didn't want anything. He stood far enough down the counter that another body could have fit between him and Janet.

David wolfed his food. Though he'd thought his hunger had gone numb, the first bite of the hot dog brought his body to sharpened, salivating life. He devoured it and Janet ordered him another one. He finished off the french fries while they were waiting for the second hot dog. He gobbled it down and could have eaten a third and a fourth with no trouble, but they had to go catch his plane.

With food inside him he felt less dazed. The three of them passed through the metal detector and found his gate. It was only as Janet was checking him in that the full weight of his failure settled down on him. He was being sent home, having done nothing more than make himself ridiculous. Nothing was changed. There was nothing much you could do about anything.

Janet told the man at the desk, "Nonsmoking," then turned to David and said, "You don't smoke, do you?"

"No," he said.

She handed him his boarding pass. "Now let's get you on that plane before you get into any more trouble. March."

"You sound like Mom," he told her.

"Well, I am like Mom."

"No you're not."

"Now you sound like Lizzie."

"I'm like myself," he said, and realized it was true.

Janet bent over and kissed him on the forehead. "Call me when you get home, okay?"

"Okay."

They went to the gate, where a sign said PASSENGERS ONLY BEYOND THIS POINT. Rob came up behind Janet and took her hand in his.

"Bye," she said. "Don't hijack the plane."

"Bye," David said. He went several paces into the boarding tunnel, and turned to face them again.

"Hey, Rob," he said.

"What, David?"

David raised his right arm, thumb and index finger erect, and fired three shots. He made the sounds. *"Pshiew. Pshiew. Pshiew."* He shot Rob straight in the head.

An unmistakable look of fear skated over Rob's eyes before they hardened in anger. He strode up to David as if to knock him over. David stood unflinching, his feet planted wide apart and his finger still cocked.

"You watch it, you little psychopath," Rob said in a whisper. "Watch it or I'll have you put away in an institution. You're about this far from juvenile hall right now." He held his thumb and finger an inch apart.

David poked his finger into Rob's shirted belly, looked deeply into Rob's face, and said, *"Pshiiiieeeeew."* He said it this time in a whisper to match Rob's. Then he turned around and walked, without hurrying, down the boarding tunnel and onto the plane. He was able to keep himself from looking back.

Mom stood off to one side of
the crowd at the L.A. airport, in her light blue jacket with the
big collar. When David reached her she held him a moment,
her thin hands pressing hard on his shoulders, and he thought
it was a different sort of hug from the ones she usually gave
him. It was more the kind of hug you'd give a man, respectful
of his body.

She reared back and held him at arm's length, and shook
him. "You're okay?" she said.

"Yeah."

"Tomorrow I'm going to kill you."

"Okay."

They walked together down a long tiled corridor and out of
the terminal. Mom said, "I'm not going to ask you for the story
right now because you'll just have to tell it again to Lizzie.
She's in the car, sleeping. I tried to wake her up but you know
how she gets, like a ton of bricks."

"I know," David said.

"Be ready, she'll be mad when we get to the car."

"Yeah, she will." He could not remember Mom confiding to

him about Lizzie before. She had always treated him and Lizzie as a unit, so deeply linked in their quarrels that blame was impossible to fix.

The car was parked under a shaggy palm tree which looked, from across the street, like it grew out of the hood. Lizzie slept on the back seat, in her robe and nightgown, her hands fisted like a baby's.

She woke at the sound of Mom's key in the lock. As Mom opened the door, her voice was already up to full volume.

"—didn't you wake me up?" she said. "You promised you'd wake me up."

"Look what I have here, Lizzie," Mom said. "Your brother, back from the crusades."

She let her face settle into neutral. "Hi, David," she said.

"Hi, Lizzie. Are you glad to see me?" he asked, just to hear what she would say.

"You were only gone one day," she told him.

The information was startling. It was true, he had only been gone a day. "You haven't gotten any more ugly since I left," he said.

"You have," she replied. He had to give her credit for picking up a straight line.

Mom started the car, and they headed for home. As they drove, David told the story of his trip. He told it pretty much the way it happened, except that for Warren he substituted a dark-haired, foreign lady who took him over the Bay Bridge and had to leave him at Van Ness because she was late to meet her husband. It pleased him to know that a small part of his life was completely unverifiable; people would have no choice but to believe whatever he told them about his doings from dawn until after eight. As he described the dark lady to Mom and Lizzie he could see her so perfectly—hooked nose, hair pulled back tight, a white scarf around her neck—that she blended with the truth. He knew ten times more than he told: she drove a white Fiat, she used to give ballet lessons, her husband was a famous psychiatrist. After he was done telling about her it seemed impossible that she didn't exist.

Lizzie fell back to sleep before he was finished talking. She lay slumped against the back door with her legs tucked under her and her mouth hanging open. She made a hushed growling noise that was like a bow being drawn back and forth and back again over a violin string.

"Is she out?" Mom asked.

"Uh-huh."

"I've never seen anyone sleep like that," Mom said. "She could win a blue ribbon at a county fair."

"She snores," David said. He couldn't take his eyes off Lizzie. She was astonishingly small. Folded up like that, she looked like she'd fit inside a suitcase. He watched her sleep until Mom asked whether Janet had fed him before putting him on the plane.

"Yes," he said. "But I'm still hungry."

"I'll fix you something when we get home. I'm glad you're back."

"Me too," he said.

"David, did you really think you could get Janet to come home with you?"

He turned back to the front seat. Mom drove straight-backed, her eyes fixed to the road, like an illustration of right driving technique, her hands on the wheel at two and ten o'clock.

"I don't know," he said. That wasn't enough. "I guess I just wanted to *do* something," he added.

"Did you talk to her about it?"

"A little."

"What did she say?"

"Well, I guess she wants to stay with Rob."

"She's an adult," Mom said. "Maybe I helped give you the wrong idea about Rob."

"Do you think she doesn't love him?"

"I think she's confused. I think you may have to help her out later on, if she gets even more confused."

"Will you help her too?" David asked.

"I sure will. If I'm around, I'll do anything for her."

"Where else would you be?"

"I don't know," she said.

"Oh."

A moment passed. David lightly touched her knuckles on the steering wheel. She looked at his hand in surprise.

When they pulled into the driveway at home, Lizzie woke up as if she'd been pinched. "Last stop," Mom said. "Wake up, everybody."

"I wasn't sleeping," Lizzie said. "Oh, *look.*"

"What?"

"Over there." She pointed to the trash cans that were lined up at the curb, waiting to be emptied. A coyote stood on its hind legs at the farthest can, its long snout poked under the lid.

"Pretty soon they'll be turning up in the living room," Mom said.

David opened his door and jumped out onto the driveway, yelling and waving his arms. The coyote dropped onto all fours and trotted off up the street in an annoyed, unhurried way. David stopped at the sidewalk and watched its shaggy white hind end retreating. The coyote glanced over its shoulder at him, showing a serene, wolfish profile. David shouted as loud as he could and ran after it. It broke into a run without looking back.

It cut across a lawn and darted under a hedge, its bony back feet scrabbling in the dirt. David sprinted to the hedge and wriggled under, right where the coyote had gone. Twigs scraped his back, and a sharp branch cut him below the eye, as neatly as a razor slicing a peach. He crawled through on his belly and came out the other side, onto the front lawn of the next house. The coyote was there, not ten paces away, its big, nicked ears perked up and its yellow eyes staring. It seemed surprised to see him. He paused, also surprised, held by the coyote's perfect round eyes, the unreasonable life in them. He and the coyote stood through a long moment of mutual shock and recognition. Then he yelled again, a war whoop he pulled up from deep in his gut. The coyote turned and ran. A man in white pajamas appeared in an upstairs window and called sternly, "Hey, what's going on out there?"

The coyote darted across the next two lawns and turned down a side street, running with its tail between its legs like a beaten dog. David kept after it. He ran so fast he knew, for a dizzying moment, he would catch the animal and wrestle with it.

When he reached the side street the coyote was gone. It had melted back into the shadows like a cup of water poured into a lake. David sprinted on anyway for another few blocks, screaming into the night, until he ran out of breath. When he stopped and turned around he saw that he had set off a string of house lights. As he walked back he waved to the houses and said, "Just a coyote, everything's all right. Go back to bed."

Mom and Lizzie were waiting for him on the front stoop. Mom had her hands on Lizzie's shoulders, and Lizzie's robe belled slightly in the breeze. She was holding his pack in front of her like a shield.

"Did you get him?" Mom asked.

"No," he said. As he strode up the walk he felt proud and light-headed.

"What happened to your face?" Lizzie said.

He touched his cheek. His finger came away dotted with blood.

"It's nothing," he told her.

"Well, I know," she said.

"Come on," Mom said. "We'll get you patched up and feed you and then I want you both in bed."

"Okay," he said tolerantly, though he knew he didn't have to go to bed until he decided to. Lizzie handed him his pack. Tomorrow he would carry her outside and throw her in the pool, no matter how she screamed and hit him. If she sank when he threw her in he'd pull her back out, wait for her to catch her breath, and throw her in again. She would not escape him until she'd learned to swim.

They all went into the house. Mom looked at the cut and told him she thought he'd pull through. "I know I will," he said. "It's nothing."

Mom and Lizzie did the cooking, and David set the table. Forks, knives, spoons. He watched them go down in their correct order, as though he was watching somebody else do it. A fog was rising inside his head, a lazy shimmering fog that was hunger and exhaustion and something else too, like a second intelligence, that saw everything a half size smaller and made him feel peaceful and in control. Fork, knife, spoon. His hands knew the business. His arms and legs felt heavy and far away, as far away as San Francisco. Someday he would go back to San Francisco. Warren would still be there.

Mom brought over plates of bacon and eggs, and Lizzie brought a platter of toast. She had made eight pieces. The three of them sat down to eat.

"I don't think I like these eggs," Lizzie said.

"Eat them," David told her. "They're just passing through."

"We may all need our strength," Mom said. Her eyes were sunken and bruised-looking from tiredness. "The weatherman says there may be more rain coming down from up north."

"It's not going to rain anymore," Lizzie said.

"I don't think so either," David said reassuringly. "There won't be any more rain for a while."

"Yes there will be," Lizzie said. She was so sleepy she was losing track of herself. In her confusion, she ate a forkful of eggs. "Was that thunder?" she asked with her mouth full.

"It's only an airplane going by," Mom said. "Keep eating."

"Hey, I just remembered. I brought you something from San Francisco," David said.

"You brought who something?" asked Lizzie.

"Well, both of you. Just a second, I'll get it."

"How about waiting until after you've eaten?" Mom said.

"No, I want to give it to you now. It'll just take a minute." He got up and went out to the hall for the umbrella. He could hear Lizzie say, "I bet he doesn't really have anything."

He unzipped his pack, which he had left slumped by the front door. Once he'd gotten the umbrella out he realized how small it was—not much use in the rain, really, except to keep your head dry. It would melt in the first good storm. Still, it was funny to have something like that just when everybody was talking about rain. He opened it, to make it look more impressive.

He went to the kitchen doorway and called out, "Okay, close your eyes. Are they closed?"

A moment's silence passed. "Lizzie, close your eyes," he said. He was surprised at how definite his voice sounded.

"Okay," she called back.

"We're ready," Mom said.

He walked into the room, followed by the umbrella, which caught a moment in the doorway. Mom and Lizzie were sitting at the table with their eyes closed. Mom's face was calm and pale; her hands lay folded in her lap as neatly as a pair of gloves. Lizzie sat with her chin resting on her fists, her eyes and mouth squeezed tightly shut as if she expected something to fall on her. David came and stood between them, holding up the umbrella. Light from the fluorescent ceiling shone through the thin green ribs and the brown paper. He might have been a tightrope walker standing in the spotlight, perfectly balanced. He held the umbrella over Mom's head and then over Lizzie's. They were circus performers too, a family of acrobats who walked blindfolded from one spangled crow's nest to another on a silver wire. The blindfolds kept them from knowing how high up they were. He watched Lizzie's shaded face in wonder, until she started to squirm. "Come on," she said.

He held the umbrella over her head. For the first time in memory, his arm felt strong. "Okay," he said.

He waited for them to open their eyes.